A High Stakes Game

Cori peered into the darkness outside the boathouse. "That's weird. How come I can hear a boat, but not see it?"

Max leaped up and tackled her, tumbling her to the floor just before the window cracked like fireworks and shattered.

"Oh my God!" Her cry was muffled by his hand, protecting her face as they hit the floor.

"Stay under me!" he ordered.

She squeezed her eyes shut, her hammering heart sending a deafening rush through her ears. "What is it?" she demanded, her voice strained from terror and the crush of his body.

She heard the click of his gun cocking. "Shhh. Listen."

The motor _____ and she felt Max lift his _____ til I know it's clear," he _____

When she _____ ss looked like a five-foo_____ web, perilously suspended in the woodwork.

Max gently turned her face toward his. "You okay?" Their faces were inches apart and the thud of his pulse vibrated through her body.

"I think so. Thank you, Max."

"Thank whoever was smart enough to put bullet-proof glass in this place. They saved your life—because someone just took a shot at you, kid."

Also by Roxanne St. Claire

Kill Me Twice
Killer Curves
Hit Reply
French Twist
Tropical Getaway
I'll Be Home for Christmas with Linda Lael Miller, et al.

THRILL ME
TO
DEATH

Roxanne St. Claire

Pocket Books

New York   London   Toronto   Sydney

An *Original* Publication of POCKET BOOKS

 POCKET BOOKS, a division of Simon & Schuster, Inc.
1230 Avenue of the Americas, New York, NY 10020

ISBN-13: 978-1-4165-2185-3
ISBN-10:   1-4165-2185-2

This Pocket Books paperback edition August 2006

10 9 8 7 6 5 4

Cover design by Jae Song
Cover photograph © Holger Scheibe/Zefa/Corbis

Manufactured in the United States of America

For information regarding special discounts for bulk purchases, please contact Simon & Schuster Special Sales at 1-800-456-6798 or businesss@simonandschuster.com.

ACKNOWLEDGMENTS

My heartfelt appreciation to the experts and loved ones who stand behind me:

No man is an island, but if I were, it would be Star Island. Special thanks to the real estate professionals of EWM in south Florida who provided in-depth information about this exclusive address and offered an insider's view of how the other half lives.

Now I know why I spend hours at malls—the terrific people behind the scenes. A grateful thank-you to the public relations team at Simon Property Group, especially the generous individuals who run the Simon Youth Foundation for their quick responses and great work.

My deepest thanks to Osa Mallow, the spa director at the Mandarin in Miami Beach, for going above and beyond the call of duty to return my call just hours before a hurricane evacuation, providing the rich details that helped me bring this world-class destination to life.

Much gratitude to Joe Shepherd, Law Enforcement Investigator for the State of Florida, for offering key facts and reality checks on marine security, investigation, and police procedure in the sunshine state.

My bodyguards Gavin de Becker and Associates, and author Leroy Thompson, who make sure the Bullet Catchers are the real deal—thanks for the guidelines on guarding.

To Micki Nuding, who is simply an editor without equal. Max and Cori would never have come alive without your vision.

To Chris Michocki, who holds my hand, makes me laugh, spreads my good news, and helps me think of creative ways to kill people. You're just a little too good at that.

Lastly, as always, my bone-deep appreciation to the little family of four who surround me with laughter and love. When I go live with the other half on Star Island, I'm taking you with me.

For J., who heals; for Gregg, who inspires; for Deborah, who empathizes; for Jeffrey, who delights. It's an honor to be your little sister, who (still) tells tall tales.

THRILL ME
TO
DEATH

CHAPTER
One

Not much impressed Lucy Sharpe. But when she told Max Roper his next assignment and he didn't even blink, her respect for his famous self-control ratcheted up a notch.

Unless he didn't recognize the name? Perhaps he hadn't kept track of his former lover. Maybe he didn't realize that Corinne Peyton, widowed billionairess, and Cori Cooper, DePaul law student, were one and the same.

Lucy slid a large color photo from a dossier, placing it so that the light caught the gleam in the subject's midnight blue eyes and captured the sheen of her long black hair.

"Here's a photo of Mrs. Peyton," Lucy said, lifting her gaze to gauge his reaction. "Lovely, isn't she?"

He barely nodded. Maybe an eyebrow moved a millimeter, but she couldn't be sure. Anyone would think this was the first time Max Roper had laid eyes on Corinne Peyton. Anyone but Lucy, who made it her business to know everything about every man and woman who'd earned the right to be a Bullet Catcher, her top-notch cadre of bodyguards and security specialists.

"This was taken on the day the Peyton Foundation was launched, shortly after the Peytons were married. Four years ago."

No response.

"The organization is the largest philanthropic endeavor of the multibillion-dollar Peyton Enterprises. Mrs. Peyton was instrumental in creating this foundation with her late husband." She paused long enough for him to look up from the picture. "The Peyton Foundation provides complete financial support and legal services to the families of fallen law enforcement officers."

Nothing. No giveaway pulse in his muscle-roped neck. No change in his carved-from-granite features. Max remained stoic and still, as always. A quality that made him an outstanding bodyguard, but one that rarely endeared him to clients who wanted to know what made this calm giant of a man tick.

She leaned her elbows on the table and repeated her earlier statement. "I'm assigning you to protect Corinne Peyton."

He merely flicked the picture to the side and pulled the rest of the paperwork closer, skimming his fingertip down the key points on the top sheet. He lifted the page and studied a photo of William Peyton, taken on his sixtieth birthday. And another, picturing the mall magnate in his Star Island home on the cover of *Fortune* magazine.

"As you can see by the date, that article ran last year," she added. "Just months before Peyton died, at sixty-three years old."

Again, Lucy paused, waiting for Max to reveal his connection to the widow.

He simply pushed the file aside and leaned back to deliver one seriously disgusted look. "Miami? In August, Luce? Why not just send me to hell?"

She smiled. "Next time, Alaska. I promise."

"That's what you said after Madagascar. Put Jazz and Alex Romero on this. They live there."

"They're on assignment in Helsinki."

He snorted softly. "That lucky bastard."

"You won't melt in Miami, Max." Or *would* he?

He reopened the folder, as though he couldn't resist another look at the man with a shock of white hair and a set of black eyebrows. The man who'd dotted the nation with ultraluxurious shopping complexes and reaped considerable wealth in the process. The man who got everything he wanted out of life . . . including the woman Max loved.

"So, did you know this guy?" Max asked casually. "Is that how the Bullet Catchers got involved?"

"No. This is a referral from Beckworth Insurance. Mrs. Peyton's had a situation recently and asked the insurance company for security recommendations. They put her in touch with me."

"Beckworth?" Max looked up, curious. "Is it a kidnapping threat?"

The Bullet Catchers routinely worked with Beckworth in areas with high incidences of kidnapping, such as South America. "No, but evidently someone tried to kiss her with the fender of a car while she was shopping. On the surface, this is a standard VIP protection."

The crease in his forehead deepened at her pointed tone. "And below the surface?"

She leaned her chin onto her knuckles. "I've spent most of my adult life as a spy, Max. You know that I know you have a history with this woman."

"An ancient history."

She arched one brow. "Ancient enough for you to protect her with your life?"

He met her gaze. "If you ask me to."

"Ancient enough for you to regain her trust?"

"If I had to."

"Ancient enough for you to quietly determine whether or not she killed her husband?"

"What?" He blew out the word. "He died of a heart attack. That's right here on page one of your file."

"That's the *official* report."

Max waited a beat, his expression asking the obvious question: What was the unofficial report?

Lucy pushed her chair back from the Victorian writing table that served as her desk. At the mullioned window that filled one wall of her library, she stared at the Hudson River Valley and the manicured acres of her estate, lushly green from the summer rain.

"No formal investigation is being launched into William Peyton's death. His heart failure was confirmed with an autopsy. But . . ." She turned to look at him. "Beckworth Insurance investigators are not entirely certain. It's very neat, this young woman being handed billions and the power of all her husband's voting shares on Peyton's board of directors. Yes, the autopsy was clean. No one is filing charges and no law enforcement has been notified. But you know how thorough Beckworth is. Since they handle the insurance for the entire Peyton Enterprises, they want the truth, whatever it is."

"She didn't really inherit control of the company," he told her. "Just that Foundation, and I believe it was one billion, not two."

She couldn't resist a wry smile. "So you have been keeping tabs on Cori Cooper."

He glanced at the magazine cover. "I read." His brow furrowed as he gazed at her. "This is no random assignment, Luce. Why me?"

Lucy locked her hands behind her back and looked hard at him. "You bring some critical elements to the party."

A smile threatened. "Other than my boyish charm, they would be?"

"You are a superb bodyguard, you are an excellent interrogator thanks to your years in the DEA, and you have a personal relationship with the principal, making it easier to access private information." He also had charm, in spades. He just didn't dole it out liberally. "I do, however, have one major concern."

He looked at her expectantly.

"Can you leave your emotions out of this, Max?"

His lip twitched and for a moment, she thought he was going to laugh. "You're kidding, right?"

"Unfortunately, I'm not."

"Lucy." He shook his head, a gleam in his chestnut brown eyes. "Of all things to get in my way, emotions would not be one of them."

"I've never given you a responsibility like this, protecting and investigating a person you were involved with."

He stood to a height that dwarfed her own six feet, his face still unreadable except for the tiny scar above his right eyebrow, which paled as he gathered the papers together.

"Not an issue. Considering I just got back from six months in South Africa sucking up to an arms dealer, I'd call babysitting some trophy widow a walk in the park."

"Parks can be deadly places."

He smirked. "Luce, this is Protection and Investigation 101. And I know Cori Cooper: That girl's an open book."

"That *girl* is a very rich woman under a cloud of suspicion for murder."

His eyes shuttered momentarily. "If she's guilty of anything, I'll know it in five minutes." He closed the folder and slid it into a soft-sided leather bag.

"Money—and murder—can change a person," she warned softly.

He crossed the twenty-foot oriental carpet in just a few steps. At the door, he slowly turned back. "Have you considered the possibility that she had nothing to do with her husband's death? That it was a heart attack, pure and simple?"

"Defending her already?" That was the risk in assigning him to the job: He couldn't be objective.

He finally gave her a long, slow smile. "Just considering every possible outcome."

"You do that. And try to stay cool down there."

As he disappeared into the hallway, she could have sworn she heard him laugh softly.

Every Bullet Catcher was tested once in his career. Lord, she hoped that this Rock of Gibraltar, with a mile-wide moat around his heart, could pass his test.

"You know what I hate most about you, Mrs. Corinne Peyton?"

Cori turned to see her closest friend descending three stone steps to the lower lawn, moving in beaded evening pants as gossamer-like as her nickname. "I'm sure the list is long, Breezy, but what is it now?"

"That death becomes you."

Cori drew back, offended. "That's not funny."

"I'm not, for once in my life, going for humor." Breezy slid a well-toned arm around Cori's waist and tugged her closer. "I watched you work that party for the last hour. You manage to exude grace, class, and radiance, with just the appropriate amount of grief and *ennui*."

Cori tilted her head and laughed. "*Ennui?* Now there's a word you don't hear thrown around too often."

Breezy shrugged. "Occupational hazard of being married to a lawyer who likes expensive words."

"Hey, you're lucky to have him," she said softly.

Breezy's whole body softened next to Cori. "You miss your man, sweetie?"

"I do," Cori admitted on a sigh. "Especially on a night like this." She swept a hand toward the uplighting surrounding the tropical estate, the pool, and pavilion area trimmed with stately royal palms and littered with overdressed guests and obsequious waiters. "I turn around and expect to see him wearing that special look he saved just for me."

"I'm going to be sick."

Cori prodded Breezy's ribs. "Did you come out here to abuse me or give me the latest numbers?"

"Neither, but I can do both. We passed two hundred thousand dollars on the last of the silent auction items. Some fool bid twenty-five thousand for a weekend on Lulu Garrey's yacht."

"Really? That's great, Breeze." Cori leaned her head toward Breezy's thin but supportive shoulder. "God, I can't believe how much work you did to pull this fundraiser together. I'd be so lost without you."

"Oh, please. I had fun. My goal was to make it so that all you had to do was slide your sexy self into that eye-popping Valentino, and show up to answer the one question on every collagen-enhanced lip in Miami."

"Which is?"

"Did he really die in the sack?"

Cori tried to laugh. "You know he did. But in his sleep."

He died in his sleep of natural causes.

How many thousands of times in the last three months had she uttered those words? And how many times had a little voice responded in her head: *No, he didn't?*

She turned to Breezy. "What they really want to know is if the trophy wife has turned into a merry widow."

"Screw 'em. You never were a trophy wife." Breezy pulled a cigarette out of her tiny bag and shot a glance toward the house as she lit and inhaled sharply. "Anyway, I came down to tell you that you have a guest."

"I have two hundred of them. Is there one in particular I'm supposed to see right now?"

"This one claims to be your bodyguard." Breezy exhaled, her green eyes tapered by smoke and accusation. "So you really did it, huh?"

"I had to," Cori said. "That little scene up in Bal Harbour convinced me."

Breezy nodded knowingly. She hadn't been shopping with Cori the day a menacing black Jag swiped her so close that the side mirror knocked her handbag to the ground, but she'd shared the postevent trauma.

"Where'd you find this guy?" Breezy asked. "He's smoldering hot."

"The insurance company hooked me up with some high-end security operation, and I requested someone intimidating and visible. I want to send a message to that weasel that I'm not afraid of him." She had deeper reasons than that, but her stepson had unwittingly offered her the perfect excuse to beef up security.

Breezy snorted. "I notice that weasel hasn't made his appearance yet."

"Thank God." The last thing Cori needed on her

first major social outing as the widow of William Peyton was a run-in with the *son* of William Peyton. "After contesting the will, I doubt even he has the audacity to show up tonight."

"If he does, you've got one sizeable stud up there being paid to protect you. Here, he gave me his card." She snuffed her cigarette in a planter and reached back into her bag.

Cori started toward the steps. "I thought he was coming tomorrow, but Marta's already set up the guest house. I'll go talk to him."

"Trust me, it won't be painful."

"No thanks, not interested. I've only been widowed for three months."

"But you haven't been laid in three years. So you might change your mind when you see . . ." Breezy tilted the card toward the light to read it. "Max Roper."

Cori's foot slipped off the limestone step. "What?"

"Executive protection and personal security. Max Roper."

Cori seized the card, the blood draining from her head so fast the letters danced. "No. The universe could not be so cruel and twisted."

At the top of the stairs, a shadow eclipsed the glittering party lights. She didn't have to look and he didn't have to speak.

She knew who it was.

"The universe is most definitely a cruel and twisted place." His sinful baritone rumbled right through her. "You of all people know that, Mrs. Peyton."

She looked up and swayed a little. But that was surely from her high heels sinking in the lawn—not the impact of a man she had loved and hated at the same time.

"What are you doing here, Max?"

"Lucy Sharpe sent me."

"You?" She injected a healthy dose of disgust into the syllable.

"Me." He descended two steps, which did nothing to diminish the sheer size of him. Maximillian P. Roper III was six feet four inches of unforgiving muscle and man. No doubt he made an excellent bodyguard.

But he wouldn't be hers. Never, never, never.

"Cori, do you know this man?" Breezy closed in as though her wispy one-hundred-and-one pounds could actually keep Max Roper at bay.

"We knew each other in Chicago," Max said.

"I knew her in Chicago," Breezy insisted. "I never met you."

Cori cupped Breezy's elbow to urge her away. "I'll talk to him alone, Breeze. Then he'll be leaving."

Max's gaze never wavered from Cori, those hundred-proof eyes refusing to reveal anything as mundane as a *feeling*. A tailored sports jacket covered what she knew to be a Herculean chest, and in that chest pounded a heart that she'd once considered her most treasured possession.

"There must be a mistake," she said. "I arranged for a bodyguard, not a DEA bloodhound."

The corner of his mouth quirked—a full-fledged

grin for Max Roper. He reached out a hand for a formal shake. "I'm here to provide you with unparalleled personal security."

She backed away. Touching a charged lightning rod would be less dangerous than touching Max again. "Let me get this straight. You're one of the Bullet Catchers?"

"Yes."

"And Lucy Sharpe sent *you* to protect *me*?" She shook her head in disbelief.

"Lucy has her reasons and we rarely question them, Mrs. Peyton."

The emphasis on Cori's married name wasn't lost on her. Did he believe what everyone else did: that she'd married an older man for his money, and won the lottery when he died in their bed, leaving her an heiress to a big, juicy estate and a seat in the Peyton Enterprises boardroom?

Surely Max, of all people, knew her better than that. Maybe not, though.

And she wouldn't explain. She stopped caring what Max Roper thought about her a long time ago, and he'd be gone before her party ended. "I'll call Lucy and make other arrangements," she said simply. "Perhaps she doesn't realize we have a—"

"Conflict of interest?"

Is that what he'd call it? The memory of soul-soaring kisses and heart-cracking tears and gut-wrenching accusations flashed in her brain. "That assumes *interest*, Max."

"Still the lawyer, I see."

She jutted her chin defiantly. "I never finished law school, but I can still argue."

"I'll look forward to that." His eyes danced. Curse him.

"Don't bother." She tried to sidestep him. "I'll go call your boss and tell her you're not what I had in mind." Now there was an understatement.

He pulled out a cell phone and held it toward her. "Just press one. It's programmed to Lucy's private line."

She took the phone, regarding him closely for signs of a bluff. He was so very, very good at that.

If he'd spent the last five years chasing evil drug lords, the job hadn't ravaged his handsome face; if anything, he looked better. Older. Wiser. Scarier. His dark hair was just as thick as it had been back in the days when Cori's fingers explored it endlessly, but he'd grown it longer, letting it touch his collar and dip farther over his ominous-looking brow. A brow that still knotted at the sight of her, as though he could never figure her out but refused to stop trying. His strong jaw remained set and unyielding, but she knew how to slacken it. She knew every weak spot on his body.

"Or you could just stare at me."

She narrowed her eyes, pointing the phone at him. "You still think you're a world-class bluffer."

"Anytime you want to play a hand . . ." He leaned an inch closer. "You can find out."

She didn't move. "The last time I bet you, I lost."

He dipped one millimeter closer, blocking all the light behind him and sending a whiff of a familiar, musky scent right down to her toes. "The last time you bet me, I made you come using nothing but a two of diamonds and this." He blew softly on her face, fluttering her bangs. "Wanna bet, Cori Cooper?"

She locked her knees, refusing to give him the satisfaction of a reaction. "I go by Corinne Peyton now."

"So I read in *Town and Country*." At her surprised look, he added, "The clipping was in your file."

"You knew who I was when you accepted this assignment?"

"Of course." He angled his head. "And, by the way, my deepest sympathies on the loss of your husband."

There was no indictment in his voice; none of the veiled resentment at her fortune. Another bluff? Or was that the gentleness he rarely displayed? God, Max could always get her with softness. No matter how big and tough and mean and bad he was, when he turned soft, it killed her.

No, she reminded herself sharply, it killed her *father*.

She opened the skinny silver phone and pressed the TALK button. The screen lit up. "You said press one?"

Max flipped the phone closed. "I'm the best she's got, kid."

She looked up and met his gaze. "I hear the Bullet Catchers are all the cream of the security crop. I'm sure we can find a suitable replacement."

He reached for the phone, but she tugged it toward her chest.

He relented and let her have it. "Before you call, why don't you tell me exactly what your problem is," he suggested. "Then I can help Lucy pick the right bodyguard for you."

The shatter of glass on metal reverberated from the patio. In one split second, Max whirled around, blocked Cori with his massive body and whipped out a handgun.

"I just want to talk to her!" The strident voice echoed across the lawn, loud enough to hush two hundred inquisitive guests who peered at the scene from around the pavilion and on every balcony. "I don't need a fucking invitation to my own father's house."

Oh, God. *Billy.*

"Don't shoot him, Max," Cori said, stepping away from the human wall he'd made. "He's my stepson. And *he* . . ." she added with a definite edge, "is my problem."

Billy Peyton easily pushed past Breezy's ineffective arms and ambled across the lawn, drawing every eye to the luster of his long, platinum blond hair. Cori knew what the cellular buzz from South Beach to Coral Gables would be tomorrow: Billy Peyton was wasted. Not exactly news.

She squared her shoulders, bracing for the worst. She'd become adept at acting like his behavior was normal, a trick she'd used to keep William from getting enraged over his only son's antics. "I'm right here, Billy."

As she took the steps to the upper lawn to meet him, Max was right beside her.

Billy stumbled as he approached her and she reached out to steady him.

"What do you want?" she demanded.

He leaned back and even in the dim party light, she could see his enlarged pupils and pink-rimmed eyes. What was it tonight? Weed? Coke? Ecstasy?

His eyes swept over her. "That's a pretty stupid question, *Mom.*"

Disgust roiled, but she kept her tone modulated. "I received the papers, and my attorney will contact yours. There's nothing else to discuss. Especially not tonight—this is a critical fund-raiser for the Foundation. Please. Do me a favor and leave."

He lowered his head in a bull-like gesture that might have been threatening, if he wasn't just this side of throwing up and his floppy surfer locks didn't ruin the whole effect.

"I don't want to discuss shit and I couldn't give a rat's ass about your Foundation. Where's the bar?"

"It's closed."

"Open it."

"Get out of here," she said through gritted teeth, vaguely aware that Max had moved behind Billy. "Without making a scene."

As he opened his mouth to argue, Max seized him around the neck. Billy tried to lunge, but Max easily overpowered him with his left hand.

In his right, he held up a sleek black gun.

"Holy fuck—" Billy's eyes widened in terror and he jerked again, but Max immobilized every muscle with one squeeze.

"Watch your language around the lady," Max growled, pointing the gun straight up.

"Who the hell are you?" Billy grunted, twisting his head to see Max. "Get your fu—"

Max yanked tighter. "I said, watch your language."

Cori took a step toward them. "I've hired a body-guard, Billy. You're wasting your time threatening me."

He snorted. "You are swimming in delusions of grandeur, Cor. I just want what is mine. Just because you got flat on your back for—"

Max wrenched his neck, maybe a little harder than necessary. "It's time for you to leave, Mr. Peyton."

Fury flashed in Billy's pale blue eyes and he tried to shake his head. "This is my dad's house and I'm—"

Max cocked the gun. "Leaving."

Billy stared at the weapon, sweat beading over his upper lip.

"Is there another way out besides the front?" Max asked Cori.

She indicated the north lawn. "You can take him around the guest house."

Billy glared at her, his dilated pupils sparking with hatred. "Whore." He mouthed the word at her so Max didn't hear it.

"He shouldn't drive," she said quietly. "I'll meet you in the front and get a car and driver."

"No need. I'll take care of him," Max said, walking away with Billy tightly in his grasp. "Billy and I are going to have a talk."

She watched them disappear into the shadows, still able to hear Billy's protests and Max's low, single sylla-ble responses. Ironically, there was a certain comfort in the idea of Max Roper responsible for her life. After all, he owed her. Big.

But he couldn't stay. Aside from the fact that they had combustible chemistry, the real problem was that she'd never, ever been able to hide anything from him. And if he found out what she was trying to do, he'd try to stop her. He'd tell her she was crazy, stupid, and wrong, and then he'd wave the autopsy report in her face just like the police had done.

William died in his sleep of natural causes.

Until she discovered what—or who—killed her husband, she wasn't safe. She needed a bodyguard . . . but she didn't need *that* one.

Breezy appeared with two glasses of champagne and a sly smile. "Well, I'd say you made the right call on the whole bodyguard thing."

Cori reached for a flute. "Oh, I still have his cell phone."

"How clever of you." Breezy chuckled and raised her drink in a mock toast. "That guarantees he'll be back, even if you do get someone else for the job." She took a sip and winked. "Which, we both know, you won't."

CHAPTER
Two

Some idiots had all the money and none of the brains.

Max definitely put Billy Peyton in that category, especially once the worm confirmed it by whimpering at the sight of a gun, and then puking his guts out on the side of the causeway. But even before that, Max had recognized subpar intelligence when he'd taken Billy's keys and opened the door of a Lamborghini Gallardo. Only a moron would drop two hundred grand for a toy that could best be described as cute.

All right, it was fast.

Whipping the yellow sports car through the streets of Coconut Grove, Max congratulated himself on resisting the urge to let Billy Peyton drive his face into a tree. Or even better, letting him flip the cute little car over the bridge and into Biscayne Bay. Although that would have made the world a better place, it might also have left Corinne Peyton without the need for a bodyguard.

Billy managed to get his window down and hang his head out, moaning softly. Hot, moist wind gusted through the car, defeating the air conditioner, but Billy needed fresh air or he'd blow again.

"So why do you hate her?" Max asked, raising his voice above the growl of the engine and whine of the wind.

Billy ran his fingers through his unkempt mop, holding his head up enough to look at Max. "Because she's full of shit and wants me dead."

"Looks to me like it's the other way around."

He grunted and let his head fall back. "I hate to break it to you, dude, but you're babysitting a conniving, gold-digging whore."

Max twisted the knob to jack up the air-conditioning. "Oldest story in the book, huh, Billy? Rich old man, hot young babe."

"He wasn't that old. And she isn't that . . . well, yeah, she is." He closed his eyes in disgust. "She's no dumbshit, that's for sure. She blew into town and picked the richest, loneliest, most vulnerable man she could find."

Could they possibly be talking about the same woman? "First of all, she didn't *blow into town* and *pick* a rich, vulnerable guy, Billy. She met your father at De-Paul Law School and didn't move here until after she married him."

"How do you know?"

"I have a file on her." Of course, he knew this long before he read that file. He'd made it his business to find out what had happened to Cori Cooper after he got back from purgatory in the Caribbean.

Billy's lips curled in a snide grimace. "Did your file say how she fucked him blind, deaf, and dumb until he gave her everything she wanted?"

Max's stomach lurched and he blamed it on Billy's breath. Could she really have transformed from Cori Cooper, budding public defender, to Corinne Peyton, trust-fund trophy wife? Could she really have gotten over him *that* fast?

That reminded him of his real reason for being assigned her bodyguard. Billy, regardless of the fact that he was half-toasted and smelled like vomit, might have some valuable information.

"You gotta get over it, Billy," he said conversationally, just like two guys driving home from party night. "It's no crime for your father to fall in love and marry."

"The crime," Billy said, his voice suddenly lucid, "was when she got him to change his will while he was crippled with a boner for her."

Been there, had that boner. But Cori, as gorgeous as she was, had never *used* her appeal to get what she wanted. Her wits, her humor, her incredible powers of persuasion, absolutely. He'd been on the receiving end more than once and had predicted she'd make a formidable attorney. But she never was a woman to use her sexuality to achieve an end. At least, she hadn't been five years ago.

"Still," he said, keeping up the casual tone, "being hot is not a crime."

"Killing him was."

Max yanked the steering wheel to the left and accelerated around a slow-moving Lexus.

"He died of a heart embolism," Max said. "Last time I checked, that wasn't considered murder."

"My father was in great shape. He had a physical a couple of weeks before he died."

This might be easier than he expected. "So what are you saying, Billy? How did she kill him?"

"I don't fucking know. Maybe he just died of a blow job that *gave* him a heart attack," Billy spat. "All I know is she knocked off my old man and got a couple billion for her services."

Max's fingers itched for the Ruger that lay on his lap, but Billy could be a star witness someday.

"What's the deal on the lawsuit? You questioning the validity of the will or just trying to scare her?"

Billy clunked his head against the head rest. "She doesn't scare."

"Then why would she hire a bodyguard?"

"Probably because Breezy told her to. She does everything that twat and her old man the lawyer tell her to."

Max tucked that information away and stayed focused on the interrogation Billy had no idea he was participating in. "You've filed your lawsuit. Why are you trying to hurt her, too?"

"I'm not trying to hurt her."

"She thinks you are."

"Ah, man." Billy lolled his head farther out the window. "I'm gonna puke."

Max made the turn into the Grove Isle condominium and Billy suddenly sat up straight. "How the hell do you know where I live?"

"I know everything, Billy." Picking up the Ruger, Max pointed it right at the bridge of Billy's nose. "I'll hang on to your car until you're sober. You stay away from Corinne Peyton."

Billy pushed himself out of the door and barely made it to the sidewalk before Max threw the Gallardo into gear and left Cori's stepson in the dark.

For what must have been the twentieth time in the hour since Max left, Cori flipped open Max's phone but couldn't bring herself to press that button. She leaned against the stone balustrade that enclosed the second-floor terrace outside her bedroom and watched the caterers pack up the bar and fold tables, as she imagined what she'd say to Lucy Sharpe.

I'm afraid there's been a . . .

A miscommunication? A mistake? A nightmare?

We'll need to change your staffing selections.

Not only would she sound like a fool, she'd feel like a baby.

What difference did it make if Max Roper was her bodyguard? He was big, tough, smart, and mean. In four minutes he'd done what she hadn't been able to do in four years—shut Billy up.

So what if the sight of him still sent heat lightning through her body? She was paying for a service, and he was—as he so humbly noted—the best there was. She could control a little sexual zing.

Couldn't she?

She closed the phone, and breathed deeply. She'd just have to keep Max far enough away so he didn't figure out what she was doing, but close enough to keep her safe if someone else did.

Was that possible? To keep Max away?

It never had been before.

A movement on the north lawn caught her attention; the caterers had finished that section and the lights had been dimmed. But something in the shadows brushed a tree branch, then stopped, sending a heat prickle over the back of her neck.

Max.

It was as if he emitted some cosmic body-zapping signal that shot *awareness* through her veins.

He emerged from the darkness of the trees and paused in the fountain's light, taking in her house with a steady gaze. He'd abandoned his jacket, stripped down to a black fitted shirt and dark trousers. Even from this distance, he looked imposing.

She stepped back into the darkness of the overhang and his gaze locked on her. She wore white, so she'd be easy to find. But even if she'd changed into cat burglar's clothes, that man could zero in on her.

He ate up the limestone with long, silent strides, approaching the spiral steps that led up to her terrace.

She reopened the cell phone and stared at the keypad.

He'd be up those stairs in less than ten seconds. She could have Lucy Sharpe on the phone by the time he rounded the top step.

She heard the scrape of his shoe on the stone stair. Five seconds.

Lucy's phone could be ringing before she had to hear his voice again.

"Cori?"

Her finger froze on the keypad and she snapped the phone closed as he hit the top step, his movements remarkably graceful for someone of his size.

"I'm right here."

He walked across the terrace, and suddenly her fifteen-thousand-square-foot mansion seemed like a dollhouse. It wasn't just his height or solid, muscular build. His presence, his very essence minimized everything around him.

"Looks like Billy brought your party to a screeching halt after all," he said.

"That's all right. It was a success." In heels, she grazed five feet nine, but she still had to lift her chin to meet his gaze. "What did you do with him?"

"Of all my options, letting him plunge his Hot Wheels into the bay was my favorite."

He was bluffing again. "Did you take him home to Coconut Grove?" At his slight nod, she murmured, "Thank you."

"Just doing my job." His gaze dropped to the phone in her hand. "That is, unless Lucy's already dispatched my replacement."

"I didn't call." Even in the darkness she saw a glint in his eyes. "Yet."

"It's entirely up to you," he said, sliding his hands into his trouser pockets and pulling her attention to the ominous gun he wore at his hip. It looked completely at home on that body built for danger and violence. And sex. Lord, he was certainly built for that.

"I just want to be safe, Max."

"That's why I'm here."

"Yeah, right."

He shrugged as if he couldn't care less if she believed him. "If you want to be safe, then the first thing you need to do is fire that valet service."

"I've used them for years."

He moved closer, his scent drifting toward her. "And you can add more cameras along the front walkway." He crossed his arms over his mighty chest and glanced toward the grounds. "The trees are effectively blocking the house, but they also make great coverage for an intruder."

"The entire property is gated."

He started to circle, slowly, around her left. "Your security system hasn't been updated since your husband died. Tomorrow morning, we'll install a—"

"Stop it." She held her hands up.

"If you want to be safe, you need to make some changes." In one more step, he trapped her with that unrelenting gaze and that enormous body.

"I mean stop cornering me." She sidestepped him, with a little more force than she needed. "Do whatever you need to do to make the property safer."

"Then I'll be staying." It was a statement.

If she made him leave, he'd know he still had power over her. He'd have the satisfaction of knowing he still made her weak with desire—even after she'd sworn she hated him, and he'd agreed she should.

"You can stay." She held the cell phone out to him,

and managed to stay cool when their fingertips burned. "For the next several weeks, I'll be focused on a single project and I don't want Billy anywhere near me."

"What project?" he asked.

"The Peyton Foundation. We're launching new programs and it's time consuming."

She'd set up the Foundation so well, the programs could launch themselves, but it made the perfect cover for what she really needed to do. Besides, no one on the board would let her near any Peyton project that impacted the bottom line. "You don't need to know details."

"I need to know everything." He regarded her just one second too long, one drawn-out beat that sent tingly warmth through her. "Including where you'll be, what you're doing, and who you're doing it with."

"I work from home, I work on Peyton business, and I work by myself or through a network of people at various Peyton locations. Sometimes I go into the corporate office in Miami. That's when I'll need you, or if I attend a social function. But please be unobtrusive."

He almost laughed. "That's a little contrary to the idea of a bodyguard."

Leveling her gaze, she said, "I just mean I'd really prefer you keep your distance."

Then he did laugh, that soft chuckle that came from his chest. He held the phone toward her, a challenge lighting gold flecks in his eyes. "Just press one, kid, and end your misery."

"You're not the cause of my misery, Max," she told him. Not anymore, anyway.

He slid the phone back into his pocket, his attention still locked on her with that quizzical scrutiny that used to make her nerve endings sizzle. Yeah, this would be a whole different kind of *misery*.

"You've changed a lot," he commented.

She lifted a shoulder. "It's been five years. I'm older and different."

"You're reserved and tense."

"I have a lot of responsibility now."

"Was it the money?"

The *money*? "The money's meaningless without my husband."

She saw the reaction in his eyes, but he turned away into the darkness so quickly she couldn't analyze it. "I'm going to examine the security liabilities on the property."

"Now?" The thought of him creeping through the shadows of her property in the middle of the night sent a little shudder through her.

"It's best at night. That's why I arrived at this hour. I can see the place exactly as an intruder would and find the problems that we need to correct tomorrow."

"I doubt you'll find much. William was a cautious man." Not cautious enough, but she wasn't willing to show her hand to Max.

"I don't think it's all that safe," he replied. "I got in here twice in one night without telling anyone my name. The first time I climbed a fence and didn't so much as snag a thread. The second time I dangled the keys to an Italian sports car in front of a teenage valet and he never saw me walk through the open gate."

Resentment straightened her spine. "Tonight might have been an exception because there were a lot of people coming and going—"

"Precisely when you should be most vigilant."

He was right. "Whatever. Do what you need to do." She indicated the guest house with one hand. "My housekeeper, Marta, has prepared the guest house for you. It's unlocked so—"

"So someone could be waiting in it right now, in ambush."

She blew out a breath, feathering her bangs. "Then you shoot him, Max. That's what I'm paying you to do. If no one is hiding in there, then make yourself comfortable. I'm going to bed."

She turned toward her bedroom doors, but froze when his hand landed on her bare shoulder.

"I need you."

Heat pooled low in her stomach, but she didn't turn, and didn't trust herself to speak.

He inched her toward the bedroom. "Go change into something you can walk around in without tripping, and I'll give you a lesson in threat assessment."

She stood stone still. "I know enough about threat assessment." She looked down at her shoulder, where his hand touched her flesh, then into his eyes. "My father was a DEA agent—or did you forget?"

His expression softened, barely perceptible except to someone who knew him intimately. "I'll be waiting on the patio," he simply said. "Unless you're afraid."

She closed her eyes and silently cursed him. "Give me five minutes."

CHAPTER
Three

"You need more dead ground." Max slowed to let Cori catch up, drinking in the way her dark jersey clothes clung to the enticing curves of her long, lean body. Yoga clothes, he'd bet. He'd protected plenty of women who wore the stretchy knit to find their bliss.

Just looking at her was enough bliss for him.

He'd sworn he wouldn't touch, but he could still feel the gloss of her skin where he'd held her shoulder.

And not even the tropical forest that surrounded her home could erase the soft, feminine scent of her. Taking a deep breath of it, he pointed toward a cluster of trees. "To get dead ground, you'll have to uproot at least a dozen of those things."

"Are you out of your mind? Those live oaks have survived hurricanes and the most zealous developers. They've been around since Al Capone lived on this island."

He snorted. "Al Capone, of all people, would appreciate the importance of dead ground. As would any of the others on your block."

The fact that Cori lived in an ultraexclusive enclave made his job easier for the most part, but the high-profile residents also attracted their share of idiots who cruised the water hoping for a glimpse of a rock star or TV personality.

"Believe me, they all have top-level security," she assured him.

"I know how they live." Behind walls and mired in security cameras. "As far as lighting, yours is all wrong. It looks real pretty, but there are too many shadows on the house. You want to silhouette anyone nearing the structure at night. But you've picked a good color with that pale yellow on the house."

"William and I chose it for aesthetics, not security," she admitted.

William and I. An unwanted image of her sitting cozy with her husband, mulling over paint chips and sofa fabrics, flashed in his head. He punched the mental picture away and pointed to the hibiscus bushes lining the property, in front of the six-foot wall. "All along there, you need infrared cameras. They're very unobtrusive and state of the art. It's not up for debate."

She placed her hands on narrow hips and glanced around as though she were looking at her lawns for the first time. "I guess you're right." Without the trappings of jewels and an evening gown, she looked much more like the fresh, appealing law school student she'd been when they first met.

"Of course I am," he said, hoping a gruff tone covered

the little punch in his belly. "If you want to be safe, you make some compromises to your lifestyle."

She looked sharply at him. "We—William did that. But digging up trees and adding cameras seems like a wasted effort. . . ." Her voice trailed off. "Because Billy can always get in."

"We'll change that. The island guards should never give him access to your home."

"He'll find a way around that, but, yes, I'll revise the admission list. At least they'll have to call the house before letting him in."

She started toward a long, wide cement dock, secured by a wrought-iron gate topped with spiked tips and chain locked. A one-room, glass-enclosed cabana sat on one corner. A top-of-the-line cabin cruiser, forty or fifty feet long, bobbed in the water on the other side of the dock. In the moonlight, he could read *Peyton's Place* across the wide-beamed stern.

"Nothing like advertising who's on board," he said, indicating the name with a jut of his chin. "You may want to change the name of your boat."

He'd never understood the ego of men who had to advertise themselves with vanity plates and yachts named after themselves. Didn't they see the security risks?

"Not necessary; it'll be gone in the next few weeks. I just sold it," she responded.

Max gave the gate a hard shake. "This isn't much more than a decorative fence. You have cameras pointed here?"

"No. But this is kept secure at all times." She dialed a code into a keypad. "I come down here once in a while, and my housekeeper cleans the cabana. The only other people who have access to the dock is the boat maintenance service who come by periodically."

He glanced at the boat, which not only screamed the owner's name, but could be fairly easily accessed from the water.

"I hope you never come down here at night, alone," he said. "That boat is a hiding place for anyone who might want to attack, and there's no cover on any of the cabana windows. With a light on in there, you're a target to a wide open bay."

She pushed the gate open. "Star Island Security motors by here regulary, but I promise to be careful. The island isn't very big, as I'm sure you've noticed. There's only one entrance, and the guard gate is vigilant."

Rubbing his jaw, he scrutinized the area—another upscale island and the sparkling lights of Miami to the west, and the golden glow of Miami Beach's nightlife to the east. He stepped around to the edge of the dock and looked into the water below. "No underwater lighting?"

"I understand you are doing your job and I appreciate it," she said. "I'll get rid of the boat, fix the gate, and order window treatments for the cabana. But Billy isn't going to scuba dive in for a Navy SEAL attack. He's not that smart."

"But he might be that desperate." Max walked to the end of the dock, then turned to look at the back of her imposing house. There must have been twenty rooms lining the two levels that wrapped in a U shape around the pool. A dozen archways, and at least forty decorative columns.

He couldn't imagine anything about the fiery, feisty law student he'd met in Chicago that indicated she wanted this life. She wanted to help the helpless, beat the man, argue the system. After a lifetime with a mother who'd bounded from husband to husband, and movie set to movie set, she'd wanted the opposite of glitz and glamour.

Hell, she'd been planning a life as the wife of a DEA agent.

But then, people changed. And no one knew what went on behind closed doors—unless those doors were glass. He tugged at the slider to check the lock and looked at her. "So what exactly does your stepson want from you?" he asked.

She leaned against the stucco frame of the cabana. "His lawsuit is asking for a hundred million dollars."

His surprised exhale left a circle of white on the glass. "Jesus. A small percentage of that would buy him someone who is more than able to dive in for a Navy SEAL attack." He looked back at the deep, dark water. "That's quite a price to have on your head."

"He doesn't get it if I die."

"Then why would he try to hurt you?"

She walked to the other side of the dock, a soft breeze lifting her hair as she moved. "I stopped trying to figure Billy Peyton out a long time ago. And so did his father."

Max stepped close enough to grab her in an instant if he had to. "You know, Billy has a theory," he said quietly. "He thinks you killed his father."

She looked at him, a quick flash in her eyes. "Billy's

an insecure drug addict who's been handed everything he ever wanted in life. He resented my relationship with his father and his happiest moment is to see me publicly humiliated and miserable."

"Did you ever consider the possibility that your husband's death wasn't entirely natural?"

Even in the moonlight, he could see the blood drain from her face. "I consider everything," she assured him. "Which is why you are here."

He was there to find out if she killed her husband. And all he knew so far was that Cori Cooper had morphed into an uptight socialite who was working very hard to hide something from him. He'd find out what it was; he knew a million ways to get information.

With Cori, a million and one.

And he wasn't above using any of them to find out what he wanted to know. No matter how bad . . . or good . . . it made her feel.

Max hadn't expected voices on his patio so early the next morning. Emerging from the shower, he heard a woman's high-pitched tone—definitely not Cori—and a low, monotone response from a man. Staff? House-guests she hadn't mentioned?

Rubbing a towel over himself, he yanked on boxers and trousers, stuffed his bare feet into shoes, and stashed his gun in his waistband. Screw the shirt for now. It was two hundred degrees, with enough humidity to grow fungus in his ears.

On the patio, he heard determined high heels click across the stone in his direction. Cori didn't walk that way, she didn't move that aggressively and he'd bet fifty bucks she didn't wear high heels at seven in the morning. At least, she didn't used to.

Plus he always knew when she was near.

Just as he entered the main room, he saw the shadow on the other side of the glass and watched the handle of the door turn. He had his weapon ready as the door opened.

Pale green eyes flashed in horror as she held up both hands and shrieked. "Don't kill me!"

"Don't break and enter," he said, putting the safety back on but keeping his attention on the silhouette of a petite woman with the morning sun at her back.

She slapped one hand on a tiny hip and tilted her very blond head to one side. "I didn't break and enter. Try *locking* next time."

"Try knocking next time." He swept her with a quick look. "I don't lock doors—that way I can get to my principal faster."

That earned him a provocative smile, accompanied by an unabashed inspection of his bare chest. "I'll have to remember that." She held out her hand and managed to migrate that smile from sexy to friendly. "We met last night."

"Ms. Jones, correct?" Her grip was firm, with bones as narrow and delicate as she was—on the outside, at least. Something in her expression told Max she was steel on the inside.

"Everyone calls me Breezy. I wasn't sure you'd remember, what with having to take down Billy and all."

"I took him home, not down." He let her hand go before she did. "Were you looking for me?"

Her gaze dropped over his torso again, pausing just a nanosecond too long before meandering back up to his face. "Did you hurt him?" she asked with a twinkle in her eyes.

"He hurt me. I had to watch him throw up on the MacArthur Causeway."

Her sharp, birdlike features dissolved into repugnance. "Ewww. Good thing you got him out of here." Then she laughed, and looked at him like she expected a comeback.

He merely stared at her.

"So. Max." She laughed again, a little self-consciously, and tucked a lock of hair behind her ear as she perched on the edge of a sofa. "Tell me about you and Cori. She seemed a bit uneasy when you showed up."

"I didn't realize you were on the interview committee."

She jutted her chin and met his gaze. "Even better. I'm the best friend."

"Then ask your best friend." He looked pointedly at the door, then back at his guest.

"She's not saying much today. Of course, she's in the jungle, counting money with my husband." Breezy arched one perfectly waxed eyebrow. "If you're going to be her bodyguard, you better get a handle on her daily schedule and a map of the manor, big guy."

He remained rooted, staring down at her. Breezy

Jones could be a fountain of information and she certainly looked ready to spout. And not the least bit intimidated by the way he towered above her.

"Is counting money the first thing she does every morning?" He dropped into the chair across from her, hoping the height equality would get her to stop flirting and start talking.

"When you have that much, you gotta keep track of it or people will take it when you're not paying attention. Gifford helps her count it." A devilish grin played at the corners of a well-glossed mouth. "I help her spend it."

He leaned his elbows on his knees, relaxing his face into a look he used to get scumbag drug dealers to trust him. "Ms. Jones, do you—"

"It's *Mrs.* Jones." She inched forward, just enough to let her pale yellow sweater drape at her cleavage. "Like the song. You know, the one about adultery?" She punctuated that with a wink. "But I really prefer to be called Breezy."

"Breezy." He nodded. "In order to ensure complete protection of Mrs. Peyton, I'll need to know about any and all threats to her. I understand that a few weeks ago someone tried to hit her in a parking lot."

Breezy wrinkled her flawless nose. "Billy's an asshole. Excuse my French."

He angled his head in agreement. "Can you think of anyone else who might want to hurt her?"

The twinkle disappeared, replaced by warmth and admiration. "Nope. Everyone loves Corinne Peyton."

"What about her husband?"

Her eyes widened. "What about him?"

"Did he have any enemies?"

She leaned back, tugging a little bag from her shoulder onto her lap and flipping open the top. "Can I smoke?"

"Sure." Smokers were talkers. He'd learned that his first year with the DEA. While she lit up, he rose to get a glass in the kitchen and filled it with an inch of water. He set the makeshift ashtray on the coffee table in front of her, and sat down.

She shivered and rubbed a bare arm. "It's cold in here."

"I like it that way."

She puffed again, regarding him. "You're not from around here, are you? Chicago, did Cori say?"

"I'm from Pittsburgh," he said, noting that she made the same face that she had for Billy's causeway dinner toss. "I live there when I'm not on assignment."

"Really?" She held the cigarette to her right in a vain attempt to keep the smoke from going into his eyes. "Have you ever killed anyone?"

"You were about to tell me about Mr. Peyton's enemies."

"I bet you have. Killed someone, I mean." She sucked in another puff, squinting at him as she blew out a cloud of gray smoke. "I'll have to ask Cori. She'd know, wouldn't she?"

"You can ask."

"No, William didn't have any enemies, either." She waved some smoke away. "Why do you ask?"

"None? A multibillionaire who orchestrated massive land deals and reshaped the landscape of suburban America? No one disliked him?"

"Nope." She flicked an ash into the glass and crossed long, thin legs clad in more yellow. "William Peyton was the nicest guy in the universe. Well, he has an ex-wife who might disagree, but she's in Dallas or Houston, with enough money to stay real quiet."

"Were they married when Mr. Peyton met Cor— the current Mrs. Peyton?"

She barked a surprised laugh. "Are you asking if Cori broke up their marriage? Not a chance. William was well and truly divorced. I know that because Gifford handled the settlement." She smiled with pride. "My husband was William's personal attorney then, and I introduced William to Cori at a party. They played 'That's What Friends Are For' at their wedding and I danced with both of them. It was sweet."

He templed his fingers and rested his chin on them. "And what about their marriage? Pretty remarkable age difference, don't you think?"

"Not in my circles." She popped off the sofa, picked up the water glass and dropped her cigarette in, the hiss matching the look in her bright green eyes. "You'd be amazed at how the years disappear when there are billions of dollars in the air."

"So, Cori married William for his money?"

She set the glass on the table with nearly enough force to break it, the humor disappearing from her expression as she transformed into a tigress protecting a cub. "That woman loved William fiercely, much more than anyone realizes. She adored her husband and was devastated by his death."

She leaned back on her high heels, jutting a bony hip in his direction and staring down her manmade nose. "Her only problem is that drug addict stepson, believe me. You should make him disappear. That's what you were hired to do, not ask intrusive and inappropriate questions about the state of her marriage."

He stood, opening the French doors in a silent invitation for her to leave. "Thank you for your candor, Mrs. Jones."

She whipped the gold chain of her handbag over her shoulder and followed him across the living room. At the doorway, she slid between him and the doorjamb, so close he had to suck in a breath to prevent her breasts from brushing his chest.

She looked up at him. "You're quite welcome. As you can see, I don't mince words and I don't care who I impress or piss off."

"Yes, I see."

"You don't scare me, big bodyguard." She still didn't move away, but her gaze became more curious than accusing. "But my rock-steady friend sure lost her balance at the sight of you."

"I have that effect on some people."

She raked his bare chest with a slow gaze. "I bet you do." Smiling, she clattered away on her gold spikes, leaving him to wonder about Cori's taste in husbands *and* friends.

CHAPTER
Four

"Take a deep breath, Corinne. Calm down and listen to me."

"I am calm, Giff." Cori lifted her bare feet from the silken fur of a snow leopard that had the misfortune to become an area rug, and tucked them under her on the butter-soft leather sofa.

Cori hated the animal prints, loathed the dead-cat carpet, and particularly disliked the dark hickory paneling of the room her designer had called "a walk on the wild side." But William had found the African theme soothing and masculine and she hadn't had the heart to change his sanctuary.

"I can tell you're upset," Gifford said, dropping his elbows to the desk he'd covered with an array of documents and folders. He peered over rimless reading glasses, a deep crease dividing his forehead clear back to the balding patch that Breezy liked to rub. "You're just like my wife, you know. Breezy's voice gets higher and higher when she's frustrated."

Damn it, she wasn't whining. "I'm nothing like Breezy, and you know it."

"You're right, my dear. You are your own woman." His brief smile was annoyingly patronizing.

"And I am a board member, a shareholder, and a very interested party where Peyton Enterprises is concerned."

He fly-swatted the air. "The last thing you need is to go to a board meeting where nothing of any consequence is going to happen."

"The status on the Petaluma Mall in Sonoma County is of consequence," she argued.

Giff lifted a pack of documents and tapped them on William's beloved hickory desk to straighten them. "Not to worry. I'll vote your proxy. I know exactly how William wanted to proceed on that property."

"That's pretty remarkable, considering William and I had precisely one conversation about the property and he wasn't sure which way to go."

Giff sliced her with a look that had silenced judges, juries, and a few witnesses. "We talked about it," he said simply.

"I'm not willing to give you my proxy on the fly, Giff. I need to study the reports and talk to the directors before I vote. This is a controversial property in a high-profile community."

"Petaluma is not high profile."

"Wine country is."

Gifford inhaled the deep breath he'd been advising Cori to take, his ruddy complexion darkening. "You don't need to vote. That's why I'm here. That's why you gave me power of attorney. You are far too busy with the Foundation to worry about the business, which practically runs itself."

Even on a good day, Peyton Enterprises didn't run itself. She knew that from long, candid cocktail hours with William. "I don't need to exercise the power of attorney now. That was just for last quarter's board meeting." It had taken place just days after William's death and Cori had been in a fog of grief and shock. "But I'm ready now. There's a great deal at stake with this mall."

"Millions."

"I was thinking of William's reputation."

Gifford nodded thoughtfully. "And so you should. Which is why you should put every ounce of your energy into the Foundation." Removing his glasses, he stood and circled the desk, moving toward her with a slow, confident stride that he'd perfected in his years of litigation. "Malls will be built. Stores will open. People will shop." He continued past the sofa, behind her, building drama with his voice. "But only you can help those families who suffer and grieve because they've lost their brother or son . . . or a *father*."

God, he was good. Well into his fifties, he could not only swim with the sharks but spear them when they least expected it. No wonder William plucked him out of the courtroom and set him up as the lead attorney for Peyton Enterprises. William had been a consummate talent-spotter, and Gifford was oozing with legal skill.

Cori leaned her head back, closing her eyes. "I am giving the Foundation all my energy, believe me.

But . . ." She ached to confide in him, but something, some sixth sense she didn't understand, stopped her. She didn't have enough information or facts to make a case, and Gifford would demand them. As he should.

Gifford's thin fingers suddenly pressed against the tense muscle that ran between her shoulder and neck. Cori's eyes opened in surprise, but he merely kneaded with the gentle touch of a concerned uncle.

"William had his reasons and we can't question them now, Corinne. He loved you and he trusted you."

She gave into the comfort of a friend who also loved her husband, patting his hand. "He loved you, too, Giff."

"Then we can't let him down. Let me handle the business complications, and you focus on the Foundation."

She didn't answer and she sensed him dipping closer to her. Ever the actor, going for the dramatic impact.

"This is what he'd want," Gifford said softly in her ear. "I know that."

The sound of a throat clearing jerked Cori to attention, and Gifford whipped his hands away.

"Who are you?" Gifford demanded.

Max filled the doorway of the library, his golden brown eyes rich with misgiving, his V-shaped athletic body braced in accusation.

"Excuse me," he said, looking from one to the other. "I'm starting a security analysis of the residence and the housekeeper told me Mrs. Peyton was in a meeting that could be interrupted."

Cori stood, not even wanting to imagine how that

scene looked to Max. "Gifford Jones, this is Max Roper, who has been retained as my personal bodyguard."

"Oh." Gifford brightened and came around the sofa, hand extended. "My wife mentioned meeting you last night. Welcome to the Peyton team, Mr. Roper."

They shook hands, studying each other.

"You must have played some football in your day," Gifford said with a laugh, pounding one of Max's shoulders. "Linebacker? Defensive end?"

"I played a little."

A *little?* Cori opened her mouth, then closed it as Max quieted her with a glance. Of course, neither one should reveal that they'd known each other in the past.

"I didn't realize there was such a thing as a Peyton team," Max said.

Cori circled to the other side of William's desk, separating herself from the men. "Gifford is the chief attorney for Peyton Enterprises. My husband liked to think of the whole company as a team and the phrase has stuck."

"And how did you land this plum job, Mr. Roper?" Gifford asked, still eyeing the bigger man with admiration. "Must be a coup for a bodyguard to get to spend time with a beautiful woman in a luxurious waterfront estate."

Max cut him with one disgusted look. "I view every principal I protect the same. And as high-end as the house is, it's full of security holes, which I intend to fix."

Gifford frowned and looked at Cori. "I take it he came on a referral."

"From Beckworth Insurance."

"Beckworth?" Gifford pulled back. "Why would you go to them? Why didn't you ask me?"

She bristled at the question. "Giff, William has been dead for three months. I appreciate your concern, but you don't have to make every decision for me anymore." She closed her eyes, corralling her anger. "Beckworth specializes in protection and security. It made perfect sense to contact them."

If Giff was irritated by her chastisement, he was too professional to show it. Instead, he turned to Max. "So you work for Beckworth? Good man, Thomas Matuzak."

"He is, but I don't work for him. I'm with a private firm. Beckworth refers security business to us." Max reached into his pocket and handed Gifford a card.

"Max comes thoroughly vetted and referenced, Gifford. We'll hardly know he is here." She shot Max a deliberate look. She didn't want Giff to start poking into Max's background and find he'd been a DEA agent in Chicago at the time of her father's death. It wouldn't take one of his legal investigators long to connect point A to point B. "He is going to upgrade the security, and accompany me in public. Keep Billy in line until we get through this business with the will."

Gifford nodded, studying the card. Then he slipped it into his pocket and gave Max a tight smile. "I've no doubt you could keep anyone in line." He stepped to the desk, picked up his glasses and began to slide his files together. "Now you remember what we decided, Cori. I'll call you after the board meeting tomorrow with a full report, and you keep your focus where it belongs."

They hadn't *decided* anything, but she wasn't about to fight him with Max's unwavering eyes taking in every detail of the exchange. "I'll be in touch, Giff. Is Breezy still here?"

"I'm right here, darling." Breezy swept into the room, as bright as the buttercup St. John knit that clung to her tiny frame. "I was just coming in to break up your business meeting. Gifford, my love . . ." She glided to her husband and threw her arms around him with enough force to flutter the papers on the nearby desk, kissing his cheek noisily. "Go to work and make scads of money." She nudged him toward the door and pointed at Cori. "You, woman, are going for the super-deluxe-ultra-overpriced fabulous day package at the Mandarin Oriental Spa *avec moi*. And you," she turned to Max and fluttered one of her hands like a bird, "go stand at the gate like a gladiator and step on Billy if he shows up."

Cori stifled a laugh, watching little Breezy wave at big Max. "I'm not going to the spa, Breeze. I have too much work to do."

Breezy's face melted in disappointment and she looked accusingly at her husband, who was stuffing papers into his briefcase. "I told you to free her up, Giff, not bog her down. I need my gal pal."

"She's got a mind of her own, as she likes to remind me," Gifford said with a wry smile, closing his briefcase over the papers. "And I need to get to a meeting. Max, good to meet you."

When he left, Breezy slapped both hands on the desk, staring at Cori and jutting her rear end out just inches from where Max stood.

"If you stay in here and work when I have set up a full treatment for us at the Mandarin, I will make you suffer so badly that your very own bodyguard won't be able to protect you."

Cori laughed. "He's going to work on the security of the house, and I'm going to work on the Foundation launch. And Swen will work on you. Give him my best."

Breezy let out a moan. "I hate you, Corinne Peyton."

"So you've said."

Standing straight, she tossed her hair over her shoulder and grinned at Max. "But I do like Swen."

Cori saw the light in his eyes and knew he was on the brink of smiling. No one was immune to Breezy's charm. Knowing what it took to coax a smile from Max, she swiped at a bubble of jealousy that floated around her chest. "Tell Swen I'll be in for a full treatment very soon."

Breezy waved over her shoulder. "Yeah, yeah. He could be deported back to Finland at any minute, then you'll be sorry you missed the magic hands."

When she left, the room felt empty.

"She makes me laugh," Cori said, watching the sunshine yellow disappear.

Max leaned on the edge of William's desk and regarded her. "She certainly stood up for you."

"She did? When?"

"When she broke into the guest house and interrogated me."

"*She* interrogated *you*? Why am I having trouble believing that? You could make a waitress confess her sins before she even took your order."

His eyes crinkled in a smile, popping that bubble in her chest.

"Your friend didn't confess a thing. But she told me plenty about you."

Cori shrugged off the implication in his tone. "I'm not worried about anything Breezy would say. She has a heart ten times her dress size."

"Oh, yeah," he agreed in a dry voice. "A big enough heart not to care when her husband has his hands all over you."

She burned him with a warning look. "He did not have his hands all over me. We're friends; he's like a— a father to me."

As soon as she said it, she wanted to seize the words back.

Max said nothing, bending over and picking up a piece of paper so that she couldn't see his face. "If you're going to be in here for a while, I'll start the security inspection here on the first floor. You may want to clear it with any housekeeping staff you have around."

"You've met the staff. She's an army of one: Her name is Marta Gaspero and she really runs the place, not me. If you're nice to her, she'll cook you insanely delicious food."

Now he smiled. "You know my weaknesses."

God, did she ever. "You don't still eat raw meat, do you?"

"Only when provoked."

The innuendo shot a high voltage charge through her. "Go ahead," she said. "Go shore up the place."

He didn't move, reading the paper that had fallen to the floor. Then he frowned. "When did your husband die?"

Her chest squeezed at his tone. "In May."

"What day?"

"May seventh."

He set the paper on the desk, flipping it around so she could read it, pointing to the bold, angular signature at the bottom. "Then either the date is wrong on this conceptual design approval, or your husband signed it posthumously."

"Good God," she whispered. She blinked at it, unable to believe what she was seeing, then looked up at Max. "That's not his signature."

He just lifted an eyebrow.

Across the top of the form, she read the property information. The Petaluma Mall. Sonoma County, California.

"I'm sure there's an explanation," she said quietly, though her heart was pounding. She took the paper. "By the way, I'll need you to accompany me to a board meeting tomorrow."

The bedroom was ridiculous.

From the coffered ceiling with a chandelier that could light Versailles to the over-the-top Renaissance bed fit for an empress, every corner screamed luxury and decadence and silly money.

But it was Cori's bedroom, so Max was drawn to it.

He'd finished a survey of the first floor of the house, working to see the whole place as a security challenge instead of the palace where the princess lived. He'd scrutinized the rooms for the basics, from the curtains to the chimney access, but found it nearly impossible not to pass judgment on the resident of a home where no detail was spared in the design and finishes.

The place was so incredibly perfect that it looked like *Architectural Digest* would be arriving for a photo shoot any minute.

And that's what really bothered him. Why, he wondered as he entered a closet the size of Milwaukee, had she stayed there all alone after her husband died? What kind of life was that for a beautiful, smart, twenty-eight-year-old woman? Was her joy in running her husband's business? She hadn't wanted to blow off work and go to the spa like most trophy wives, and she'd never been a shopper.

At least, she didn't used to be. With a low whistle of disbelief, he pivoted in the massive closet, his gaze falling over an endless rainbow of shades and fabrics and dozens of shoes.

"Looking for a particular style?"

He completed his turn to find Cori leaning against the doorjamb, arms crossed, with that sneaky little smile she got when she was holding a couple of fours and trying to act like it was a royal flush.

"Exactly how many handbags does one woman need?"

She shrugged. "Comes with the job."

"Oh, yeah, I forgot you own malls."

She took a step into the closet, and shrugged. "Not technically. Peyton Enterprises holds the REIT—the real estate investment trust—on one hundred and forty-eight properties, in its aggregate of ninety-nine million square feet of gross leasable area in twenty-two states plus Puerto Rico."

He dropped his hands into his pockets and eyed her. "You sound like an annual report."

"Some days I feel like one." She fingered a beaded, shimmery gown, tugging at the pale blue silk. She probably looked insanely gorgeous in that thing. "I guess this does look like a disgusting display of consumerism, but William bought me beautiful clothes and," she laughed softly, "my best friend likes to shop."

She dropped the fabric and looked at him. "What are you doing in here? Installing cameras?"

He rubbed his jaw, considering the illicit benefits of that. "I'm still surveying the residence. I'll give you a complete analysis of what you need when I've finished the house. That could take a while in this place."

"Stop making digs at how I live."

"I'm making observations, not digs. You live in a six-zillion-square-foot house with a theater and two kitchens and more open terraces than the palace at Monaco—I know, because I did a security detail there last year. But I'm not casting aspersions on your lifestyle, Cori. I think you're overly defensive."

He expected a spark of denial, but got a sigh instead. "Then stop observing. I've had a lousy morning."

With the surprisingly open admission, she kicked

off her shoes and pushed them toward the shoe department, then dropped onto a creamy chaise along one wall. She wore a pale pink sleeveless top with matching pants, and looked like a model for the designer label he suspected he'd find inside.

"You don't look like you've had a lousy morning."

That earned him a quick glance as she pulled her thick hair back and twisted it into a makeshift ponytail, a move he'd seen her do a hundred times. She rubbed the back of her neck with both hands. "I should have gone to see Swen."

This was the first time since he arrived that she'd sounded like the girl he remembered.

"Did you figure out how that document got signed?" he asked.

She closed her eyes. "Working on it."

"Want help?"

"No." Then she glanced sideways at him. "What could you do?"

"The Bullet Catchers have great resources. We could do a lot of things to trace a forgery."

"Maybe," she said. "First, I'll exhaust my own resources and talk to some people at Peyton."

"What else has you so unhappy?"

She blinked at him, her lashes grazing the fringe of bangs. "You want to know the truth?"

That's why he was there. "Hit me."

"The weight of what William left me really hurts sometimes."

"You sound surprised," he said, leaning against a granite-topped center island that housed dozens of drawers and cubbies. "Didn't you know you'd inherit this kind of responsibility? I assume you discussed his last will and testament."

She shook her head. "He didn't like the topic."

"Come on, Cori. The man was sixty-three and worth billions. And you seem pretty tight with the family attorney. Surely you knew that if something happened to your husband, you'd be in charge. Surely you discussed that with him and planned for it."

She looked up at him, her eyes suddenly dark with emotion. "He discussed those kinds of things with Giff."

He looked at her for a long moment, taking in the shadows and tiny lines of exhaustion around her eyes. Lots of things could make a woman that tired. Grief. Stress. Committing murder. For all he knew, she was having an affair with her husband's attorney.

He had a long way to go before he got behind Corinne Peyton's mask.

"And didn't you discuss those things with the lawyer?"

"Let's get back to the house," she said, crossing her arms and shutting him down. "What did you find?"

He had to remember, she knew he was a skilled in-terrogator. "I found that your architect thought of everything but a safe room."

"You mean, like a panic room?"

He nodded. "We prefer to call it a safe room. It needs to be an interior room, not too big, with a single entrance. I haven't seen anything that qualifies."

"There's a room exactly like that."

He scoured his mental layout of the house. "Where?"

She pointed over her shoulder. "It connects to my bedroom, and isn't accessible from any other place."

"Is it bulletproof, blast resistant, and stocked with first-aid and emergency supplies?"

A wistful look briefly crossed her face. "It's empty. You can stock it with whatever you want."

"Good. I'll check it out and add it to the list of recommendations." He waited for a second. "Want to show me, or should I go exploring?"

Her hair untwisted as she stood, falling over her shoulders like a black velvet drape. He followed her out the door, his gaze traveling down her backside, taking in the way the expensive linen rode her hips as she glided through her bedroom.

He stared at her ass, her waist, her hair, a powerful, familiar clutch in his belly and balls. *That* hadn't changed.

But everything else had. Where was the easy laugh? Her quick wit? Where was that face so open that reading her was easy . . . and so damn fun? Something had made her closed and insulated.

Money . . . or murder?

She opened a door that led to a small hallway and another door, then took an unsteady breath before she turned the handle and revealed a small empty room, unpainted, uncarpeted, and unadorned.

"I didn't want to decorate," she said, seeing his surprised look. "It seemed like bad luck."

"Is that some kind of feng shui thing?"

She laughed softly. "No. I just didn't want to jinx it. I kept . . . hoping."

He stepped inside, looking for a clue to what she meant, but saw none. "Hoping for what?"

She lifted her chin and squared her shoulders. "A baby. We'd been trying for a baby when we built the house. This was designed to be a nursery."

He didn't like the impact that came along with the image of her trying to have a baby. It was one thing to think about Cori having dinner parties or going to functions on the arm of her rich, older husband. But that's as far as his imagination wanted to go.

"So, what was the problem?"

"None of your business." Her response was clipped and, he had to admit, justified.

"Fair enough," he conceded. "We'll have to seal the room, close off the window, and reinforce the walls with steel or concrete. We'll need a metal door with a keyless dead bolt."

"Whatever you like."

"Of course . . . " He took a few steps, his shoes echoing on the hardwood floor. "If you think you're going to use this room for its intended purpose someday, we could build a bunker downstairs."

She shook her head. "No. I won't."

Suddenly feeling way too big for the little room, he stepped past her and back into her oversize bedroom where he fit. "I'll add the necessary supplies for a safe room to the security analysis. And I'm done in here."

But she was still back there, and didn't seem to notice him leave.

Was she sad about wanting a baby that she'd never had? Or was that guilt in her eyes? How desperately were they trying to have a child? Enough for her to want to end her marriage when William couldn't make her pregnant?

He blew out a breath and headed down the hall. And he'd thought this would be a cakewalk.

Gifford Jones rubbed his throbbing temples and squeezed his burning eyes shut.

The pages of black print swam before him, torturing him like pinpricks on his irises.

Key points, he told himself, just read the key points.

Peyton Enterprises mandates that the majority of its directors be independent . . . replace the Company's inside director with an independent director . . . prohibits repricing of stock options . . . no outstanding loans to officers. . . .

The last one was what caused the searing pain in his head.

If he had to, could he convince the board that the money had been a loan? If William the Great hadn't insisted on rules of corporate governance stricter than the SEC's, maybe he could.

He took a long slug of the Scotch Breezy had thoughtfully brought into his office when he told her he'd be working late. God, if she knew that he was really covering tracks . . . That's all he ever did now. He couldn't even imagine the look of disappointment, of horror for what he had done. It wouldn't matter *why* he'd done it, it would only matter that he'd done it to her dearest friend.

Ignoring the pain in his temples, he opened his fountain pen and initialed the draft in front of him. Screw it. His head hurt too much to try and think of a way to fix this right now.

He reached for the next file, expecting another contractor agreement, then blinked and stared at the document. The menu for the board of directors meeting? Micromanagement was definitely the cause of this headache.

But if he didn't micromanage, someone could find his trail.

He started to scratch his initials on the page, but as he read the names of the meeting attendees, he exhaled a quiet curse.

Corinne Peyton.

She was the *real* cause of this headache. She was the root of all his problems. She was the one who should have died, not William.

He scrawled his initials, blood pounding behind his eyes as a shadow crept in his peripheral vision. His headache-darkened vision. He'd tried and tried to ignore it, but something was very, very wrong with his sight.

Rubbing his temples, he knew it would clear with sleep. But he hadn't slept well in a long, long time. And he wouldn't until he came up with some way to keep Cori Peyton out of the boardroom tomorrow— and out of the picture for good.

CHAPTER
Five

Max opened the French doors of his living room so that he could hear any unusual sounds during the night. A wave of August humidity rolled in, and he peeled off his T-shirt.

In his opinion, the biggest sacrifice a bodyguard had to make was sleeping in clothes—and in this swamp it was torture.

Grabbing an ice-cold bottle of water from the refrigerator, he positioned himself at the kitchen counter so he could see through the open door, then flipped up his laptop and scanned the message he was about to send Raquel Durant. Lucy's assistant would arrange for the materials and construction necessary to secure Cori's mansion, magically using her ability to Make Things Happen. They'd all be lost without her and, feeling magnanimous, he added that in a PS at the end of the e-mail. No doubt that would elicit her classic New Jersey eye roll.

That done, he roamed the guest house, glancing out

the windows and the open door, counting the lights still burning in Cori's house. When did she go to sleep? The office and master suite were the only rooms still lit; the rest of the place was dark and hopefully sealed for the night. He'd already checked every door once, around eleven.

It was midnight now.

He picked up the remote for the TV, considered trolling for sports, then flipped it back on the table. He opened up a magazine about Florida living and fluttered a few glossy pages full of sun and fun, but some sixth sense pulled his attention to the open door.

In less than a second he had his Ruger in hand and was crossing the patio, scanning the doorways and windows, surveying the shadowed lawns. He circled the main house slowly, his bare feet making no sound on the damp grass as he darted in between Al Capone's trees. Every few steps, he stopped, listened, smelled.

He saw nothing unusual, heard the constant whir of crickets, and smelled only the sweet musk of oleander and mangoes. Heat and humidity bore down like a steam iron over everything. Wiping his brow, he returned to the back of the house, looking up to the terrace outside Cori's bedroom.

Was she in there? Showering? Undressing?

His body tightened and hardened and he swore at his shitty luck in assignments.

Not that it was the hand of Lady Luck that had sent him back into Cori's world. No, that would be the hand of Lady Lucy. Ms. Machiavelli.

He started another lock check of the French and

sliding doors along the back of the first floor. Every one clicked and tightened at his touch, assuring him they were bolted. A guest room, the living room, the dining room, the game room, the main kitchen, the butler's pantry, the laundry . . . swung wide open.

"Damn it," he muttered. He stepped into the utility area, moving from there to the main kitchen, which was dimly lit by the halogen bulbs under the cabinets. Granite counters and stainless steel appliances gleamed, and the aromas of dinner were masked by something like oak and vanilla.

Furious, he headed for the office at the front of the house, expecting to find Cori working where he'd left her earlier that night.

He crossed the main foyer and strode through the enormous living room, his path colored blue and green from a gigantic saltwater aquarium built in one wall. Around the dining table that sat more people than were in his entire family, to the entrance of the office, a room full of dead animals and dark wood.

He waited outside the door, listening for the click of a computer key, the turn of a page, the scratch of a pen. A whisper of her sigh.

Heat and anticipation rumbled through him as he stood stone still.

Nothing.

Clearing his throat in warning, he stepped into the doorway and met the eyes of a spotted-leopard rug. The room appeared to be empty.

"Cori?" The desk was cluttered with papers and a pamphlet, a laptop humming softly, featuring a screen saver of the Chicago skyline. Why would she leave her computer on, her files out, the lights on?

He glanced at the papers, noting a stockholder's report with multiple sections highlighted in yellow, a spreadsheet with handwritten notes in the margin, a file marked PETALUMA MALL/SONOMA COUNTY.

He called her name again, glanced in the bathroom, then barreled through the rest of the rooms on the first floor. He took the main stairs two at a time, pausing at the top to listen for sounds of life. A TV, music . . . nothing.

He headed toward the light that spilled from the double doors at the far end of the hall. "Cori? Are you in there?"

He waited a second, then entered. Her bed was made, the room virtually untouched. Everything was as he'd last seen it, although the pink outfit she'd worn was draped over the chaise in the closet.

Where the hell was she?

And then he knew. The nursery.

Taking a quiet, slow breath, he paused before he tapped on the door to the tiny room. "Hey, kid, you in there?"

Nothing. He pressed his ear to the door, then slowly turned the brass handle. It was pitch black and empty.

A hot spurt of fear shot through him. Where the hell was she?

He moved like lightning from room to room, without even pausing. He knew damn near every inch by now, and he retraced his steps, all the way back to the guest house, in the off chance she went to find him.

He tried the garage—all cars accounted for.

He combed the north and south lawns and finally jogged toward the dock, his imagination in way too high a gear, a sheen of sweat covering his whole body.

The gate was unlocked. Throwing the bars back, he devoured the concrete dock in a few strides. The cabin cruiser rolled on its moorings, dark and abandoned.

But there was a flicker of light in the cabana at the end. He moved silently toward the building, his hand on his pistol. All four walls were floor-to-ceiling glass, enclosing a room that was only a couple hundred square feet. He saw the back of a white sofa and an empty one facing it, but he couldn't see the floor between them.

A pinpoint of light flickered momentarily, maddeningly out of sight. Was she hiding? Was someone else?

Weapon drawn, he curled one finger around the handle of the sliding glass door, and slid it carefully so that it didn't make a sound going over the track.

Someone was on the other side of that sofa, on the floor. He stepped into the cool air, purposely scuffing his foot in warning. "Who's in here?"

"I am."

Raw, rough relief coursed through him. He came around the sofa and found her sitting on the floor. A tiny flashlight propped next to her illuminated an extensive game of solitaire spread out in front of her.

"Cori, what the hell are you doing?"

She looked up, her eyes a little red, her features

drawn. Her gaze dropped slowly over him, then she looked back up and half-smiled, a familiar mix of surrender and warmth in her eyes.

"I'm trying to beat the devil." Her gaze turned dark. "But he's really on his game tonight."

He fell onto the sofa as the adrenaline gushed through his veins like a waterslide. "Jesus Christ," he whispered. "I thought something happened to you."

She slapped a card on an ace pile. "Something did," she said, so quietly he could barely hear her.

Every defense was down, her emotions had lost control, and she was tired. Classic conditions for a good interrogator to pluck out the truth.

"Wanna tell me about it?" he asked softly.

She nibbled on her bottom lip and studied her cards, then dealt three more, scanning the field of play without moving her head. She let out a soft breath, and dealt three more. Then three more. She flipped the final set down to her side and held up her empty hand.

"I guess. The devil has me but good."

Max braced himself. "Then it's time to talk."

She scooped up the cards and slapped the deck on his thigh, her hand hot through the thin cotton sleep pants he wore. "No, it's time to play." Her look was pure challenge. "Deuces are wild."

She'd lost her mind—Cori could think of no other explanation for issuing the invitation.

Max sat, crossing his legs Indian-style, like hers. The position pulled the drawstring pants tight over his thigh muscles and all but dared her to look between his legs.

She willed herself not to, instead lingering on his chest. Bare, magnificent, cut with muscles, dusted with a rough patch of dark, curly hair. God, she loved that chest. Loved to lay her cheek right in the middle and count the beats of his heart. Loved to thread her fingers through that hair, following the straight line over the ridges of smooth stomach muscles that used to clench, then relax, at her touch.

And below that . . .

A twisting ache coiled low in her belly.

"You want to deal or size up the competition some more?" He didn't hide the amusement in his eyes.

"You deal."

He made a bridge and fanned the deck with practiced ease, looking around the cabana. "So is this your secret hiding place?"

"One of them."

He glanced at the end table, narrowing his eyes to read the title of the book she'd left there. "I remember that about you. You like to find . . . spots."

She smiled. "Guilty."

As he shuffled, she studied him in the shadows of the flashlight beam. His cheekbones formed hollows darkened by stubble. She instantly remembered the scratch of that beard on her cheeks, over her breasts, between her thighs.

"Feels different down here," he observed, looking around again. "Not so glitzy as the rest of your place."

"I decorated it," she said, as though that explained

the lack of glitz. She looked impatiently at the deck. "Are you ever going to deal those?"

"When I'm ready." He divided the deck, and shuffled some more. "Are you down here in the dark because you listened to my warnings?" he asked.

She picked up the flashlight, repositioning it so it wasn't washing him in an artist's light. "I'm trying to be a good client for you," she said, feigning an agreeable voice.

"Principal," he corrected. "We refer to the person we're guarding as a principal."

"We? How many Bullet Catchers are there?"

"It varies. Some are permanent. Some are consultants. There are a few guys I work closely with."

She shifted, the marble floor hard under her bottom. But she didn't suggest they move to the sofa. There was something too intimate, too familiar, about playing cards with Max on a sofa. Or a bed. Or, like they once had, on the roof of his Chicago apartment on a hot summer night. "Are all the Bullet Catchers like you?"

He chuckled, a low, rumbly tone that made the hair on the back of her neck rise and fall. "No one's like me. But one of them is Dan Gallagher. You remember him?"

"Your friend from Pittsburgh? Of course I remember him." Dan's startling green eyes and rapier sense of humor were unforgettable. "Wasn't he an FBI agent?"

"He's a security specialist, and he still does a lot of undercover work." A hint of a smile deepened those hollows; Dan was one person who could always make

Max smile. "He brought me into the Bullet Catchers."

"When was that?"

"A while ago." He leveled the deck on the marble floor with a crack that sounded like a door, slamming the subject closed. Then he held the cards to her. "Wanna cut?"

She tapped her fingernail on the top card, the way she always did. *I trust your shuffle.*

"You keep any chips down here in your haven?"

She laughed lightly. "No. I only play solitaire."

"Cash?"

"Not on me."

He dealt one card to her, slow and deliberate, facedown. "I don't play for fun."

"Yes, you do." Her heart thumped a tattoo on her rib cage.

"You mean strip or favors?" His sexy half-grin sent a wicked craving straight up her middle, like liquid fire. "Too conventional. It always ends up the same."

Yeah, horizontal.

"I have a new game for you," he said, dealing the next two cards. "We'll play for answers. The winner gets to ask anything. Loser has to answer."

She took her cards and fanned her hand open. "So no one gets naked or sweaty."

"Guess that depends"—he raked her with an evil, teasing look—"on what you ask. No topics are off limits."

"Some topics are off limits," she volleyed. "I'm not going to answer personal questions."

"Then you better win." He checked his cards. "This is five-card draw, but you know that."

She pulled a pair of eights and some junk. His expression was as blank as a dead man's.

"How do you keep that straight face?" she asked.

"No questions unless you win. Rules of the game."

"Fine." She flipped out the three useless cards and set them down. He handed her three new cards, including another eight. She bit her lip, but consciously let no muscle move in her face.

Yet she must have given away her triplets, because he zipped his cards together and folded. "Ask away." He shifted on his haunches.

"Are you uncomfortable on the floor?"

"Nope." He scooped up the cards and held them out to her. "Your deal."

"Hey, that wasn't a question."

"Sounded like one to me." A smile threatened, an infinitesimal rise at the corner of his lips. Once, long ago, she could coax a full smile from him with just a look or, even better, a touch. Back then, she could make him laugh. That deep, sexy, from-the-heart sound that rolled over her and made her weak and dizzy and in love.

She shuffled, cut, and started the deal, but her concentration was waning fast. In her fingers, she held a pool of black and red, picked a few lousy cards and folded.

"Can I take a bye on a question?" she asked.

"Sure. I'll buy your shirt." He didn't even blink, but a tiny glint in his eyes gave away the joke.

She laughed and shook her head. "Never mind. Ask me something. I have nothing to hide."

His quick look surprised her, but then he asked, "How's your mother?"

Why, of all the stupid questions, would that one twist her heart a little? Because when Max got *nice*, she got . . . gooey. "She's fine. Got a job at Paramount Studios as an assistant to an assistant to an assistant. Still only wears purple. Temporarily single after her fourth divorce. Well, fifth. But twice to the same guy, so we only count it as four."

He nodded and dealt again. She concentrated and won easily, this time with a juicy full house.

"My question." She pulled her legs up and wrapped her arms around them, enjoying the fun of their play. Max's gaze slid over the skin revealed by her denim shorts, as warm as if he'd touched her. That would be a whole different kind of fun.

She forced herself to focus on a good question. If she could ask Max anything, what would she want to know?

Have you thought of me every single day?

Have you ever been in love again?

Did you let my dad take that shot on purpose?

"You're staring at me again." His voice was soft, no more than a breath escaping his lips.

"Then we're even."

Electrical impulses jumped through the cabana as each second dragged by. "Make it easy on yourself, kid."

Kid. God, she loved it when he used that nickname.

It was so . . . protective. But the time for that kind of admission was long gone. "Tell me, Max, why'd you leave the DEA?"

"Sucky assignments in places like Grenada and Guatemala. Hot places. Like this."

She knew why he'd been sent to Grenada and Guatemala. She'd been in the room with the men who'd loved her father nearly as much as she had, and they all needed to blame someone, to hurt someone for the indescribable pain caused of losing Paul Cooper. She'd given them what they needed. She'd handed them the head of Max Roper, and ensured that he'd never get any higher in the DEA than where he was. Lower, in fact.

So, really, that was a waste of a question. She knew why he left the DEA. Because of her.

She started the shuffle without comment. There wasn't really any safe topic or impersonal question with Max. She won the next hand way too easily, certain he'd let her.

"How are the Steelers going to do this year?" she asked.

He lifted his chin, an acknowledgment of the ideal impartial question. "Going all the way again."

She slid the deck his way. "Ever the fan. You get to see them play?"

"One game, one question."

She leaned her arm against the seat of the sofa, propping her head on her hand as he dealt. "Could be a long night."

He took another visual journey over her body, then

glanced at the windows. Pointedly. "When are you going to get those drapes in here?"

The implication was obvious. She stared at her cards, her pulse racing, her imagination slipping into places it had no business going. She took two cards, hoping for a straight that never materialized, and lost to his pair of nines.

"So, Cori." He repositioned himself on the floor again, a tad closer, his gaze direct, his voice low—the master interrogator. "Why did you stop trying to have a baby?"

She blinked at him. "What?"

"You said 'when we built this house we were trying to have a baby.' That gives me the impression you stopped trying at some point. Why?"

She shook her head, then reached down and looped a finger around the back of her sandal. "Since you said I could strip instead of answer"—she flipped the shoe off—"that's my answer."

He grinned. "I said I'd buy your shirt. You're forgetting our rules."

"We have no rules anymore, Max."

"Fair enough," he said. "Your deal?"

She took the cards and dropped them. "I don't want to play anymore."

"But I have more questions."

She smiled a little. "So ask them. You think we have to play poker to communicate?"

She heard his slow intake of breath, the first sign that Max was fighting for control.

"What I think," he finally said, very slowly, "is that

it might be hard as hell to be this close to you, for this long, and not . . ." He put one finger on her knee, then traced a single, burning line up her thigh. "Lay a hand on you."

She glanced at his long, strong finger against her bare skin. "You are laying a hand on me."

"No, I'm not. I'm laying a finger on you." He spread his hand, the large span of it practically covering her whole leg. "Now I'm laying a hand on you." He glided that hand an inch higher.

Goose bumps rose over her skin and it felt like all her blood raced to a single, throbbing place in her body. Max swallowed, then wet his lips with the tip of his tongue.

That would be the next sign of his losing control. God, she knew every expression, every gesture, every inch of his body.

If she dropped her gaze, she knew she'd see his erection, ready and straining the fabric in its way.

She did.

It was.

She closed her eyes as desire slammed through her whole body. "Max—"

His mouth was on hers, harsh and hot, before she could take another breath. And when she tried, he just kissed her deeper.

Fire whipped through her veins. His kiss was as unrelenting and arousing as she remembered, and she opened her mouth to his demanding tongue, which glided between her teeth without hesitation.

Deep in his chest, he let out a low groan, plunging

one hand into her hair while the other still burned like an iron on her thigh. She slanted her head to get more of him, clenching her fists to keep from grabbing handfuls of him and touching all that mountain of muscle. Once more, his tongue took over, slick on the roof of her mouth, exploring and tasting.

Then he pulled away as quickly as he had started the kiss, his eyes nearly black as he seared her with a look, his fingers still knotted in her hair. "One word, kid. All it'll take is one word."

Yes.

Her eyelids fluttered with the weight of wanting to say that word.

Yes.

Her throat was so damn dry, she might not have been able to say that word.

Yes!

"But first you better answer one more question, Cori Cooper."

She inched away, but not too far. "First? You're that sure of me?"

"Doesn't matter. You'll change your mind when you hear the question."

"I don't like that tone. What?"

"I want to know . . . I *need* to know something." He threaded his fingers and tightened his grip on her hair ever so slightly. "Was it the money or the power?"

She jerked a little in response, pulling her own hair. "Excuse me?"

"That attracted you to William Peyton. Money or power?" He narrowed his eyes and she could see that little scar above his right eye throb. That was usually the last sign when Max lost his control—but right now, he looked very much in control. Despite the scar, despite the tightness of his breathing, and despite the erection still throbbing between them.

Why would he ask a question like that right now? "If you're looking for something to cool you down, Max, there's a shower in the guest house. The right knob is ice cold."

He released his grip, dropping back against the sofa, and she took that as a silent acknowledgment that, once again, she'd nailed him. "Why did you marry him? I have a right to know."

She coughed in surprise. "Since when?"

"Since you got married less than a year . . . after . . ."

"After what? Come on, Max. Say it," she demanded, taunting. "I got married less than a year after we broke up."

"We didn't break up," he almost spat. "You disappeared in the middle of the night."

"You killed my father in the middle of the day."

He let out a dark curse under his breath. But not, she noticed, a denial.

She pushed herself up in one move, needing to get away from him. "We're not going there. Screw your games and your answers, and screw you, Max. We're *not* going there."

She turned toward the window and placed both hands on the cold glass, staring out at the blackness of the bay. "You don't have a right to know," she finally said, softly. "But I'll tell you anyway. You wrecked my life, broke my heart, and stole my joy, and I found someone else. It happens a million times a day to a million different couples."

"He was a father figure to you."

She snorted softly. "If you already know why I married him, why the hell are you asking?"

"Am I right?"

"I met him at DePaul." She dropped her head against the glass and closed her eyes. They had to talk about this, eventually, otherwise they'd both go crazy. Just like they had to get that kiss out of the way. "There was a fund-raiser held at the Law School, where he had made an endowment."

"I didn't ask *how,* Cori. I asked *why.*"

She didn't reply

For a long time, the only sound in the room was the soft, indistinguishable hum of a tiny refrigerator and the growl of a motorboat in the distance. Cori peered into the darkness, unable to see the lights that went with that sound.

"Your friend, Breezy, told me she introduced you two," he said.

Good trick, Max. Change the subject . . . just a little. "She might have made the actual introduction. I don't remember, I'd just met her that night, too. Giff is a DePaul alum." She lost her train of thought, watching a shadow in the bay. Was that the boat? No more than a hundred and fifty feet away. "That's weird."

"What is?" She sensed, rather than saw, Max square himself and follow her gaze.

"How come I can hear a boat, but not see it?"

He leaped to his feet so fast that she didn't even get a chance to turn, but simply tumbled as he threw her to the ground at the precise moment that the window cracked like a firework and shattered.

"Oh my God!" Her cry was muffled by the force of his body, his hand protecting her face as it hit the floor.

"Stay under me!" he demanded.

She squeezed her eyes shut, her hammering heart sending a deafening rush through her ears, Max's weight pushing her against the floor so hard that pain shot into her hipbone and her breasts as they smashed on the marble.

"What is it?" she demanded, her voice strained from terror and the crush of his body.

Over her raging pulse, she heard the double click of an automatic pistol. "Shhh. Listen."

The motorboat raced into the night. She felt Max lift his head an inch, snapping his attention from window to window.

She tried to rise up, but he pushed her head down with his chin. "Wait," he whispered. "Wait until I know it's clear."

"What happened?" she demanded again, a tremble starting to overtake her.

He eased off to her side, his thigh still over her lower back and one strong arm across her shoulders. His other hand held the gun, aimed out and ready to fire.

When she lifted her head, she saw that the glass looked like a five-foot-wide spiderweb, perilously suspended in the woodwork.

He slid his hand under her throat and used one finger to gently turn her face toward his. "You okay?"

"I think so." Their faces were inches apart; she could practically count his eyelashes and the thud of his pulse vibrated her body. She closed her eyes and steadied her breath. "Thanks."

"Don't thank me. You can thank the person smart enough to put bulletproof glass in this place," he said.

"William did it," she said softly.

"Then he saved your life," Max said. "Because someone just took a shot at you, kid."

CHAPTER
Six

Max blessed the shadows he'd cursed earlier, whisking Cori into the guest house through the full-coverage foliage.

"Why here?" she asked as he locked the French door behind her.

"You're a target in your house. Did your husband install bulletproof glass there, too?"

"No." She curled onto the sofa, still looking a little dazed.

He snapped the plantation shutters closed, then moved to the kitchen and turned off the light. "Do us both a favor and don't stand in front of any more windows." He could still hear the sound of the glass pop just as he landed on her. So close, so damn close.

The thought of almost losing her the same way he'd lost Coop landed like a boxer's punch to the head. Could a person endure that twice?

"Any chance I can go home? I mean to my own room?"

"That's exactly where they'd expect you to be."

She dropped her head back on the sofa, and even in the dark he could see her chest rise and fall with uneasy breaths. His hard-on threatened to make a return visit, so he left the room long enough to case the house, and cool off.

Somehow that interrogation had gotten way too personal. Of course he didn't get any worthwhile intelligence about her husband's death. He got all tied up in knots over why she married William Peyton before she ever even *talked* to him again.

Can you keep your emotions out of this?

Shut up, Lucy.

"Does Billy have a key to this house?" he called as he checked the window locks in the downstairs bedroom.

"He doesn't have a key to anything on this property. I had every lock changed after William died."

"Why?" he asked pointedly as he returned to the room. "I thought the first threat to you just happened, up in Bal Harbour. Was there something else?"

Her head was still back, her eyes closed, her throat exposed. He went to the French doors to listen for any unusual sounds on the patio and maybe look at something, anything, that wasn't going to light his fuse again.

"Gifford Jones suggested it. Or maybe the insurance company. I don't remember. I was still in a bit of a fog, then. Still in shock."

"I gotta say," he mused, opening one shutter an inch and peering into darkness. "Shooting you from the bay just doesn't strike me as Billy's MO."

She choked a little. "Billy's MO? You met him once. He was totally wasted. How would you know what his MO is?"

"Because totally wasted drug addicts are my specialty, remember? First of all . . ." He closed the shutter and walked closer to her. "He never got his car. It's still in the drive outside your garage."

"This guy was on a *boat*, Max," she said.

"But the fact that he didn't bother to get his car tells me he may have spent the day as high as he was last night."

"Drunk enough to go out and do something really stupid."

"No drunk took that shot. Does he own a boat?"

"No, but he has a zillion friends who do."

"Friends who would escort him into the bay to shoot you? That's some pal."

She pulled her legs in tighter and with a small sound, buried her face in her knees.

She was hiding something. Max knew it, as well as he knew she was freezing. He got up and went back into the bedroom and tugged the pastel comforter from the bed. Obviously, the maid didn't get the message when he'd tossed it on the floor the night before. He dropped it on her lap. "Here."

"Thanks."

While she gathered the down comforter around her, he settled on a bar stool where he could see most of the rooms and the only entrance. Questioning her would be a hell of a lot easier ten feet away, and with her covered by a blanket.

"Tell me about the night your husband died."

Even in the dark room, he could see her expression turn wary. "Why?"

"Because I want to know." Adrenaline and fear and survival instinct made his tone sharp—along with disgust that he couldn't ask her a question without getting emotionally involved in the answer. "Somebody just tried to kill you. If I can help figure out who, then I can do my job, which is to stop them."

She stiffened, opened her mouth to say something, then shut it just as fast. Hiding, hiding. But what?

Son of a bitch, he didn't want this woman to be guilty of murder.

"He had a heart attack. In his sleep."

"And you were there."

"Of course I was there." She pushed the comforter off. "When can I go to my room?"

"You can't." He pushed off the bar stool and went to the refrigerator to get water. "What were you doing in the cabana?"

"Tonight? I needed to relax and get away from the office. I wanted to think about the board meeting and . . . a bunch of stuff."

"Did you tell anyone you were going there? Or is this something you do regularly, on scheduled nights?"

"No and no."

He held up a bottle of water. "Want one?"

"Please."

He tossed it over the counter and she caught it with one hand. "Forget about the board meeting," he said. "You're not going."

"Yes." The hiss of her word matched the air suction when she opened the bottle. "I am."

"Cori, rule number one of security is: Don't make it easy. Don't be exactly where you're expected to be." He opened his own bottle and took a swig. "Can't someone vote proxy for you?"

"Giff can, but I want to be there." She pulled the comforter around her again. "No one knows I'm going except Gifford's secretary. I called her late in the day and told her. As of yesterday he was attending as my proxy, so no one would have any idea I'm going to be there. The agendas were already printed and distributed by the time I reached Gifford's secretary. I planned it that way."

The admission snagged his attention. "You did."

"I have to find out why William's signature was on that paper."

"And no one else knows you'll be there?"

"Marta arranged for my driver to come early tomorrow, but even he wouldn't know where we were going."

"In that case, maybe you can go."

"Maybe?" She almost choked on her drink. "Isn't that the whole reason you're here, so I can go wherever I want? So I can go on with my life? That's *all* I need you to do."

He caught the tiny emphasis in her voice, but it was too dark to read her expression. All, as in *no poker, no kissing, no sex*? Or all as in *stay away from my secrets*?

"A big part of personal protection is being prepared for anything. You can go tomorrow, but tonight, I don't want you crossing that patio or standing in front of your bedroom window or . . ." He froze at the sound of skittering steps across the patio. "Get down," he barked, pulling out his weapon and walking toward the door. "On the floor."

She froze as a sharp rap hit the glass. "Mr. Roper? Mr. Roper, are you awake?"

"It's Marta," Cori said.

"Stay there." He halted her move with one hand held out. "What is it, Marta?"

"I can't find Mrs. Peyton!" The woman's voice was tight with panic. "I've looked all over the house. Something's wrong."

He took four quick steps to the door and opened it just a crack. "She's okay," he assured her.

He'd only met the housekeeper for a few minutes that day, but he could tell by her face that her fear was genuine. Her dark eyes blazed with worry, and she hadn't even taken the time to tie her bathrobe.

"Are you sure?" Marta asked. "We just received a phone call from the Star Island security about a shooting. And I can't find her anywhere."

"I'm right here, Marta. I'm fine." Cori was beside him in an instant, and Max let her pull the door open wider. "What did they say?"

Marta's narrow shoulders shuddered with relief. "Oh, Mrs. Peyton!" She reached for Cori, and Max stopped her with one hand.

"Max, please." Cori pushed him away. "Come here, Marta. Look, you're shaking."

"Thank God. I'd thought I'd lost you both."

For a moment, Max thought she meant Cori and him, then he realized she meant Cori and William.

"Tell me what they said," Cori prodded. "About a shooting."

Without makeup and curly hair falling loose, Marta looked younger than he'd first thought, with unlined olive skin and a full lower lip, which she bit as she looked from one to the other.

"They called to say that there had been some vandalism around the island; some kids in a boat with a BB gun were shooting at the houses and boats. The Security Force is alerting everyone on the island."

That was no flippin' BB pellet.

"Really?" She sounded as disbelieving as Max. "Kids fooling around shot at the cabana." No, she didn't buy it either.

Marta's eyes widened like two black olives. "Were you down there, Mrs. Peyton?"

"Yes, but I'm fine. We're fine."

"Fine enough, but she'll stay here tonight," Max announced.

For a moment, Cori looked like she'd argue, then she relented with a tilt of her head. "Thanks, Marta. Keep the doors locked and the alarm on. Max will walk over with you." She looked up at him and added, "I'll be right here. I swear."

He stepped outside with the housekeeper, but gave Cori a sharp look. "Don't move until I come back."

By the time he returned, not forty-five seconds later,

the comforter was gone and the bedroom door locked.

As if that could keep him out.

"What do you think you're doing?"

Cori jumped at Max's demand, the comforter she'd wrapped around her falling to the floor as she peered at the thermostat on the wall. "I can see my breath," she answered, pressing the set button to read the tiny digital gauge. "And no wonder, since you have it set to fifty-five."

"Fit for humans." He pulled himself up from the way-too-small sofa to let her know where he was. He could see in the dark; but then, he'd been lying awake for hours. Had she, on the other side of that door?

"Fit for Eskimos." She tapped the button several times and the soft hum of the air conditioner stopped, leaving the room bathed in silence.

"C'mere."

She froze at the command, then scooped up the blanket and turned in the direction of his voice. "It's almost dawn. I can go back to my room now."

"Come here. You're barefoot and in shorts. I'll warm you."

She pulled the heavy comforter around her like armor, then approached the sofa. "Did you sleep?" she asked.

"I rested." He tapped the seat next to him. "Come on. I know your feet are like ice cubes."

She sat sideways on the sofa, leaning against the armrest and lifting her legs. As she settled the blanket around her, he took her feet and pulled them onto his lap. "You should wear socks."

"We're in the subtropics, Max. And I thought I'd be in my own bedroom where the temperature is a healthy seventy-two degrees."

"Shhhh." He leaned his head back and closed his eyes, rubbing the soft skin of her instep and letting the heat of his hand warm her chilly flesh. "Don't talk."

"Why not?"

"I'm still resting."

Max concentrated on her feet, fighting his body's reaction to the contact. Everything was tight, pulled and strained, but not hard. Not yet.

"Max?"

"Hmm?"

"Why did you take this job?"

His fingers stilled.

"Don't stop." She wiggled her toes. "This is no co-incidence, is it?"

He circled his thumbs against the balls of her feet. So smooth. He didn't answer.

"Since I never met Lucy Sharpe I can't say for sure," she continued, "but I'd bet nothing that woman does is accidental."

He let his right hand slide up her ankle. Delicate. Narrow. Satiny. "Good bet."

"So she didn't just flip open an employee roster, slide a finger down a list of supermen and say, 'Oh, Max. He'd love Miami in August.' "

That made him laugh. "We did discuss the undesirable geography."

"And not the undesirable client?"

His hand slipped higher, to her calf. To the little

muscle that looked so neat in high heels. "First of all, you're not a client, you're a principal." He moved both hands to the other leg, following an identical path. Just as nice. "Second, 'undesirable' is just about the last word in the dictionary for you."

She actually slid a little deeper into her blanket and the move forced his hands an inch higher. Almost to that tender spot behind her knees that he used to—

"Are you looking for my forgiveness?"

He glided both hands back down to safer territory, rewarming her feet. "No."

"Because I—"

He squeezed. "I know you won't." Hadn't he begged once before? Begged? Hadn't he fucking *cried*?

"Okay, then why?"

His fingers moved independently of his brain. Back up the calves, around that sleek shin. He kept his eyes closed, breathing evenly, his whole body nicely under control. "It doesn't matter."

"Did you think we'd have another chance?"

Control slipped. "You really would have made a good lawyer, Cori. Why did you quit?"

Under his palms, he felt her muscles tense. "We're not talking about me. We're talking about you."

"We're not talking at all." He gave in and slid his hands to the back of her knees. God. Like velvet. Control slipped further. "We're resting."

"Sex." She said the word so softly, he wasn't sure he'd heard it. But his body heard perfectly.

"Sex?" he repeated. "Is that an order?"

She almost laughed. "Is that why you took the job? You want sex?"

"Sorry to disappoint you, kid. But I do okay." Contrary to the growing ridge between his legs.

"I'm sure you do." She tortured him by shifting enough to put a little weight on his lap.

He smiled in the dark. "That's because I'm irresistible."

"I resisted you."

He snorted softly. "Not for long."

She didn't bother to argue that fact. Their chemistry had been flammable from the moment they'd met, a month after she arrived in Chicago to attend law school and live with her dad.

"But you were the one who lost fifty dollars within ten minutes of my crashing your poker game," she reminded him.

Max smiled, seeing the aqua linoleum floor of Coop's undersize kitchen in Berwyn, Illinois, smelling the aroma of burned Jiffy Pop and beer. "Oh, you crashed it, huh? I thought we were so loud you couldn't study."

"You remember that?"

"As if I'd forget." The memory was branded into his brain. Looking up from what was a fairly decent hand to see all that black hair, a yellow top clinging to perfect breasts, endless legs—these very endless legs that his hands currently roamed—in tiny running shorts. Oh, and eyes so navy blue and intense that he thought he'd drown.

Mind if I deal my kid in?

He could still remember leaning back on the two legs of a maple chair, a beer to his lips and raw lust thumping straight through him.

That's no kid, Coop.

"You distracted me," he said huskily, vaguely aware that his hand had traveled higher up her tight, silky thigh, and wildly aware that her hips stirred . . . just a little.

"And I held out for a whopping twenty-four hours." She laughed lightly.

"It was inevitable," he whispered. His fingers took two steps closer to the softest skin, the warmest place. Inevitable.

He could feel her pulse under her skin, matching the thump of his. She moved one leg over him. He grew harder.

"What was inevitable," she said, "was the end."

The end. The dark, miserable night when she'd fought so hard with her father, and Max had punched the wall and left, furious with Coop. Then that night morphed into a bright, blue morning . . . except there was nothing bright about the look in her eyes when she opened the door and met his anguished gaze.

There's been an incident, kid.

A good two minutes passed before either one moved, or spoke. Finally, she scooted up an inch and locked him in her gaze. This would be the look she would have saved for the most difficult witness, had she ever made it into the courtroom.

"So if you're not looking for redemption, a reunion, or a repeat performance, why did you take this job?"

He wasn't about to tell her the whole truth. "Very simple. My boss said you needed a bodyguard and I already knew you."

"I would think that would hurt your chances of getting the assignment, not help them."

She was so smart. "You have to know how Lucy thinks. She's former CIA and a spook to the bone. She knows everything. She probably figured—"

"You know damn well I didn't ask for her background." Cori took her feet from the nest of his lap and leaving him, for once, feeling cold. "And if she knows everything—and by that I assume you meant that we were lovers and how and why we split up— then why would she pick you to protect me and . . ." She held her hand out to stop him from answering before she finished her question. "Why would you accept the job?"

It wouldn't be long before she knew his ulterior motive. If he didn't have any information on her or her husband's death by the time she did, she'd send him packing.

He pulled her back in place, gliding his hands greedily over her legs in the process, returning easily to the soft curve of her inner thigh. "Come back here and calm down," he urged, pulling her closer, letting her feet tuck back into his lap.

"I am calm."

It took very little movement for him to be sure she felt the strain against his sleep pants. "I'm not."

He heard her breath catch. "Don't change the subject," she said softly. "You're hiding something."

"Not hardly." He rocked his hips and let his erection press against her legs. Then he leaned over her and lowered his voice. "If anyone's hiding something, Cori, it's you."

"I am not."

"No?" He grazed the edge of her shorts with his fingertips. "You sure are different than you used to be."

"Because I don't go all melty when you touch me?"

"You don't?" He dipped his hand right under the hem, sliding onto the silk of her panties. She sucked in a breath, but he felt the damp material and that nanosecond of touch shot fire into his balls. "Feels pretty melty to me."

The phone jangled next to her head, and she lifted the handset and pointed it toward him. "You haven't answered my questions. You haven't done anything but prove I'm human." She purposefully rubbed his erection with her calf. "Just like you." Her gaze on him, she stabbed the button and held the phone up to her ear. "Hey. You're up early."

Cori blessed and cursed the distraction, willing her blood to cool and her head to clear. What the hell was she doing playing feelie with him?

She'd lose for sure. She always did.

"You're in the guest house?" Breezy's voice rose in implication. "That didn't take long."

"You're awake at six thirty," Cori said, easing her body away from the warmth and hardness of Max. "That's a first."

"You really should teach your maid some discretion, hon."

Max stared at her, questioning. She covered the receiver. "It's Breezy."

Even in the dark, she could see him roll his eyes. What was his beef with Breezy?

"We had an incident here last night," Cori told her. "I stayed here for security reasons." Not that she was all that *safe* here.

"Marta told me." Breezy sounded like she'd smoked a pack of cigarettes the night before. "She's gossiping because she's still trying to get back in my good graces so I'll hire her sister. So what happened?"

Cori relayed the story, minus the poker game.

"That little prick fired at you from the bay?" Her voice cracked in fury and shock. "What the hell is the matter with him?"

"I don't know. I'm just glad Max was there."

"I bet you were," Breezy said pointedly. "And where is the big bodyguard now? Underneath or on top?"

"Neither," Cori insisted, pulling away completely so that it wasn't a lie. Breezy knew nothing about her history with Max and, for the moment, Cori preferred to keep it that way. "What's going on? Why are you awake at dawn?"

"My husband's been up all night getting ready for the meeting."

"I'm going," Cori said. "Giff doesn't have to vote my shares."

Breezy made a soft sound, then porcelain clinked in the background. "That's too bad," Breezy said, after a sip.

"Why?"

"Swen has an opening. Marc Jacobs has a trunk show. Lulu Garrey is having a tea on that insane yacht she snagged in her last divorce. I can think of twenty reasons why it's too bad. I want to hang with you today."

"I need to be there. It's important."

"Cor, I need a friend. It's more important."

Cori tapped down a flash of guilt. It was a cold day in Miami when tough-as-nails Breezy admitted she needed something.

But then Cori thought of that signature—that forgery. Maybe if she told Breezy the truth, if she shared her suspicions . . . But, no. Then Breezy and Giff would turn the company upside down trying to find out who signed William's name, and whoever it was would hide the trail. The trail that Cori had a hunch might lead to the answers she wanted.

"We'll get together," Cori promised, hating how vague it sounded. "Just let me get some things straightened out. What about tonight? Come over and we'll have girls' night in. I'll kick Marta out and we'll make pizza again. That was so much fun."

"Can't. Julius Escaya has a showing at the Stone Art Gallery. I promised Giff."

The magic words: *I promised Giff.* She knew better than to argue with that. "The next night?"

"Dinner party. Something I don't remember or care about."

"Children's Hospital fund-raiser," Cori reminded her. "I sent a check but I'm not going."

"Giff wants to make an appearance." There was no

cigarette smoke behind Breezy's long, slow sigh. Just sadness. "Never mind, Cor. You're busy and so am I. I really wanted to see you today, that's all."

"Listen, let me just get through this, Breeze. I'll call you this afternoon."

"All righty, then." She'd copped a cavalier voice, but it sounded hollow.

"I'm sorry, Breeze. I promise I'll call you this afternoon."

"I might not have cell service out on Lulu's tub," Breezy said. "But you can try."

Breezy hung up and Cori dropped the phone, glancing at the early rays of sun breaking through the plantation shutters. "Something's wrong with her," she told Max.

"I knew that the minute I saw her." He stood up and looked down at her. "You probably don't want to hear this, but—"

She held up her hand. "Then don't say it."

"She's not your friend."

Cori shook her head. He was always jealous of anyone who got close to her. Even her father. How could she forget that? How could she come so close to trusting him again? To . .

It was inevitable.

Or was it?

CHAPTER
Seven

Max didn't have a business degree. Hell, he'd barely gotten through his liberal arts degree at Pitt on a football scholarship. But he had enough business savvy to know something seriously stunk in the mall management world of Peyton Enterprises.

After he was introduced to a few corporate officers and the outside directors, he planted himself in a corner of the massive conference room, ignoring the wall-to-wall-window view of Miami glitz in favor of the power struggle that unfolded inside the boardroom the minute the gavel fell. In no time, they'd all forgotten he was there, including Cori, who was obviously up to her swan's neck in corporate chaos.

First of all, there was no CEO. Peyton had left voting shares to Cori, but no power. There was a chief operating officer who struck Max as ineffective, and a team of three slick MBA-type guys and one hard-ass woman named Andrea Lockhart who checked him out thoroughly, then bared her fangs in defense of investor relations, which evidently fell into her cage.

As far as the business agenda, Cori rarely made a comment until they reached the last item, an update on the status of the Peyton Foundation.

"The Foundation now has an operating budget of four million dollars," she told the group. "We've awarded four hundred thousand in scholarship funds this year, as well as two hundred thousand in legal services, health care, and housing support."

The barracuda, Lockhart, closed her eyes. Another one of the MBAs tapped his pencil and glanced at his papers. Only Gifford Jones watched with rapt attention.

When she finished, Jones all but clapped, beaming his approval from across the table. "Well done, Mrs. Peyton. We have no doubt that Foundation will continue to be a huge success, one that highlights our company in a glow of corporate goodwill and ingratiates us into the many communities where we do business. We're all deeply indebted to you."

"Why do we need an outside PR agency?" the investor relations woman asked Cori, propping her elbows on the table. "I have a team of communications specialists in my department, so there's no reason to outsource that function. You can cut that line item."

"Your team of communications specialists are very busy, Andrea," she responded. "I requested assistance, but no one was even able to draft a press release, let alone set up interviews with national media. This firm has guaranteed us coverage in all of the major national newspapers and the morning shows."

Andrea raised a sharp brow. "I'm thrilled that you

get to be on the *Today* show, Cori, but our stockholders are already at work by the time they run the fluff segments. Did your spin doctors think about CNBC?"

Cori leveled her gaze at the other woman. "The agency has already scheduled a live interview in early September, just in time for the shareholders' meeting. Perhaps you didn't read the e-mail I sent to you last week, asking if you'll be available to go to New York for that."

"That's wonderful!" Gifford interjected. "I think the outside firm is a perfectly reasonable expenditure. William Peyton wanted this Foundation to be run as independently as possible and it's obviously in good and caring hands with Mrs. Peyton."

"Obviously," Andrea muttered, moving some papers around.

"Then we can close the minutes of this meeting," Jones announced.

"No, we can't," Cori said.

All the attention returned to her.

"I want to open the discussion of the Sonoma County property."

A few people glanced at their paperwork, and Gifford glared at Cori. "The executive committee has taken that off the agenda, Mrs. Peyton. It would require a mandatory motion of the board to reinstate the item."

"I so move." Her gaze slid from one to the next as she remained standing. "Will anyone second?"

For a long moment, no one breathed. Who, Max wondered, was really Cori's ally? Their resentment was as obvious as Gifford Jones's sucking up. The sound of that bullet rang in Max's ears. Did someone want to lower the population of the boardroom so badly that they'd take her out?

"I second." The motion came from an outside board member, a banker, if Max remembered correctly.

After a bit of murmuring and some shared looks, half the room stood, and Max realized that only the board of directors would vote on the issue, and that included Cori, but not Gifford, who was only on the executive committee.

"I'll handle it," Cori said softly to Jones, who remained seated. "You can leave."

His face paled slightly but he nodded. "Of course. Come and see me in my office when you're finished here." He glanced at Max on the way out. "You need to wait outside."

That was exactly the out he needed. "Cori," Max said, approaching her, "I need to talk to you."

He shot Gifford Jones one look and the man backed away, giving them privacy.

"What is your password to the computer system?" he whispered to her.

She glanced at him. "Why?"

"While you're in here, I'm going to make some copies of files." He looked around the table, and lowered his voice. "To help with that forgery."

She regarded him for a moment, then nodded. Tearing a corner of paper from a pad, she wrote on it and handed it to him. "I'll find out what I can from this group, then meet you in my office."

Jones walked out with him. "She's amazing, isn't she?" the lawyer asked as the doors closed behind them.

Max gave him a questioning glance. "I suppose."

But Jones lingered, glancing toward the doors as though he longed to go back inside. "This Foundation is very, very important to her," he said. "Nothing should distract her from it."

That sounded oddly like . . . an order. "I'm afraid my capabilities don't extend to managing her schedule, Mr. Jones."

Jones drew back. "But surely, with your close personal relationship, you can convince her of what's important." At Max's incredulous look, he added, "My wife tells me you two knew each other before. Before William."

Max glared him down and ignored the implication. "I'm not here to convince her of anything, but to keep her out of harm's way."

A young woman approached, looking at Jones. "Mr. Nash on line two," she whispered.

Gifford Jones turned and walked away, and Max headed in the opposite direction to Cori's corner office, where he'd been earlier. The assistant's desk was abandoned, so he entered the office, closed the door and locked it.

He sat at her desk, opened the folded piece of paper, and read the single word.

Euclid.

Interesting choice of passwords. Either she had a fascination with the father of geometry . . . or she remembered the name of the street he'd lived on in Berwyn. In a Chicago-style bungalow where they'd spent almost every night for a year.

Well. He had only a few minutes to dig through her computer and look for evidence. And while he was there, he'd grab the files on the Petaluma Mall for cover.

Cori stared out the sedan window, a thousand miles away.

Max turned around in the passenger seat. "You want to talk?"

She blinked at him, visibly pulling herself into the moment. "Not here," she replied. "Not now."

The driver, David, stared ahead and said nothing.

"How about lunch?" Max suggested.

She brightened a bit. "Yes, I'm starved," she agreed, and leaned forward to address David. "Azul, at the Mandarin." Then she resumed her study of Miami traffic, elevating an invisible wall as effective as privacy glass. Max knew when to wait out an interrogation.

Half an hour later, seated at a wide table for two surrounded by six fawning servers flipping napkins and opening menus, Cori finally focused on him.

"Did you get what you needed from my computer?"

No. "I found the files on that mall and copied them."

She tilted her head to the side. "Good. Did you scan the forged signature and send it to your 'resources'?"

He nodded. "Of course."

"What did you think of the board meeting?"

He notched an eyebrow. "You're not the most popular girl in school."

She barely shrugged. "Look at it from their perspective. I'm the dead founder's trophy wife with too much voting power and no business degree."

"I thought you had the chops." But then, he was biased. "Your buddy Breezy told me that everyone loves you."

"She likes to forget Andrea Lockhart exists. And Breezy refuses to acknowledge that a whole lot of people dislike me because I married well."

"Or because you widowed well."

A young Asian woman approached their table, her saffron-colored dress matching the sunshine outside. She bowed, welcomed them, and then shared a long list of specials that included something she called "a study in the tuna roll." Max resisted rolling his eyes, but shared a quick look with Cori.

"No cannibal sandwiches," she said with a wink.

He just smiled and after they ordered, leaned closer. "Tell me what you found out today."

"Absolutely nothing. No one knows much about that property. The person managing it is out for a few weeks, ostensibly in California at the site. I did talk to his assistant who showed me the original document. It had the same date, but was signed by Giff on William's behalf."

"Is that normal procedure?"

"Absolutely."

"Then why don't you ask Giff about the signature?"

She hesitated just a moment too long and Max

remembered the affectionate way the lawyer had touched her. Avuncular, yes. But could there be more to it? Could Cori be involved with her best friend's husband? *No.*

"Giff is thinking like a developer, not a lawyer."

"How's that?" Max asked.

"The Sonoma property is a highly controversial development in the heart of wine country. There's this incredibly picturesque town called Petaluma, and Peyton Enterprises has put a bid in for a five-hundred-thousand-square-foot mall, which will essentially change the town."

"The locals are fighting it?"

"Oh, of course, some of them. Others recognize the positive economic impact a giant Peyton mall brings to an area, especially one that, despite its location, is floundering. We own a home not far away, in Healdsburg," she said. "The project was personal. I love the area and, although he hadn't spent much time there, William knew that. He didn't want to ruin the town, but help it. He'd mentioned alternatives, including donating the land to the county as a reserve."

"A move that probably doesn't sit well with the executive committee of Peyton."

She shrugged. "Some are for, some are against. William ran a very democratic company, but always made the final decision. He died before making this one. So, Peyton owns the property, and I learned today that all of the permits have been pushed through and a vote is moot, because they've broken ground already. Construction's started. I talked to people, but it was all a dead end. If I want to stop it, I'd need to go out there. I might."

"So what happens if you don't? The mall goes up?"

"I made a motion to stop construction temporarily. We voted, but tied." She smiled wryly. "Seems like we needed Billy after all. Without his vote, we had a stalemate. Can you tell they'd like me to stick with the Foundation and nothing else?"

"You're obviously very good at that job."

"It's dear to my heart. It's the closest thing to what I wanted to do with my life."

"Help the underdog," he said. "So why don't you sell the company or your shares and go back to law school?"

She gave him a wistful smile. "Because William wanted a Peyton at the helm and Billy is MIA."

Their food arrived on wide, white platters containing minimal portions. He thanked the waitress and touched his sirloin with a fork. "Grilled, out of deference to you."

She picked up a seared scallop, the smell of sea and butter wafting toward him. "I'll ask Marta to make you some meat dishes. She'll be delighted. I don't eat red meat."

"You used to."

She held a bite of scallop midway between her plate and mouth. "I used to do a lot of things."

"Yeah, like drive your own car. Cook your own food. Laugh and make jokes."

"I laugh and make jokes," she shot back. "And I lost my husband three months ago, in case you forgot. I haven't exactly felt lighthearted."

"Think you'll remarry?"

The look on her face confirmed he'd caught her off guard. "I don't know."

"Think you'll date?"

She shrugged. "Maybe. Sometime."

"You will." Her sexuality was too powerful. He swallowed a bite of meat, along with the memory of her response to his touch early that morning.

"You seem sure."

"I know you."

"You used to know me," she corrected. "I've changed."

"You're more guarded," he noted, stabbing at some greenery in his salad. "That happens when people get money."

"That happens when people get hurt." She put her fork down to take a sip of water. "Honestly," she mused. "I'm not really comfortable with anyone but Breezy anymore."

"You were comfortable last night. Playing poker."

A soft flush colored her cheeks. "Okay. Breezy and you."

A direct hit, delivered with an enticing sparkle in her eyes, riveting enough to keep his attention from the room behind her. But instinct took over, pulling his gaze to a large man who moved purposefully toward them. Max dropped his hand to his lap to be nearer to his weapon.

The man, damn near as tall as Max, sported shoulder-length blond hair and a single diamond earring. He nodded to a patron but continued a dead-on

approach, his brilliant blue eyes locked on Max, un-
smiling.

Max's fingers inched closer to the Ruger.

"What is it?" Cori asked, glancing over her shoulder. "What's the—oh! Swen!"

Max put his napkin next to his plate and stood
swiftly, stepping away from the table in a move that
was both polite and protective.

But Swen didn't notice him. He'd zeroed in on Cori
and in a flash, she was wrapped in a tight embrace.
Max's fingers twitched toward his holster.

He kissed her, just a millimeter off the mouth,
then pulled away to grin and bare a perfect set of
bleached teeth. "So this is where I have to come to
find you." Swen squeezed tighter and *tsk*ed, adding a
slow shake of his mane. "Eating and drinking with
another man."

Cori laughed lightly, pulling back but keeping her
fingertips on his shoulders. Shoulders that had definitely seen some gym time.

"I've been very busy, as I'm sure you've heard."

"Oh, yes," Swen answered, his accent about as real
as the model in a Finlandia vodka ad. "By the way, I'm
so sorry I missed the fund-raiser the other night. I hope
you got the check I gave to Breezy."

"Of course, and that was extremely generous of
you." She frowned and asked, "Was she in today?"

"No, I didn't see her. Why?"

"I don't know. I'm a little worried about her. She
seemed . . . off this morning. Never mind." She let go of
him, and turned toward Max. "This is Max Roper. Swen

Raynor, the manager of the Mandarin's world-class spa."

Max shook his hand, unsurprised by the power in the man's grip. Swen gave him an approving nod, but quickly turned his attention back to Cori. "Are you almost done? I have a suite upstairs and a bed waiting for you. Let's go."

Cori looked at Max, then laughed. "It's not how it sounds," she assured him.

"I'm serious," Swen insisted, then ran a possessive finger along her jaw. "You look very tense, Corinne."

Max clenched his jaw, keeping his expression blank.

Swen glanced at Max, then his gaze dropped to his plate of half-eaten steak and a salad he'd barely touched. He whispered something that made Cori smile, and then ran his hand over Cori's back, settling way too close to her backside.

Maybe it was time to open his jacket, reveal the Ruger and suggest Finlandia was a little too close to his principal.

"Come and see me after lunch," Swen said to her, his accent rich with invitation as he patted her hip. "I can heal you." Then he looked pointedly at Max. "You're welcome in the spa anytime, Mr. Roper."

"I don't need healing."

"Is that so?" Swen's blue eyes sparked in amusement, then his gaze dropped to Max's salad plate. "Must be all that red clover."

With one more kiss on Cori's cheek, he ambled away, and Max stood watching him leave, guessing he was at least six two and two hundred pounds. No match for Max, but no doubt he appealed to the ladies.

"You were rude," she said, sitting back down and glaring at him. "He's been good to me and only has my best interests in mind."

"He's got more than that in mind."

"Swen?"

"He's . . . touchy."

"Touching me is his job, Max. He's my massage therapist."

Max stifled a grunt, picked up his fork, and stabbed the offending pink flower in his salad. "What is he, an herbalist *and* a masseuse?"

Cori stifled a laugh. "Nobody calls them that anymore. He's a *massage therapist*."

"Oh, excuse me."

"There's no need to be sarcastic. And yes, he is an herbalist. His mother was a well-known Finnish chef who wrote books on spices and herbs, so he's very smart about homeopathic and holistic treatments."

After their plates were removed, Cori opened a compact and discreetly reapplied some lipstick.

"So what does red clover heal?" Max asked. "A bad mood?"

She smiled at him over the edge of her mirror. "Come to think of it, it might."

"Seriously, what did he mean?"

"I think it does a lot of things. Makes you relax. He's had me take it in the past because it's supposed to enhance fertility." She snapped the mirror shut and tucked it in a side pocket. "Obviously it didn't work."

"Maybe the problem wasn't your fault," he suggested. She kept her attention on her handbag, her head still down. "Our fertility problems had nothing to do with William. I'm the one incapable of conceiving. He was fine."

There went the theory that she wanted to get rid of the husband who was too old to make a baby. And she certainly didn't hasten his death so she could take over the boardroom. That left only *money* as her motivator, which didn't fit at all.

Maybe Beckworth Insurance was sniffing around for the wrong reasons. Maybe William Peyton died of a heart attack, just like plenty of other sixty-three-year-old men.

But that didn't explain who shot at Cori, he thought as they strode over the black river rock that decorated the oriental-themed lobby.

"Maybe we ought to pay Billy a surprise visit," Max announced.

She stopped midstep. "Are you crazy? I don't want to see him."

"I'd like to see the two of you interact when he's sober."

"Trust me, it's not pretty." She nudged him toward the lobby doors. "You go grill Billy, I have something better to do." She headed in the other direction and he watched her disappear around a corner.

He knew where she was going and who she was going to, and swore under his breath. That long-haired Viking wasn't going to *heal* her.

"Is it so bad that you need to eat meals with your bodyguard?" Swen had rubbed oil on his hands for a full minute before he touched her, and still his fingers weren't as warm as Max's had been that morning.

"Is what so bad?"

"Your love life."

Cori smiled into the soft suede cushion that surrounded her face, looking through the hole at the single orchid in a vase, a signature symbol of relaxation that could be found in every nook and cranny of the four-story, five-star spa. "I don't have a love life, Swen. I'm a widow who likes to play solitaire and do charity work."

He pressed the muscles along her spine, rolling his thumbs. Still not as comforting as Max's touch behind her knees.

"Oh, I see." Swen kneaded gently. "Your bodyguard didn't like me."

"Charm isn't his specialty."

"He was jealous."

Something dangerously close to satisfaction hovered over her heart. "He's protective. That's his job."

Swen was quiet for a moment, knuckling the knots between her shoulder blades. "So," he finally said. "What do you think is wrong with our little summer breeze?"

"I don't know. She just seemed . . ."

"Off. You told me." Swen's hands paused for a moment. "Sometimes she gets moody, you know that. Last week she said—" A soft, digital beep interrupted him and he let out a frustrated sigh.

Could that be a phone? In the middle of her massage? It beeped again.

He swore softly. "I am so, so sorry, Corinne. They

would never call me unless it is an emergency. I am very sorry."

"It's okay, Swen. Answer it."

He pulled the sheet over her shoulders and picked up a cell phone while Cori settled deeper into the memory foam of the massage table. If it were a spa emergency, wouldn't they have called on the house phone that hung on the wall?

"I'm very, very busy," he said, his Finnish accent lilting over the words. "I see. Yes. Oh. That is a problem."

Part of her resented the intrusion, but Cori reminded herself that not only was she a walk-in, but as the manager, Swen took very few clients. She was here to relax, not get more uptight.

"I really can't do anything now," he said harshly into the phone. No, this was not going to be relaxing.

She looked up from the doughnut hole. "That's okay, Swen. I'll wait."

"All right, all right," Swen said, irritation growing. "I'll be there in a moment." He hung up with barely disguised disgust. "No one is capable of making a decision around here, and I think there is a very upset client downstairs who is about to ruin the Zen of my spa. I promise this will take ten minutes. Then we'll start all over and I won't upset you by talking about your bodyguard."

"That didn't— Just go, Swen. I'll wait. If you're not back in fifteen minutes, I'll just make a real appointment when I leave."

He bent over and kissed her on the head. "*Kiitos.*"

"You're welcome."

"Try to meditate. Inhale the patchouli and reverse the stress damage. I'll be back to finish this, I promise."

"All right." After all, where was she going to go? She had no idea if Max had taken her car and driver or waited for her in the lobby.

She eased her face back into the headrest and closed her eyes. Why had she run away from him? *Again.* It was easy to use the excuse of not wanting to see Billy, but she knew it was more than that. She wasn't scared of Billy.

But Max . . . Her mind drifted back to the kiss they'd shared the night before. The searing heat of his hands on her legs this morning. He'd been aroused and, God, so was she. Past aroused and dipping into desperate.

How long could they deny the chemistry that still crackled between them? A warm, sexual tingle pulled at her body, the feel of the cool cotton and the aromatic scents of the room sending waves of sensuality over her.

What was she doing here? She didn't want therapy. She didn't want to be healed. She wanted Max—the way he used to caress her and cover her body with his, filling her up with the length of him, groaning her name as he exploded over and over again.

She clenched her stomach and thighs, growing moist and taut and achy. She moaned softly, imagining Max sliding the sheet down, trailing her skin with his magnificent fingers, and his delicious, creative tongue. Heat rocked her hips in a move so natural she couldn't have stopped it if she wanted to.

Years melted away and she gave in to the memory of making love to Max. If she were on her stomach, like this, in her sleep, he would kneel over her, pulling her backside into his stomach and opening her gently before sliding into her.

She could feel the heat of his hips, the tickle of his sack as it thumped against her, arousal and need and hunger driving her insane, making her clutch the sheets and bite the pillow as he took her harder and faster and . . .

The sound of the rice-paper door sliding open doused her fantasy.

Cori froze, holding her breath and clinging to the tingly sensation. Had someone walked in, or was that her imagination? What if Max had stepped into the darkened room? What if the next hands to touch her were his . . . what if he'd come to her, as hungry and hot as she was?

She squeezed her eyes shut and listened, unwilling to lift her head and end the thrill of her daydream.

She heard a loud tap, then a scuff, a breath.

Someone was in the room. Apprehension tightened her belly, and she started to raise her head, to turn and look.

The *thwack* on her back was so ferocious, it forced her breath out with a grunt. Something hard immobilized her, pressed down on her, like a giant slab of cement. She groaned with the pain, and the vicious whip from fantasy to horror.

"Give it up!" Hot breath burned her ear, no more than a low growl full of threat and darkness.

She pushed, but something held her down. Hands? Iron? She couldn't catch her breath enough to scream, her limbs jerking helplessly. The pressure increased.

"Give it up or you'll be sorry!"

Fury and denial and the bone-deep instinct to survive bolted through her like an electrical charge, but she couldn't fight the power of what pressed down on her back.

"Give." The weight increased. "It." The pain intensified. "Up." The voice burned her ear. "Or you'll regret it."

Suddenly agony cracked against the base of her skull, sharp and blinding. In the moment it took for the blackness to descend, Cori knew she was about to die.

CHAPTER
Eight

"What the hell kind of bodyguard are you, any-way? Why weren't you in here with her?"

Pain shot through Cori's entire body with a high-pitched screech. Or was that Breezy's voice, an octave higher from panic? Breezy . . . screaming at . . . Max.

She tried to open her eyes, moaning with the effort, and an image of a man swam before her.

Max, leaning over her, holding her down with one hand . . . and holding off Breezy with the other.

"Get back," he ordered. "She's waking up."

Cori groaned as a wave of pain rolled from one side of her head to the other.

"Cori!" Breezy exclaimed, coming closer despite Max's command. "Oh my God, I thought you were dead."

"Me, too," she managed, her voice sounding far away.

Max's grip tightened on her shoulder. "You okay, kid?"

She tried to nod.

"Breathe," he ordered. "Slow, deep. Get some oxygen."

She did her best, smelling something spicy and sweet. *Patchouli.*

The scent brought everything back.

"I was getting a massage," she muttered, trying to sit up, but it felt like a knife was planted in her skull. Someone had attacked her.

"Easy, easy." Max guided her back.

"What happened?" Breezy demanded. "I came in here to talk to you and you were out. I couldn't wake you! Did you faint? Swen told me you were waiting for him and I—"

"Shhh." Max quieted her with a raised hand. "Give her a second. It'll come back to her."

Even the dim light of the massage room hurt her eyes, so she closed them and silently blessed him for silencing Breezy's voice.

"Everything . . . hurts."

"I'll call for an ambulance." Breezy whipped out a cell phone.

"No." Cori managed to rise a bit, but then realized Max was lifting her shoulders. She squinted for focus and her gaze landed squarely on him, locking onto the concern in his eyes, and something else. Anger? Was he mad at her for taking off and not telling him where she was going?

Or was it guilt for not being there when she'd been attacked?

"What happened?" Breezy begged again.

"Swen left to do something," she said foggily. "How long was I out?"

"I don't know," he admitted.

"I saw Swen downstairs, about ten minutes ago," Breezy said, snuggling into Cori's side. "He said you were up here in room four, and he had to calm down an upset client, but that you were waiting for him. I came in here to talk to you, and you were . . . totally out." Breezy's voice cracked as she gripped Cori's hand.

"Someone attacked me." Cori looked at Breezy, then Max. "Someone came in here and held me down, then hit me."

"What?" Breezy was incredulous, then she whipped around toward the dressing table. "Is your jewelry here?"

Cori sat up, cringing and barely holding the sheet over her breasts. "It didn't have anything to do with my jewelry. Someone sat on me and—"

"Sat on you?" Max demanded.

"Something strong and solid held me down," she recalled, thinking of the slablike weight on her back.

Max reached toward the floor, picking up a blue padded board no bigger than a throw pillow. "Could this be what felt like someone sitting on you? This, pressing on your back?"

She imagined the pressure, the flat weight of the reflexology footrest. "Yes. But then . . ." Slowly, she reached up to touch her head, wincing at the egg-size lump. "I was hit."

Max touched the spot under her hair and she winced. "A rabbit punch," he said. "Well placed, too. Someone knew exactly what they were doing."

"Oh, my darling," Breezy crooned. "We have to get you out of here. You need to go to the hospital."

"No," Cori insisted. "I'm fine. I just want to know who was in here and why."

Breezy sucked in a breath. "Do you think they . . ." She looked deliberately down the outline of Cori's sheet-covered body. "Touched you?"

"No." She didn't know how, but she just knew. Her attacker was trying to scare her. To *stop* her. She knew what and why . . . but not who.

"Who knew you were in here?" Max asked.

"No one, really." She looked at him. "It was a totally impulsive decision. The only person who knew was Swen and—"

"And I just saw him downstairs," Breezy said. "What did this guy say, Cor?"

"He said 'Go away.' No, no. Something like . . . give it up. Yes, that's what he said. 'Give it up.'" *Or you'll be sorry.*

"Oh, you poor thing." Breezy wrapped her in a hug. "I'll get you home and safe."

"I'll get her home," Max corrected. "Get her dressed. I'm going to question everyone in this spa. No one leaves. No employee, no guest."

"Good luck with that," Breezy said with an eye roll. "The place is a small city with four floors full of suites like this one, a health club, a sea of saunas and steam rooms, and about a hundred Chinese-speaking employees."

"I can handle it," he said, shooting her a hard look.

Cori grabbed his hand and he stopped. "Max, where were you?"

"In the lobby making a phone call. Then I tried to find you, but no one in the reception area knew where you were." He stood up and went to the door, sliding the rice-paper panels back and giving Breezy a measured gaze. "Don't leave her alone." Then he left.

Breezy patted her arm, her sympathy palpable. "Maybe you should listen."

"To him?"

"To whoever came in here and told you to give it up."

But Breezy didn't know what he was asking, or why.

"I want you to be safe," Breezy continued. "Although lately, even shopping isn't safe for you. Do you think Billy sent a thug?"

"I don't know," Cori said, finally sitting up. "What are you doing here? I thought you were going yachting with Lulu Garrey."

"Too hot. Too dull. And Swen called and told me they found my diamond earrings here from yesterday, and I had been so afraid I'd lost them. The ones Giff got from Bulgari."

"Oh." A memory of their morning conversation trickled through Cori's dazed mind. "Is that what was wrong this morning?"

Breezy shrugged. "Among other things."

Cori fought a wave of nausea. She'd talk to Breezy about whatever it was later. "Can you get my clothes?"

"Of course." Breezy pulled a suit off the hanger and smoothed the white silk blouse before handing it to

Cori. "Why would someone do this to you? And here of all places?"

"I don't know," she whispered as she buttoned her blouse with shaky fingers. Her bare foot stepped in something wet and she looked down to see the tipped-over vase, its flower crushed by someone's foot.

Whoever had been in that room may have—probably had—killed William.

The thought made her dizzy. "You sure you didn't see anyone leaving, Breezy?"

"Not a soul." Breezy handed her the skirt and when their hands touched, she held on to Cori for a moment. "If I were you, I'd be scared."

"I am."

But not scared enough to back down.

"So were you wrong about the walk in the park, Max?"

Max hated that Lucy knew him so well. "I'm only calling to see if there's any progress on the background checks I ordered and the signature scan I sent. Don't need a lecture."

God knows he'd kicked his own ass plenty for taking one ten-minute break from his bodyguard work to do investigative work, and his principal had paid dearly.

"Raquel is gone, but she left me a note that said our team in Helsinki is working on Raynor. There's nothing on Andrea Lockhart, except that she's been investigated once by the SEC for her involvement in insider trading, but she was exonerated. This was a few years before joining Peyton."

"All right. Thanks. I gotta—"

"Wait."

He closed his eyes and suppressed a groan.

"I have new information," Lucy announced.

He adjusted his position on the balustrade so he could see better into Cori's bedroom. The doctor was still sitting with her.

"The ME who did the autopsy on William Peyton has disappeared," she told him. "He resigned his job and left with his family on a flight to Kyoto, Japan. Beckworth Insurance thinks that's very odd."

"They're right. It is. But not illegal or suspicious. The guy performed hundreds of autopsies. What makes them think this move has to do with Peyton's death?"

"Timing."

He considered that. "Are we investigating? Are they?"

"I don't know what they're doing. I don't have anyone free at the moment, but I might in a week or so. In the meantime, what have you found on the widow?"

Her sweet spot. "No motive except inheritance, but she's always been ambivalent about money."

"No one is ambivalent about billions."

"I met a woman once," he said quietly, turning toward the pool area below, "who told me sweeping generalizations are always wrong."

Lucy laughed softly. "I'm never sure if you're listening. But I'd like to find out why she ordered cremation just hours after the autopsy report was filed, before another pathologist could confirm."

"Because the guy died of a heart condition, not a

stab wound, and there would be no reason for a second opinion."

"You're defending her," Lucy said.

"I'm considering every angle," he replied. "Including who and why someone attacked her today. I hit nothing but brick walls when I talked to employees and patrons of that spa." The doctor was heading for the bedroom door. "I gotta go, Luce."

He snapped the phone shut and trotted down the back spiral staircase to meet up with the doctor just as he got to the bottom of the main stairs.

"Dr. Mahesh," Max said as he approached. They'd met earlier, but the diminutive doctor still looked warily at Max. "How is she?"

"She does not need X-rays," the doctor said, his voice thick with an Indian accent. "She will be fine. Just rest."

"Does she have a concussion?"

He shook his head. "No. She can sleep now. It's been four or five hours. She needs three things: a warm bath, a light meal, and a good night's sleep."

He said it as though he knew her very well. "You've treated her before," Max said as he fell into a slow step with the doctor.

"Yes, of course. And Mr. Peyton, as well." There was just enough of a note of pride for Max to know that having the billionaire businessman as a patient was an honor.

"I imagine a man in his position monitored his health closely," Max said.

"I have not treated Mr. Peyton for several years," he

admitted. "But I believe he was in perfect condition and his death was a shock."

"He was at least healthy enough to want to start another family," Max noted.

Dr. Mahesh looked up at Max, a question in his eyes. "No."

"He wasn't? Was something wrong?"

The doctor slowed his step. "Nothing was wrong. He had a vasectomy years ago."

A vasectomy? Had Cori lied to him . . . or had she been lied to?

"I see," Max said as he opened the door. "I must have misunderstood."

When Dr. Mahesh left, Max closed the door and looked around Cori's estate.

All he had were questions. He wanted answers. Maybe he needed to call in a little backup to get some.

CHAPTER
Nine

"This better be good, Roper." Dan Gallagher put major irritation in his voice when he flipped his cell phone open with one hand, but he grinned at the woman in bed next to him. Tenderly, he thumbed the sweet pink nipple he'd been nibbling when the phone rang. "Just a sec, *ma cherie,*" he whispered to her.

She giggled at his lousy French, but arched her exquisite body into him.

"Where are you and what are you doing?" Max demanded.

"I'm in Paris, which means it's . . ." Dan paused, then rocked his very ready body against the concave of her stomach as he squinted at the clock on the nightstand. "What time is it, honey?"

"Can I safely assume you're not asking me?" Max deadpanned.

Dan's laugh was quick. "Actually, that was my polite way of answering the 'what are you doing' question. I'm busy." Her fingers encircled his erection and

Dan winced as pleasure shot through him. "*Très* busy."

"Aren't you working? Lucy said everyone's booked right now."

"Gig's up, but Lucy doesn't know yet," Dan said, straining to keep his voice steady as Monique stroked him. "And if you tell her before I'm done getting to know my new friend from the embassy, I'll have to kill you." He winked at the doe-eyed beauty with the magic French fingers.

He heard Max grunt a little, which probably accompanied an eye roll. Dan scooted up and gave Monique a pat. *"Attendez, cherie."* Not that he wanted her to wait, but he'd known Max for thirty years, and Monique for about thirty hours. Although they were really good hours.

"I need help," Max announced in a voice that was, if it was possible, more serious than usual.

"Hang on." Dan covered the mouthpiece of the phone and reached down to kiss Monique. "Call. Phone. Friend."

"I'm your friend, too," she whispered in charmingly accented English, punctuated by a squeeze on his cock.

Dan groaned. "I know, baby. *Attendez, s'il vous plait.* That means wait, I'm begging you."

She giggled and trilled something delightful in French, then slipped out of the bed, giving Dan a nice view of her ass as she tiptoed toward her bedroom door. He situated himself on the fluffy down pillows and held the phone to his ear with one shoulder.

"Roper, you owe me so big. What's up?"

"You know where I am?"

"Swimming with a few alligators in Florida." Lucy told Dan more than she told other Bullet Catchers. He knew where everyone in the organization was, and why. "Since it's August, I can only imagine how much the polar bear loves that."

"Did she tell you who I'm assigned to?"

"Uh-huh." Dan considered a wisecrack, but knew from experience that Cori Cooper was no joking matter. "And how's that going?"

"Interesting." Max, being Max, offered no more.

Dan, being Dan, couldn't let it go. "Interesting like you're pretending nothing ever happened and she can't keep her hands off you?"

"Just interesting."

"Interesting like she's forgiven you and you two have finally acknowledged that you were both wrong and still love each other?"

"You're worse than a freaking woman, you know that?" At least Max had a little humor in his voice. "I need a favor, not an advice column."

Dan grinned into the phone. "Oh, you need more than that, buddy, you just don't know it. What's up?"

"Can you get away for a few days?"

"Can I bring Monique the *Magnifique*?"

"No."

"Bastard. What do you need?"

"I need you to find a missing person and get some intelligence from him."

Dan sat up, Monique forgotten. "Who and where and about what?"

"A doctor, an ME, who might be in Kyoto."

"Japan?" Dan half-laughed. "Maybe you didn't hear me. I'm in Paris."

"Closer to Japan than I am."

Dan had to agree. "What's his name and what do you want to know?"

"I can't go into details right now. My principal is in the bathroom and could emerge at any minute." Max paused and Dan imagined him checking for the all clear. "I'll e-mail it all to you tomorrow. I just needed to confirm you could go, 'cause I can't leave here. She needs round-the-clock protection."

"I thought she needed investigation."

"You know everything about this?" Max sounded miffed.

"Hey, I'm watching your six, buddy. Will this take more than a few days? I don't want Monique to forget me. Not that it's possible, but hey."

"Listen," Max said. "When you find this guy—"

"When? You either have a lot of confidence or a lot of information on him."

"How many American pathologists can be running around Japan?" Max asked.

"It depends on whether or not the guy wants to be found. Is he hiding or sightseeing? And are you sure you don't want Lucy to know what's going on? She probably has some CIA connections in Japan to speed things up."

"We'll bring her in when we have to. Now listen, I need to get some information about a Finnish guy, too. Is Romero still in Helsinki?"

"You'd go to Alex Romero for help?" Uneasiness stirred in Dan. "Man, you are in a bind."

"I need information. Alex's wife is very good at getting that."

"Alex and Jazz are both in Helsinki and should be there at least another month," Dan told him. "You can e-mail him."

"I'll e-mail *her*," he said emphatically.

"And who am I looking for in Japan?" Dan asked.

"The ME who performed an autopsy on William Peyton. The only one, because there was no second opinion."

"Cause of death?" Dan asked.

"Sudden cardiac failure. So, no reason to do a second. But Cori ordered an immediate cremation."

"Still not unusual," Dan suggested, "for a grieving widow."

"If she's grieving." He waited a beat before continuing. "Now the ME has disappeared. Resigned his position, left the country with his family. I want you to find him and see if there was anything unusual about Peyton's autopsy that didn't get into his report."

"What do you suspect?"

"All I know is this: This woman is married to a sixty-something billionaire, who happened to be in perfect health when he drops dead in her bed. She gets all the money, voting shares on a highly competitive company board, and several luxurious homes in the process. The stepson gets nothing. And now I find out from their GP that the old man had a vasectomy, after she tells me they were trying to have a baby." Max lowered his voice even more. "There's some other stuff going on around here and it stinks. The whole thing doesn't add up right and

I'm starting to agree that William Peyton's death was just too damn convenient."

Dan waited, but Max was suddenly silent.

"Who are you talking to?" The demand from a female near Max came through Dan's end loud and clear.

The connection died and Dan rose reluctantly from the comfortable bed. Mad Max was busted. But he'd handle it. In the meantime, Dan had just enough time for a shower with Monique before leaving for Japan.

"Who are you talking to?" Cori repeated, but all Max did was close the phone, facing away from her. He had to come clean and tell her the truth. Had to turn around and admit that he was conducting a very preliminary, but very real investigation into her involvement in her husband's death.

What would he find when he turned around? Angry sparks? The palm of her hand whipping in his direction? Tears, denials, and demands that he leave?

Or would she just do what she'd done the last time they'd clashed . . . run away?

He pocketed his phone and slowly pivoted to face her. Instead of furious she looked . . . hopeful. Relieved, even.

"I was talking to Dan Gallagher," he said, his gaze flitting over the thin robe she had wrapped around her.

Her fist clutched the knot at her waist. "I heard you say something about Beckworth. That William's death was too convenient. What did they find? What do you know?"

He glanced at her skimpy cover-up again, and the

tenuous hold she had on it. "You want to get dressed or have this conversation in a robe?"

"I don't want to have this conversation at all," she said. "But I can't put it off any longer."

"What do you mean?"

She studied him for a long time, then wet her lips. "I think my husband was murdered."

"You do." He purposely didn't show any surprise. "Why?"

"I'm first with questions. What were you talking to Dan about?"

"My objective here."

"Your objective? Other than keeping me alive?"

He leveled his gaze and didn't blink. "I've also been asked to investigate your role in your husband's death."

Her eyes widened. "That explains a lot."

He watched every infinitesimal change in her expression, waiting for a telltale sign of guilt. But she never looked away, never paled, never even tugged her robe with nervous fingers.

And Cori never could bluff, either.

"Have you found anything?" she asked. "A single clue to prove I pulled off a perfect crime to inherit a few billion dollars?"

In truth, no. "I think it's odd that your doctor told me your husband had a vasectomy."

"Mahesh hadn't treated William in years. His vasectomy was reversed after we were married, and there's a microsurgeon at Mercy Hospital who'll confirm the reversal." She lifted one eyebrow. "And by the way, that's not exactly a smoking gun."

"I just found it surprising since you said you were trying to have a child."

"But not relevant," she said dismissively. "Any other reason to suspect me?"

"You were the last to see him alive."

"And I inherited a ton of money," she agreed. "And Beckworth is scared of pissing off a major client."

"Probably." He took a step closer. "Okay, my turn. How long have you suspected foul play?"

"From the minute he died."

He tried to process that. "What? What happened? And why didn't you tell anyone?"

Her jaw set. "I didn't know who to trust."

"Trust me."

She looked doubtful, then nodded. "I guess I don't have a choice now." She tilted her head to the sofa in an invitation. "Sit down. And don't interrogate me, Max," she warned. "I'll tell you the truth."

"Okay," he agreed. "But start from the beginning."

"The beginning was the end," she told him, sliding down the edge of the armrest to sit on the sofa with him. "The night he died. There was nothing leading up to it, no clues, no indication. Yes, he'd gotten a little more safety conscious, as that bulletproof glass indicates, but he was a wealthy man with vast holdings. That didn't set off any alarms."

"What did?"

"His last words." Her voice was soft, and ominous.

"Tell me everything that happened that night."

She lifted a shoulder. "That's just it. Nothing happened. It was the most uneventful evening. William hadn't worked late and, for once, we had no function to attend. Marta had the night off and had gone to her sister's house. I made dinner, we each had a glass of wine, and we watched television. The most mundane evening imaginable, watching Larry King and the news."

"What time did you go to bed?"

"I made some lemon balm tea and went upstairs around eleven."

"And William?"

"I think . . ." She drew her mouth in a tight line. "I think he went down to the boat."

He waited for her to elaborate.

"I was in the bathroom washing up when he said he'd be back in a little while, and I'm almost certain that's where he said he was going. On another night he might have gone into his office to work, or to the kitchen for a late snack, but he and Giff were planning to go offshore fishing early the next morning. So I think he went to the boat, probably to program the chart plotter for their course, or check the fishing gear and weather reports. I honestly never really knew."

"How long was he gone?"

She thought for a moment. "It could have been a half hour, an hour."

"Were you awake when he came in?"

She shook her head. "The tea makes me sleepy."

"Did your husband drink it?"

"No. He hated the taste of it."

"More wine?" Max leaned forward. "Did he finish the bottle?"

"Nope. He wasn't a big drinker."

"So then what happened?"

She exhaled and wrapped her arms around her waist. "Maybe an hour later, midnight or one, he got up to go to the bathroom. I didn't hear him or wake up. I heard water running—the toilet flushing or the sink. But I'm not sure. The next thing I knew, he was in bed, moaning and gripping me."

"What did he say?"

"He said . . ." She looked at him, raw pain in her eyes. "He said, '*Cara*—that's what he called me—'this wasn't meant for me.' "

"What wasn't?" Max urged.

"I don't know; I was half asleep. I sat up to turn on the light and he stopped me. Held me, but his hands were so cold and shaking." Her voice cracked and he saw her swallow. "Then he told me to be careful. He told me that . . . I couldn't be too careful. Then, he said it again. 'This wasn't meant for me.' Then he died."

Her eyes glistened with unshed tears.

She loved him. The knowledge punched him and Max stood suddenly. "That could have several meanings," he said. "Like his death was too soon, or not meant to be."

"I thought of that," she agreed, tucking her feet under her. "But there was something in the way he said it that . . . that made me distrustful of everyone."

He paced across the patio, then looked at her. "Why didn't you tell the police? Why haven't you done anything?"

She pulled the robe over her exposed legs. "Because

the autopsy said he died of a thrombosis and emboli, and there was nothing in him or done to him to cause a blood clot to the heart. It was pronounced a natural death."

"Did you consider a second opinion?"

She shook her head. "Those first few weeks, I was in a fog. In shock. Billy was wild, making insane accusations, and I just tried to shut everything out. I wasn't even thinking straight until about six weeks ago."

He waited a moment, considering what to tell her. "I just found out that the medical examiner is missing."

"What? The doctor who did the autopsy? Yakima Bauer?"

He frowned. "What's his name?"

"Yakima Bauer. He's half German, half Japanese."

"Half Japanese?" He recalled his blithe promise to Dan. "He might be more difficult than I thought to find in Japan."

"What do you mean?"

He briefly explained that the ME had left the country and that he'd asked Dan to track him down.

"I have a copy of the autopsy," she told him. "Would it help to look at it?"

He nodded. "And make a list of anyone who would want your husband dead."

"I tried. I couldn't come up with anyone, honestly. I'll show it to you." At his curious look, she added, "I've been very quietly checking out every board member, reading their personnel files, and old e-mails to and from William. I haven't hired investigators because I wanted to be able to give someone specific direction. Of course, the deeper I look, the more vulnerable I am."

"That's why you hired a bodyguard."

"Exactly. Billy's antics and big mouth provided the perfect excuse to hire protection while I try to figure this out. But I know this in my heart—it wasn't Billy."

Max happened to agree. "Someone knows what you're doing." He crouched down in front of her and put his hand on her leg. "You realize that, don't you? Whoever took a swipe at you in the parking lot and a shot at you in your cabana and clocked you in the spa. He knows."

She nodded slowly. "I'm going to find him, Max."

"No," he corrected. "We are."

"Why aren't you wearing the Bulgari earrings, Breezy?" Gifford lifted a strand of blond hair and peered at his wife's bare earlobes.

She flicked at her hair and took in enough of a breath to lift her well-exposed cleavage an inch.

"I thought your other gift would distract you enough not to notice."

His gaze dropped to her bosom, round and high and glistening with a golden sheen. "If you lost those fucking earrings, I'm not going to notice anything."

"Chill out. They're in a safe."

"Where?"

Breezy grabbed a silk wrap and her evening bag from the vanity, knocking over an open lipstick that hit the white carpet. Swearing softly, she scooped up the gold tube.

"I told you this afternoon. Swen has them in a safe at the Mandarin."

"I know you told me," he said, examining her face for signs of a lie. "But when I called you, you said you were on your way there to pick them up."

She sighed. "I got distracted. Let's go."

Giff followed her out of the bedroom, pausing in front of a mirror in the hallway to check out the off-white Armani suit he wore with the open-collared shirt. He straightened his shoulders and touched the single button on the jacket, exposing the edge of his Rolex watch.

He touched the balding spot on his head before stepping away. "What distracted you?"

"Oh, Giff, it was awful. Someone barged into Cori's massage room and . . ."

"And what?" He stopped halfway down the curved stairs and glared at her. "What happened to her?"

"We really don't know. Someone attacked her."

"What?" He tried to think of a reason someone would walk into a massage treatment room and attack a client. "Was she hurt?"

"Not really. Just scared, poor thing." She tugged at his sleeve. "C'mon, we're really late."

"Billy," he said as he followed Breezy down the stairs.

Breezy opened the front door and nodded to the waiting limo driver. "Sorry, we were a bit delayed. Drinks ready?"

"Of course," he responded, opening the back door for her.

Giff followed Breezy into the back and before he'd taken off his jacket, she'd handed him a glass of Scotch and had her own champagne ready.

"Could have been Billy," she said, "trying to convince Cori to give up the fight and turn over his father's estate to him."

"Pretty stupid way of going about it," Giff noted.

"Billy's stupid," Breezy said. "To us, my love," she said, clinking his glass and taking a healthy gulp. "Drink up, because who knows what the bar situation is going to be at this gallery."

He sipped, and Breezy cuddled in next to him, sliding her hand between his legs and fondling his nuts. "You want me to relax you, baby?"

He waited for his cock to stir under her touch. But he didn't feel sexy. He felt old and bald and troubled. He sipped again, laying his head back while she stroked. His balls tightened a little and he let out a breath of relief, but then the first twinge started. Like a needle to his temple. "Shit," he muttered, slurping some Glenlivet.

"What's the matter, Giff?" Breezy asked, her fingers still for a moment. "The headaches again?"

He just groaned. The headaches he could stand. It was the other part, right after the headaches started. The scary part.

"Easy, Giff. Drink." She unzipped his pants and slid her hand into his shorts. "Just let me take care of you."

He took a solid slug of Scotch, the ice touching his lips as the hot liquor burned his throat.

The guilt started like a black ball in his gut, moving up, taking over. He shouldn't relax. He shouldn't be going to gallery openings and charity events.

He should be home figuring a way out of his mess.

He squeezed his lids as the needle in his temple dug deeper and the back of his eyes throbbed. Slowly, he opened them. Praying . . . hoping . . . oh *fuck*.

Breezy's cool, damp fingers slid over his cock but he remained limp. "Come on, baby," she cooed, stroking him. "I know you like this."

He took one more deep drink and spread his legs. He did like it. He always liked it when Breezy took care of him. That's what she did; that's why he married her. He squeezed his eyes and willed his dick to respond, but pain speared behind his eyes.

What kind of man couldn't get it up for a quick blow job in the back of a limo from his willing wife?

She stroked again, licking her fingers and sliding her wet hand over him.

A guilty man, that's who.

She dipped her head to suck him, but he pushed her away. "Not now, Breezy."

She looked up at him, her eyes glinting, then softening. "Whatever you want, baby."

Shadows darkened his peripheral vision. "Later," he murmured. When the headache was gone, if his remorse and shame and worry hadn't siphoned all his blood to his brain instead of his dick, he'd take advantage of the woman he'd selected with the same care he gave every decision that reflected who he was.

He had to *think*. No matter how much it hurt.

"Where was that bodyguard?" he asked suddenly,

causing Breezy to straighten and carefully replace him in his shorts. "He didn't go five feet from her at the board meeting this morning. How did someone get by him?"

Breezy shrugged. "She escaped him somehow and got to Swen."

Giff took a slow sip, finishing the Scotch as the inside of the limo got darker and darker at the edges of his vision. He closed his eyes to block out the reality of something that superseded all his sins and all his troubles.

Something that felt sickeningly like karmic retribution. Something he couldn't deny any longer.

"You okay, Giff?"

No, he was *not* okay. But how could he tell his beautiful, prized wife that the world she'd so carefully built with her quick wit, her model's body, and her always-ready tongue was coming to an end? How could he tell Breezy that he was slowly going blind?

CHAPTER
Ten

"Ronald Mendoza is here," Marta announced.

Cori looked up from the vanity mirror, her mascara applicator frozen mid-stroke. "The broker for William's boat?"

As it did every time William's name was mentioned, Marta's wide mouth turned downward with sadness. "He's down on the dock. With Mr. Roper."

Cori grabbed a pair of sneakers and a few minutes later, a cup of coffee in hand, stepped into the wicked summer humidity and sunshine and headed toward the dock. Men's voices floated up from the water, and as she neared the gate, she saw Max standing on the rear deck deep in conversation with the broker she'd hired to sell the forty-eight-foot motor yacht. She slowed her step and drank in the image of the man she once loved so ferociously that it hurt to look at him.

Sometimes it hurt still.

He wore a white knit polo shirt over khaki pants,

the fitted short sleeves doing just what her fingers itched to do—wrap around his sizeable biceps just for the pleasure of squeezing the granite-hard muscle. His dark hair lifted at the roots in the breeze, tempting any woman to tangle her fingers in the thick strands. He stood solid and steady, unfazed by the slight sway of the vessel in the water.

As the boat broker was talking, Max suddenly turned as if he sensed her coming. She knew the feeling . . . mutual radar.

She unlatched the gate and walked down the dock. "Good morning, Ronald."

The man turned and greeted her with a wave. "Nice to see you, Mrs. Peyton."

As she approached the boat, Max stepped up to the dock and held out his hand to help her on board.

"Morning," he said, the gleam in his eye making her dizzy even before she felt the slight pitch of the motor yacht. When she slipped her hand into his, the naturalness of the feeling rocked her.

She turned her attention to the broker, releasing her hand from Max's once she found her footing. "I didn't expect you so soon, Ronald. I thought you said next week."

Ronald Mendoza gave her a bright salesman's smile. "The buyers will be here then, but I wanted to get some paperwork done today."

"I still have to get some personal items," she told him. She'd wanted Marta to clean out the boat, but the poor woman couldn't even make it through the task of emptying her former boss's closet, let alone his beloved boat. "Did you want us to run her around the Bay one more time?"

"No need, Mrs. Peyton, but it would be nice to have her gassed up. But please, take the weekend," Ronald said with a hint of sympathy in his voice. Then he lifted a nylon briefcase. "Here's the bill of sale."

She glanced at Max and saw the sheen of perspiration above his lip. "Let me run up and get my keys, so we can work inside in the AC."

"I still have a key from the showings," Ronald said, moving toward the cabin door to unlock it.

As soon as she stepped inside, Cori remembered why she'd been on the boat only once in the last six months. The salon was drenched in William's favorite colors of tan and cream and black, with two leather divans circling a coffee table, a plasma screen TV at one end, and burled wood shelving and storage units along the whole port side.

Ronald spread his documents on the coffee table, and Max passed through the galley and disappeared into the forward stateroom. She'd never slept there, she thought guiltily. But then, William had never asked. He'd been very understanding about her seasickness.

As Ronald chatted about the buyers from North Carolina, her gaze drifted around the cabin, taking in the details of William's haven: the row of classical music CDs that he used to blare from the hidden speakers, the framed picture of her on one bookshelf.

She gazed at the photo, taken on their honeymoon. She was sitting cross-legged in the sand on the French Riviera. She reached for the picture, but the frame had been anchored into place. Of course, nothing on the boat rolled around in the waves.

Fiddling with the edges of the frame, she snapped it out of the clasps and lifted it from the shelf. A glimmer of gold tucked into a corner behind the frame caught her attention.

She picked up a sculpture of a palm tree, not much bigger than her hand, its golden fronds extended as though they were caught in hurricane winds. Turning over the thick base, she ran a finger along the letter engraved in the middle: W. Words encircled the letters, an unbroken stream of lovelovelovelove. Like an eternity circle surrounding the letter W.

What was this?

"They expect the trip will take a few days, but by the time it's over, they'll know their new ship, don't you think?" Ronald asked her.

The sculpture weighed heavily in her hand. "Excuse me?"

"The Hamilton family," Ronald said. "They are planning to cruise back to North Carolina instead of having the boat transported."

"Oh." Cori replaced the palm tree on the shelf. "I'm sorry. . . . I . . . I . . ." She smiled apologetically. "I wasn't paying attention."

He gave her an understanding nod. "We're just about finished. All you have to do is sign three more papers and *Peyton's Place* will officially belong to someone else."

She glanced once more at the sculpture, then took the pen.

"The boat is in beautiful condition," he said as he pointed to the red Xs where she needed to sign.

"The divers come every week or two to get the barnacles off the bottom and run the air-conditioning," she said absently. She'd spent only one afternoon on board *Peyton's Place* after William died, the day that she and Breezy and Giff had taken it out to dispose of William's ashes in Biscayne Bay. She'd been so sick, they'd even cut that excursion short.

She pushed the signed paperwork across the table toward the broker.

"That will do it," he told her. "The Hamiltons will be here toward the end of next week." He handed her the boat key he'd used. "And I won't be needing this anymore."

She took it, and shook his hand. After a brief discussion of logistics, he was gone. She stood on the rear deck as he disembarked, her gaze drifting to the cabana where Marta had arranged for wood boards to cover the shattered glass.

Max emerged from the salon, lowering his head to clear the threshold and nailing her with a look that sent her stomach spiraling downward in a familiar, helpless sensation. Definitely *not* seasickness.

"Are you all done?" he asked.

"I still have to clean out William's belongings."

He studied her with that furrow in his brow, then his expression softened. "You okay?"

She touched her stomach lightly. "If I can breathe open air. I prefer the deck to below."

"Why don't you stay here and let me get whatever

needs to go," he offered, taking the keys from her hand.

"I just might." She gave him a quick smile of appreciation. "But I'll have to go in at least one more time and look around, maybe get some storage boxes from the house. I have no idea how much stuff he has in the bureau and armoire. It could take five minutes or it could take two hours to unload it all."

On the way through the salon, she glanced at the palm tree sculpture, then looked away, a different kind of queasiness rolling through her as her mind raced for an explanation. Where would he get that?

In the forward stateroom, the king-size bed, covered in a navy and gold silk spread, took up most of the room. A custom-made bureau and armoire filled one wall and another plasma screen TV took up another. She slid the top bureau drawer open, surprised to find it empty. As was the next, and the next, and the next.

"That's funny," she said. "I know he kept clothes here."

But the bureau had been completely cleaned out.

"Maybe your housekeeper beat you to the job."

"I doubt it," Cori said. "She would have asked for instructions about his clothes and personal items."

She opened every single drawer, and they were all empty except for the second to last, where a quarter was lodged under the wood, along with some purplish dust.

"What's that?" Max asked, kneeling down to examine it. He ran a finger through it, then smelled. "It looks like . . ." He brushed some of the iridescent color on the back of his hand. "Eye shadow."

She laughed a little. "Not likely, unless William had a secret life of cross-dressing."

As Max continued to trail his finger over the seam in the back of the drawer, Cori turned to the armoire; it had been cleaned out as well.

"I don't get this," she said, staring at the empty rod where William's clothes would have hung. Had she done this already, in a grief-induced fog, and forgotten? "I did come down here, once. I thought I might find something, some clue. I know there were clothes in those drawers."

"Marta must have done it without telling you," Max said. "I'll check the head."

Cori stood in the middle of the stateroom, rubbing her arms against a sudden flurry of goose bumps on her arms. There was nothing on the dresser top, nothing . . . anywhere.

She turned back to the galley and salon and headed toward the wall where numerous cubbyholes opened and closed for storage. But her whole being was drawn to that strange sculpture of a wind-whipped palm tree.

"Cori?" Max stood in the doorway between the stateroom and the galley, an odd look on his face. In his hand, he held a leather case, which she recognized immediately as William's toiletry kit. "Was this your husband's?"

"If it has the initials WGP on it, yes."

Max looked down at the side facing him, then tilted the case to show her the gold letters. "Could it have been Billy's?"

"No. Billy's middle name is Hobart, his mother's maiden name."

She reached for it, but Max drew it back. Looking up at him, she scowled. "What's the matter?"

"Are you certain it was his?"

"Yes." Apprehension twisted tighter, more from his tone of voice than the words. "Let me look, Max."

Slowly, he held the case toward her. "I found it under some folded towels in the cabinet. It could easily have been missed by whoever cleaned this place out."

Max had left the zipper open and she peeked in. A toothbrush, toothpaste, aftershave, a razor and a . . . box of condoms.

"Oh." The sound was out before she could catch herself. She looked up at Max.

Why, oh God, *why* would he have the one personal item they had never, ever used?

"Was there anything else in the bathroom?" she asked.

"Not much besides towels and some cleaning supplies."

Wordlessly, she turned around. "I need to get out of here." As she hustled through the salon, she paused long enough to grab the gold statue, then rushed through the sliding doors to gulp some air.

Cori perched on the cushioned leather seat that ran around the stern, clutching something gold, staring straight ahead.

Max watched her silently until she lifted her head and stared back at him, her eyes nearly as navy as the water behind her. "There has to be an explanation."

He'd returned the bag to the stateroom, but not before checking the expiration date on the condoms. They were good for another four years, which meant they'd been purchased—and several had been removed—within the last year.

"There has to be a reason," she insisted. "He found them. Or someone left them on board. Or . . . or there's some other function for a condom. Like for fishing."

He wished he could think of one.

"A gag gift?" she said weakly.

"Cori—"

She held up her hand to halt him. "Don't give me sympathy. I don't want sympathy. I want to figure this out."

"Did you know?"

She cut him with a look. "Did I know what, Max?"

He let out a breath. "That your husband had a need for condoms?"

"I guess I didn't know everything about William," she said, toying with the small sculpture in her hand. She turned it over, and he could see it was a palm tree. "I've never seen this before, either."

He sat down next to her and took it. "Whoa. This is solid gold." He flipped it over and studied the engraving. "A circle of love," he said. "Around a W."

Yanking it from his hands, she stood up. "I'm going back in there. I want to see what else is left."

He gave her three minutes alone, then found her seated on the bed of the stateroom, the contents of the Dopp kit dumped in front of her. Holding a man's razor, she looked up. "This is all his stuff. His shaving cream. His favorite toothpaste. His travel-size cologne."

Max leaned against the doorjamb. "Was it possible your husband was having an affair?"

She picked up the condom box. "I'm not so stupid that I can sit here holding these and unequivocally say *no*. I'm just . . . I'm in shock." She picked up the empty leather bag and slammed it against the bed.

Then she swiped the spread, sending bottles, tubes, and a hairbrush flying. Her face contorted, her color high, she picked up the gold palm tree and whipped it across the room full force, where it crashed into the bureau, took a chunk of mahogany and fell on the floor with a thud. "Goddamn it!"

Her voice cracked as she fell forward, and Max rushed to her.

"Cori," he whispered as he folded her in his arms and she melted into his chest with a gut-wrenching sob. "Shhh." He wrapped his arms around her and kissed her head. "It's okay, it's okay."

"No, it's not." She was shaking so hard he could practically feel the blood boiling in her veins. "It's not okay."

He had no idea what to say, so he just held her, stroked her hair and let her cry, thinking of the son of a bitch who had Cori Cooper in his bed and wanted someone else. He kissed her hair and made small circles with his hand on her back until she stopped crying.

"I thought he was impotent," she murmured.

He pulled back to look at her. "What?"

"That's what really hurts," she admitted. "He . . . we . . . didn't. Anymore." She closed her eyes, color rising to her cheeks. "We stopped making love a few years ago. Our marriage turned platonic. Not bad, not troubled. Just not sexual."

"I thought you said . . ." Max forced himself to think like an investigator and not a former lover. "Didn't you say it was your fault you couldn't get pregnant?"

"It wasn't his," she said. "Not in the beginning. We figured it was me, although none of the preliminary tests showed why. Then, after we started formal infertility treatment, William just lost interest. It was too clinical for him. And, no, before you ask, he wouldn't take anything so that was out of the question."

"Whoever he was sleeping with probably killed him, Cori, or had him killed. You know that, don't you?"

She nodded slowly, her look still far away. "How could I be so blind? I should have come down here more often, but I always get so seasick. I never thought that when he went overnight . . . or for a weekend. Oh, God." Her voice cracked again.

"You can't beat yourself up," he told her. "You have to think about who it could have been. Who might have seen them. Where they could have gone."

She nodded, wiping some makeup from under her eyes. "Where do we start?"

He stood up. "Right here. In the water. We're going to take this thing to every gas station, every marina, and every possible place in Biscayne Bay where he could have taken this boat, and I'm going to do what I do best."

"Get people to talk."

"Yep. You can ride in the bow so you don't get sick."

"Too late for that," she said bitterly, picking up a remnant from William's Dopp kit.

CHAPTER
Eleven

When he was straight and sober, Billy Peyton could do just about anything. But when he was high, he could do anything better. At least, that's what it felt like.

Right now he was moderately stoned, but after he got his car back, he'd go deep. He'd go as far away as he could get.

"Just wait here," he said to the woman who'd driven him to Cori's house. Violet? Lily? Some flower, he vaguely recalled. It had been loud in the Ocean Drive club where he'd met her an hour ago, and he hadn't been paying much attention to her when she approached. She was a little on the chunky side, and definitely on the desperate side, but she'd said the magic words . . . *Star Island* . . . and Billy moved in with his usual finesse.

It would have been better if she lived on the Island, not worked there, but she got right past the guards and that was all that mattered.

"Are you going to call in?" she asked. "I mean, isn't it kind of late to surprise your mother?"

He loved the whole "I'm going to surprise my mom and be the first to say happy birthday" story he'd given her. It was so freaking clever and he knew this girl would have never have given him access to the Island to take a car.

"Nah, it'll be great. I'll go up first and surprise her, then I'll let you in, 'kay?"

She looked a little wary, so he leaned closer. Yes, Billy Peyton could do just about anything, and convincing this chick that he liked her was way too easy. "I have a room in this house," he said, low and sexy. "Wait for me, so you can come up for a little while." He needed her not to leave until he had the Gallardo.

Her lips twitched and for a second, he thought she was going to laugh at him. But she smiled, revealing straight, white teeth that nudged her over from fat to kind of cute. He dropped his gaze to her chest and momentarily considered fucking her, but then common sense took over.

He had a rock of gold dust at home and he'd rather fuck his head up than her.

All he had to do was get his car, drive out—the gate opened automatically from the inside—and tell . . . Daisy? Rose? . . . . to follow him to Coconut Grove. He could lose her before he hit Biscayne Boulevard.

"Stay here, babe," he said, leaning closer like he was going to kiss her, and letting some hair fall over his eye. He'd used his looks before to get what he wanted with women, usually sex or drugs. All he needed from her was a ride. "I'll be five minutes, all right?"

She ran her tongue over her lips. " 'kay."

He slipped out and jogged to a specific place in the side wall, well out of range of her rear view. If she saw him jump the fence, she might get spooked and go get the Island guards.

Once in the shadows, Billy found the piece of stucco that pointed out and formed a foothold. If Cori had that bodyguard around much longer, there'd be dogs and cameras and armed freaking guards. But until then, Billy knew every way there was to sneak into the house.

He ripped his shirt on the wall and scraped his palms, wiping his hands over his mouth and tasting a drop of blood. Stumbling on a tree root, he managed not to make any noise as he checked out the house and headed toward the driveway. He patted his pocket to make sure he still had his spare key.

Some lights were on and he couldn't see the back rooms, but she might still be awake. Then he heard voices, low and serious, from a patio on the side.

He froze for a moment, squinting into the shadows. Powered by the hit of pot he'd had at the club, he tip-toed along the wall, well hidden by the shrubs. He heard the voices again and paused. He dared a few more steps, propelled by curiosity.

"It just doesn't make any sense that no one would remember seeing them together."

A man responded, but Billy couldn't make out what he said. He waited, hearing nothing but crickets and a dog in the distance. Could he get in his car and drive it away without attracting their attention? He'd been counting on her being asleep at this hour.

"I think the guy up at the Bayshore Marina seemed more than a little surprised to see me," Cori said.

"You said you never go out on the boat."

Billy's face contorted. So she went cruising on the old man's boat, enjoying the fruits of his labor. And he recognized that voice now. The human Doberman with the motherfucker of a gun.

"What are you going to tell the insurance company?" she asked.

Why would they be involved? Christ, did she wreck the boat or something?

"Nothing until we hear from Dan and find out what the doctor says." The baritone of the bodyguard was easy to make out as Billy moved closer. "They don't have enough to open a case yet."

A case of what?

"They have enough to investigate me," Cori said. "Enough to suspect me of killing my own husband."

Billy stood dead still, excitement seeping through his veins like a shot of really good dope. The insurance company thought that she killed Dad?

"Then . . ." The bodyguard was talking, but too low to understand. "Put the suspicions to bed."

Billy squinted, swearing because he'd missed critical words.

"But what do they have? Nothing. A missing ME, and doubts. That's certainly not enough to take to a grand jury."

"You have a motive, Cori."

Oh, yeah. Now we're talking.

"I'm the one who knows the truth, Max. I'm the one who saw him die and, except for that pathologist, I'm the only one who knows it wasn't a heart attack."

Every hair on the back of Billy's neck catapulted to attention. It *wasn't* a heart attack? A *grand jury*? He inched closer, moving some shrubbery, unable to hear the bodyguard's response.

Damn. Billy eased closer to the edge of the patio, kneeling down because his legs felt shaky. If he got caught, that thug would kill him. But their voices had dropped and he had to hear what they were saying.

"Until then . . . I'm accused of murder."

Holy shit. Did he hear that right? The insurance company actually thought she killed Dad? No wonder she hired a bodyguard. All that crap about him scaring her? Oh, this was rich. This was fucking rich.

Billy tried to hear the bodyguard's response, but his pounding blood deafened him. He knew enough. He knew now that Cori killed his father, just as he always suspected. And she was scared. He could hear it in her voice.

He almost shrieked for joy. This was all he needed to change everything. He would ruin her. Even if she wasn't guilty, if anyone even suspected it, he'd get everything. Everything.

He stood up too fast, making his head reel and his legs wobble, knocking a branch against the wall.

Cori went silent midword, and a sliding door opened and closed.

Swearing silently, Billy raced through his options. He turned and peered through the bushes into the dark. What should he do? Haul ass and get shot? Come clean . . . and maybe still get shot? She'd call it self-defense. He should just walk to his car like he owned the place—which he would, soon—and get out of there. But he might still get shot. He waited, listening. Damn—if he'd only heard a little more, something more concrete to pin on her.

He had to get the hell out of there.

He bolted toward the driveway, digging for the key in his pocket, but that cost him his balance and he tripped, sucking in a breath as the ground came up and slammed in his face.

Then something hard hit his back—a shoe—and that prick's gun jammed into his neck.

"I told you to leave her alone." He seized Billy with one massive hand, yanking him up and back so hard that pain shot down his spine.

Spit flew out of Billy's mouth. "I just want my car, man. That's all."

"It's not parked on the side of the house." The gun bit deeper into his neck.

"Please . . . don't . . . shoot." Icy black fear closed his throat. "I'm leaving. I'm leaving." He didn't want to get shot. Not now. Not when everything was about to turn around.

But the bodyguard wouldn't let go. "What are you doing here, Billy?"

"I heard voices," he said, haltingly. "And I just wanted to be sure Cori was okay."

The man pulled Billy into a band of light from the front of the house. "Maybe you need to visit the Miami Beach PD now."

Billy closed his eyes. He had to negotiate. He had to buy time to figure this out. "Listen, man, I'm sorry. I really just want to get my car." He noticed the beast's grip relaxing. "Honest. But no problem, man. Forget the car. I got a ride out front. I'll go home with her. I'm outta here, man. I'm outta here, I swear."

Max grunted, pushing Billy forward to the gate.

"Just lemme go." He was begging now and didn't give a shit. "You can watch me leave. I'm with a woman, I swear. I just wanted to pick up my car."

Relief washed over Billy with each step they took, with each centimeter the gun eased up against his neck. He was going to get out. Alive. And fully armed with information.

When the gate clanged into place behind him, Billy wasn't that surprised to see the chick had left. He stumbled out to the road, pulled out his cell phone and called a cab.

Life as he knew it was really about to change. He just had to enlist the right help.

And there was someone who had as much to gain as he did—someone who would help him bring that whore down for good.

Cori dreamed that Max had slept beside her.

She'd gone to bed, nursing a headache, shortly after he'd dealt with Billy. Turning toward the nightstand, she peered at the alarm clock. Four fifty-eight. What was she going to do today? Go through William's files again? His phone book? His secret life?

Dragging herself from the comfort of bed, she brushed her teeth and rinsed her face. She pulled on silky drawstring pants under the lace camisole she'd slept in, then tiptoed down to the kitchen. As the coffeemaker bubbled and hissed, she leaned against the island, her heart heavy.

How could she ever think of William again without wondering who he'd slept with? One woman? More than one? Someone she socialized with at a fund-raiser or had dinner with as a couple?

Could he really have betrayed her like that? It seemed so preposterous and unreal.

She stuck her cup under the dripping coffee, unable to wait for the pot to finish.

They'd found out nothing yesterday. Lots of people had seen William on his boat before he died; none of them had seen him with a woman. He hadn't been having sex with someone while the boat was docked here, had he? Could a wife be that blind and stupid? He had to have gone *somewhere* with her. How did she get on board? Surely not from their dock.

She went toward his office to start digging for clues again. Now that she suspected a woman, she'd look at everything differently: credit card receipts, travel itineraries . . . She stopped at the sight of Max, bare-chested, dark-bearded and rumpled, hunched over the computer.

"You're not going to like this," he said without looking up.

Oh, Lord. "Now what?"

He turned from the screen, his gaze sliding over the camisole and sleep pants before settling on the coffee cup. "Only one?"

"We can share," she said, padding barefoot into the office. "Assuming you still take it black with a quarter teaspoon of sugar."

"Some things never change."

She handed him the cup and scanned the papers and files he'd spread out. "Don't you ever sleep?"

Half her coffee disappeared in one gulp. "I rested." He raised the cup. "Bless you."

"Any time," she said, taking in the shadows of his unshaved face, then drifting down to devour the hard muscles of his chest darkened by a tangled mess of curly hair. "So, what won't I like?"

Reaching over to the printer, he grabbed the top sheet and handed it to her, then drank more coffee. She settled her hip on the corner of the desk and focused on the pages, still warm from the printer. According to the heading, they'd been sent to an e-mail address, mpr3@bc.com.

"Maximillian Phillip Roper the third at bullet catchers dot com?" she asked.

"Guilty."

Swensen Raynor . . . standard background check . . . Helsinki, Finland. "Swen? You're investigating Swen?"

"I didn't like the way the guy touches you."

She rolled her eyes. "Trust me, it's totally professional."

"Then he's gay."

"Nope, just a natural healer." She flipped the page and scanned the words. Place of birth, last known address, schools, financial data, and . . . "Oh." Her stomach dropped. "He has a record."

Max leaned back in the chair and nodded. "Yes, he was arrested in Esbo, Finland, and charged with possession of cocaine. Not green tea and red clover," he added pointedly.

She shot him a look, then reread the second page. "It was nine years ago."

"That's right," he agreed. "And to be honest, the arrest doesn't really bother me. He was young enough to be considered naive, and stupid enough to get mixed up with the wrong people." He reached over the desk, and handed her the next page. "What intrigues me is his marriage. Or should I say, his divorce."

"I didn't know he'd been married." And didn't care. Swen was not on the boat with her husband using condoms. Swen was not the last person, other than herself, to see William alive. She tossed the papers back on the desk. "You're wasting your time."

"He's was married to a very rich widow."

She frowned at him. He couldn't be implying. . . . "Fill in the blanks, Max. I'm not following you."

Max leaned on the desk and looked hard at her. "Didn't you tell me you and William were two of his best customers?"

"Yes. In fact, William had an appointment the very day he . . ." Her voice trailed off and she seized the pack of documents again, swearing softly under her breath.

"Swen worked for a well-established drug runner when he was nineteen, but he was a low-level middleman. Nothing too incriminating, actually. But I checked into his former wife and found more information. Come here." He beckoned her with two fingers to the side of the desk and cocked his head toward the computer screen.

She studied the e-mail message, reading the sender's name. "Who's Jazz Adams?"

"A great cyber investigator. She used to be a Bullet Catcher principal, now she's one of us."

Cori leaned over toward the screen. "She must have been one happy client to join the company."

"She liked her bodyguard." He pointed to the computer. "Read."

She did, out loud. "Elina Kallarson is a multimillionairess who was widowed, then remarried to Swen Raynor. They married less than a year after her husband, Jan Kallarson, died in an automobile accident in bad weather. Swen and Elina divorced three years later, the courts granting Swen a sizeable settlement." She looked at Max. "All right, he married a wealthy woman and divorced her. How can you possibly tie this to William's death?"

"He got enough money to get him to America, gain him entrance to an elite world, and land himself a job as a manager of a highbrow spa where he could meet more rich young widows."

"But I wasn't a widow when we met. I . . ." She stopped at his look. "Are you suggesting he killed William so that I could be free for him?"

Max grabbed another piece of paper. "As you have said several times, Swen is an herbalist."

The coffee turned bitter in her mouth as she watched him pull out yet another page.

"Here's a list of natural 'remedies' that can induce a coronary arrest. Here's a few that have been used to treat a number of different ailments, from arthritis to . . ." He leveled his gaze on her. "Impotence."

She stared at the names of plants and herbs, disbelief spiraling through her. "You think William could have taken something that *induced* a heart attack?"

"It's possible."

"This is really a stretch, Max." She walked to the leather sofa, studying the paper. "Swen has never said or done anything inappropriate."

"He's biding his time. Waiting for you to get through the mourning period. But he will, believe me. I saw the way he looked at you."

"There are plenty of wealthy widows hanging around the Mandarin, if he's interested in marrying for money." She glanced at the list of herbs again, then back to Max. "He wouldn't have to kill a man to free one up."

"But how many of them are worth billions? And how many of them look like you? And who the hell else knew what room you were in yesterday?"

She nodded, considering that. "He would have to have slipped it to William somehow. My husband didn't believe in holistic treatment. He wouldn't even take vitamins, and prided himself on being sixty-three and on no medication."

"Cori, you don't know. If the man was truly impotent, you have no idea what he might do to fix that."

Truly impotent? But of course he . . . oh. Then why the condoms?

"Wouldn't something like that show up in the autopsy?" She opened a filing cabinet and pulled out a copy of the report. While Max read it, she perused the information on Swen, the herbs, and the e-mail from Jazz Adams.

"This is a copy," Max said, flipping through the pages. "It could have been altered. Dan might know more after he finds this guy. In the meantime, I'm going to talk to Swen."

"Can I come with you?"

He shook his head. "I'll get more out of him if you don't. You better stay here."

"I'll go crazy, Max. Can't I at least meet Breezy while you're with Swen?"

"Don't say a word to her," he warned. "She talks too much."

"Okay. I'll see if she can meet me at the Mandarin while you talk to Swen," she said. "Is that all you have in mind for today?"

He lifted one eyebrow. "Not all."

The way he said it made a flock of wild butterflies take flight in her stomach. "What else?"

His gaze dropped over her camisole briefly, then settled on her face. "You'll see."

CHAPTER
Twelve

"So I need to know, and I need to know *now*, Corinne Peyton. When, where, and how often?"

Cori looked across the table she shared with Breezy on the terrace outside the M-Bar, squinting at the light that glimmered off the infinity pool below and the endless blue of Biscayne Bay beyond that.

"Do we have to sit out here? I'm sweating." More important, Max would hate that they'd taken a table out in the open. But he was behind closed doors with Swen, after leaving her a corner table inside, with a simple "Be careful" in her ear when they'd parted.

"Yes, we have to sit outside. I can't smoke in there." Breezy waved her cigarette at the cherry wood and cushioned couches of the chic martini bar inside. "Do not avoid the question any longer, my love." She put both elbows on the table and leaned in with a conspiratorial whisper. "I'm dying for details."

Cori shook her head.

"Come on," Breezy urged. "Tell me something.

Anything. Is he huge? Does he growl when he comes? He looks like the type."

Cori laughed. "You're awful." The urge to spill her guts to Breezy tugged at her. She yearned to tell Breezy about William, about his dying words, about the condoms on the boat. She wanted to open up and wallow in Breezy's inimitable ability to make her feel better.

But she'd promised Max, plus Breezy would tell Giff. And Giff would be devastated.

Breezy leaned back and puffed. "So how long were you climbing Mount Max?"

Cori smiled, taking enough of a sip of her French martini to let the Grey Goose and Chambord tingle her lips. "A year."

"A year?" Breezy flicked her ash. "And this was in Chicago? Before I met you?"

"Right before. We . . . we split up just a few months before the fund-raiser where I met you." Cori frowned for a minute. "Did you actually introduce me to William? I know I met you both that night."

"Oh no, no, no." Breezy shook her head with a sultry laugh. "Thou shalt not change the subject."

Cori grinned back at her. "You're relentless."

"Thank you. Now." Breezy repositioned herself as though settling in for a good long talk. "You were together for a year, and then you broke up. Why? No, no. We'll get to that. How serious was it?"

Serious? Oh, it was rarely serious. It was fun, wild, delicious, exhausting, unforgettable. Back then, Max laughed more than he scowled. "We were going to get married," she said quietly.

"Married?" Breezy could barely keep the amazement out of her voice. "You never mentioned that you'd been engaged before." The accusation held a good dose of resentment.

"It wasn't ever official. We never had a chance to announce anything."

No announcement. No ring. No celebration. She'd told her father, he'd gone crazy, they'd argued and gone to bed. The next morning, Max knocked on her door to tell her that Paul Cooper was dead. She hadn't said good-bye to her father before he left for work. She hadn't said she was sorry. She hadn't said she loved him.

And that was the end of her brief engagement.

"So why did you break up?"

"My father was killed. I think I told you that." Cori took another sip of her drink.

"Well?" Breezy prodded, tapping her lighter with a creamy colored nail. "Weddings happen, even after funerals."

"Not in this case."

Breezy notched an eyebrow and flipped her blond hair over her shoulder. "I'll have to hate you for real if you don't tell me more."

"Max was . . . involved with my father's death. They were both DEA agents, both at the scene."

"My God. What happened, Cori?"

There was no escaping Breezy when she wanted something. "I'd just told my father we were going to get married the night before. That didn't go over big, because Dad believed that life with a DEA agent husband is the kiss of death for a marriage—as it had been for him and my mother. The next day, he and Max were arresting a drug dealer at O'Hare and my dad was killed and . . ."

"And?"

"And I believe that Max could have prevented his death, but didn't." Cori looked away, over the precipice of the infinity pool. "I told that to the DEA. Max got demoted, not punished since there was no proof. And we said good-bye. End of story."

"Until last week, when the story began again." Breezy pulled out another cigarette, rolling it between her fingertips.

"No, nothing's begun."

"Hah. You hummed like a metal detector when he showed up at your house." She stared pointedly at Cori.

Cori smiled. "I admit I was . . . surprised."

"I bet you were. What a coincidence. Of all the bodyguards in the whole world, you get your ex." She put the cigarette down without lighting it, her moss green eyes sparking. "I don't believe in coincidences, Cor."

"Neither do I." Cori swallowed another sip of her drink.

"So what do you make of this one?"

"I don't know." She lifted her glass and looked at Breezy over the wide rim. "He left the DEA, and now he works for the security firm that the insurance company recommended. I got him. Weird stuff happens."

"I think he's still hot for you and lobbied for the job so he could get back at you."

"Get *back* at me? I was the one who lost my father."

"And he lost his job."

"Not technically," Cori corrected. "He just got pushed aside. It's how the agency works."

Breezy waved her hand. "Whatever. But you shouldn't trust anyone bent on revenge. It's the worst kind of bad."

Her skin prickled, heat and alcohol mixing her blood. "Can we change the subject?"

Breezy narrowed her eyes. "And what about you, Mrs. P?"

"What about me?"

"Do you still hate him?"

She lifted a shoulder. "Seems kind of pointless now."

"Or do you still want him?"

Down to the bone. "Not in the least."

Breezy just laughed and lit her cigarette. "You can want him—it's perfectly normal. The guy's freaking gorgeous, and you've been living like a nun for too long. Maybe you need to get him out of your system with one good shot of that big gun he carries around." She gave Cori a lecherous grin. "Tonight."

Laughing, Cori rolled her eyes. "I'd rather you come and have dinner with me tonight. I'll get Marta to make something you love."

Breezy signaled for the waiter and a refill. "I can't, honey. I can't leave Giff for the night."

"Is he okay?"

Misery pulled at Breezy's pretty features, softening the sharp lines of her cheekbones and jaw. It was definitely time to get the focus off Cori and onto Breezy.

"You sounded really down the other morning," Cori said. "What's going on with you?"

"I'm just . . . it's nothing." Breezy shifted in her chair, toying with the gold lighter, her gaze flitting over the crowd.

"Hey." She tapped Breezy's hand. "You forget who you're talking to. What's the matter?"

"I'm worried about Giff." She snuffed the half-smoked cigarette. "He's really distracted these days. He's not himself. The whole business with Peyton . . ."

Discussing the company with Breezy was awkward, but sometimes it couldn't be avoided. "What business in particular?"

"The Petaluma Mall."

"What about it?"

"William talked to Giff about this property before he died." Breezy leaned over the table, her voice low. "He told me William wanted that mall to be built, without question. It was important to him. But Giff gets the feeling . . . well, he feels like you don't trust him to handle the whole thing."

"It's not that I don't trust him, Breezy, it's that—"

Breezy held up her hand. "Stop. I hate talking about Peyton stuff with you. Let's go back to the bodyguard. Give me some disgustingly personal details. Just one thing. Anything. Has he ever—"

"I'll talk to Giff about that mall property. I promise. Maybe he can convince me going forward with it is the right thing to do."

Breezy held up two hands in surrender. "Nope, no shop talk. I'm sorry I brought it up."

"You didn't," Cori corrected. "I could tell something was bothering you the other morning and I knew it was more than misplaced earrings."

"I just love him a lot, and . . . and he doesn't seem healthy. I'm afraid. . . ." She reached across the table and squeezed Cori's hand. "You know better than anyone what stress can do to a man. Look at what happened to William."

The need to share nearly buckled her. Breezy was like a sister to her; there was something fundamentally wrong about holding back the truth.

Cori folded the damp cocktail napkin into small squares. "Breezy, what if . . ." She leveled her gaze across the table. "What if William's death wasn't natural?"

Breezy's mouth dropped opened. "You were with him, Cori."

"But what if someone did something, or gave something to William that . . ." She lowered her voice. "Killed him?"

"Who the hell thinks that?" Breezy demanded.

"The insurance company is considering the possibility."

Breezy's eyes blazed. "What? Who are they accusing? *You?*"

"Nobody is accusing anyone. It's a theory," she said gently. Of course Breezy would feel this way. She tried denial, too, for the longest time.

"Whose theory? It's stupid. And it's desperate." Breezy lifted her empty glass, then slammed it down on the table. "Can't the man just rest in peace?"

Cori shifted on her chair. "Not if it's true. Maybe the insurance company is on to something."

"They should spend their time and your money chasing after real murders, not sixty-three-year-old workaholics who have heart attacks," Breezy said sharply.

"The ME is missing," Cori said.

"What's an ME?"

"The medical examiner. The pathologist who did the autopsy on William."

Breezy made a face as though discussing the details of pathology turned her stomach. "Where is he?"

Cori shrugged. "Somewhere in Japan. They don't know."

"What difference does that make? No one questioned his findings three months ago." Breezy shook her head. "Why now? What gives?"

Should she tell Breezy what William said when he died? Could she help solve the mystery? Or would she be burdening her friend, or fueling gossip—or worse, risking having someone find out? "I don't know."

Breezy stared at her for a moment, her green eyes suddenly narrowing like she was aiming at a target. "Well, I do."

"You do?"

"Of course. It all makes sense now. Your ex-boyfriend shows up out of the not-so-blue," Breezy said knowingly. "And he just happens to work for the insurance company who doesn't want to pay you, so they are trying to make a perfectly accidental death look like murder."

"William's life insurance was a small part of his estate." But Breezy's point couldn't be ignored. "And Max doesn't actually work for the insurance company. He works for a firm that the insurance company recommended."

"Same difference." She looked hard across the table. "Isn't it?" she demanded.

Yes. No. "You don't know Max."

"I know this about men: You hurt them and they'll hurt you worse. Max Roper is out to destroy you, Cori."

The hair on the nape of Cori's neck lifted, and the muscles in her stomach tensed. The image of a box of condoms in William's bag flashed in her mind. Could Max have planted them there? Was he capable of that? Did he still hate her for ruining his DEA career? "I don't think he's like that," she said uncertainly.

"You're blinded by lust. That man wants the big Get Even and he'll take you down trying to get it." Breezy tightened her jaw as she spoke. "He's out to crush you. You ought to get rid of him or get away from him. Fast."

A chill ran down Cori's spine.

She gasped as two hands landed on her shoulders and warm breath hit her ear. "Can you come back to the massage parlor with me now?"

Cori glared at Breezy, who had to have seen Max approaching from behind. "You should have warned me," she hissed.

Breezy's steady gaze remained riveted on Cori. "I just did."

CHAPTER
Thirteen

Max purposely brushed his lips against Cori's hair, close enough to warm her ear and then count the goose bumps on her bare arms. When she turned, he didn't move, so their lips nearly met.

She inched back. "It's a *spa,* not a massage parlor."

"A massage parlor?" Breezy coughed pointedly. "Wouldn't Swen love to hear it called that?"

Max remained close to Cori, ignoring the other woman. "Swen gave us suite number four." He lifted her handbag from the ground next to her. "Let's go."

Cori shot an uneasy glance at her friend.

"It'll help you remember what happened." He nudged her gently with the bag. "Let's go," he repeated a little more forcefully.

Breezy leaned forward and crossed her arms, a move she'd no doubt perfected to show off her plastic surgeon's handiwork. "This is why I hate you, Corinne Peyton. Right in the middle of a perfectly good cocktail, you get dragged off to a massage table by your personal alpha dog." She winked at Max. "Bow wow."

Max gave her a look that usually shut up a smart-ass, but this one just responded with glare equally as steely.

"I realize that compelling security business is forcing you to do this," Breezy told him, picking up an empty cocktail toothpick and sucking on the tip. "But do you have to take her just when our conversation was getting interesting?"

"I'll go," Cori said quickly, pushing back her chair.

"You know, Cor, everyone's talking about how the bodyguard is the must-have accessory this season." Breezy's smile drifted into predatory territory. "I might have to get one now."

Cori rolled her eyes, then bent over and air kissed her friend. "I'll see you soon."

The humor evaporated from Breezy's eyes as she slid thin fingers around Cori's bare shoulders. "Remember, you're still not seeing things clearly." Her gaze drifted to Max. "Especially now." She pulled Cori closer and whispered something in her ear.

Cori just stood and nodded. "I'll call you," she said, then took her bag from Max. "Let's get this over with."

At the end of the terrace, Max guided her down the stone steps that led to the spa entrance. "What were you two talking about?" he asked.

She glanced up at him. "You."

He knew that. They went past the receptionist and headed for the elevator that would take them to the fourth-floor massage suites. Once inside, Cori positioned herself as far away from him as possible.

"What did Swen say?" she asked.

"Nothing of consequence."

She looked disappointed and pressed the fourth-floor button again.

"Though he did tell me all about his marriage, it might have been to convince me he's not gay."

"What about his drug bust?"

The elevator doors opened to a cool, hushed hall. Max stepped out first, holding the elevator door. The hall was empty, lined with rice-paper doors and minimal oriental artwork. "He admitted it openly. Said it was a boyhood indiscretion."

"Did you ask him about William and the herbs?"

Max had handled the issue of William carefully, giving no indication that he suspected foul play. "A little. Swen was at a dinner with the advertising agency that handles the spa the night your husband died, but he did see him that day to give him a massage. He corroborated your statement that William refused herbs of any kind."

She froze midstep. "There's nothing to *corroborate*. And it wasn't a *statement*. I was sharing a fact with you, to figure this out. Don't . . ." She slammed her hands on her narrow hips and glowered at him.

"Don't what?"

"Don't put me on the defensive," she said. "I want to find whoever did this more than you do. Don't be an adversary."

He frowned at her. "What were you drinking out there?"

"Go to hell," she muttered, pushing him with one hand and heading straight for suite four.

He grabbed her elbow. "Seriously, Cori. Your color's up. Your pupils are dilated."

"I had half a French martini, Dr. Roper," she said sarcastically. "And other things besides alcohol can induce those symptoms."

"Such as?"

"Stress. Lack of sleep." She flitted her gaze over his face, then met his eyes again. "Sexual attraction."

He held her look, then reached for the handle to the suite door. "Then you should relax and get some sleep."

Brushing by him, she ignored the comment. "The room's been cleaned," she said, looking around. "Has it been dusted for fingerprints?"

"You didn't file charges, so it's not a crime scene." Max closed the door and turned the flimsy lock. "Swen said he cleaned it himself."

She walked to the windows, a floor-to-ceiling wall of glass that looked out over blindingly blue water. The light behind her beamed right through the pale pink summery dress she wore, outlining her long, lean thighs and the enticing little gap where they didn't touch at the top.

"This room gives me the creeps now," she said, turning sideways and changing his see-through view to a profile. "How long will this take?"

"A few minutes. Have you ever heard of forensic hypnosis?"

She shook her head. "Waste of time, Max. I can't be hypnotized—I've tried."

"Why?"

She dropped her handbag on the counter and

walked to the massage table, scooting up on the edge. "Because I just can't get into that alpha state."

"I meant why have you been hypnotized?"

"Breezy had this California hypnotherapist at a party once who was supposed to get us in touch with our inner spiritualist." She waved a hand dismissively. "It was ridiculous. And I couldn't go under."

"That's different," he said, following her footsteps to the window. "This is something developed for crime witnesses, and I'm pretty good at it. I'll need to re-create the atmosphere. Were the drapes closed yesterday?"

"Yes. Swen had lit some candles, over there. And he had music on; he likes the ocean sounds."

Max drew the heavy gold drapes, instantly cloaking the room in darkness. "Incense?"

"Patchouli, I think he mentioned. And there was a . . ." She turned on the massage table, looking down the little hole in the head support. "An orchid down there, but not today."

At a long counter that lined one wall, he pulled open a drawer, spying some incense sticks and a black lacquer urn. "What were you wearing? Do you get massaged in the nude?"

"Is that part of the reenactment?"

He flicked a lighter and touched the tip of the incense, focusing on the tiny orange dot. "If you want it to be."

In the drawer, he saw a pile of CDs and he flipped through, plucking out *Seascapes* and sliding it into a CD player. "Okay. We'll start with the moment Swen left. What were you thinking about?" The sound of a zipper jerked him around.

Her sundress hit the floor with a *whoosh* that matched the air flowing out of his lungs.

"You."

He stared at her. At the challenge in her eyes, first. Then, God help him, at her body, bathed in shadows and bared to him. Her breasts were firm and smooth, tipped with ripe, dark nipples that jutted defiantly in the air. Below them, her waist narrowed, and around it, she wore a thin silver chain that rested on her hips, touching the edge of something silky—not quite a thong, but not quite functional panties, either. At the bottom of her endless legs, the dress lay in a pool around four-inch heels.

Evidently, Cori Cooper was in a betting mood.

"Me?" he asked with as much nonchalance as humanly possible. "Why were you thinking about me?"

She kicked off one sandal, then the other. In a smooth move, she slithered onto the massage table, facedown. "I happened ๛ be thinking about one night . . . in our past."

He stared at the round curve of her ass, barely covered in pink satin, and the tight, tempting vortex of her thighs. His jaw went completely slack. His cock did the opposite.

"What night was that?"

"New Year's Eve."

The words punched him almost as hard as the provocative lift of her backside, and she turned her head so he could see the gleam in her eye.

He reached down and pulled the cotton sheet over her, committing the view to memory. "Put your face down and close your eyes," he ordered.

"What are you going to do?"

Not what he'd done on that New Year's Eve. Although his mouth actually watered for the taste of her again. "Shhh. Close your eyes *and* your mouth."

She let out a tiny sigh of exasperation.

"The first part is building rapport. I'd say we passed that stage, oh, that New Year's Eve." Her shoulders moved in a quiet laugh. "I'm going to do something called progressive relaxation, to help you—"

"Will I know what I'm saying?"

"This is no different than being mesmerized by a movie or book. You are vaguely aware of outside stimuli, but mostly you'll be deep inside the sensory memory of your brain. Our goal is to jar that memory, to get you to dig far enough into your subconscious to unearth some detail that you might have forgotten. In ten minutes, you might know who was in here that day, Cori. This is very effective."

"Okay. But I warn you, I don't hypnotize easily."

"Lift your arms." When she did, he put his thumbs on the touchpoints right between her shoulder blades and made a small, light circular motion. "I want you to go back to the day you were here with Swen. When the phone rang, he left the room."

As he concentrated on that one spot on her back, her breathing became even. Her muscles relaxed.

"He left the room, closed the door, and you were alone."

The tips of his fingers slowly moved down her spine. Her skin was hot, silky. As he eased the sheet lower arousal threatened his concentration, and he willed it away by closing his eyes and focusing on the hypnosis.

He said the same thing several times, keeping his voice low and monotone, continuing the rhythmic circles on her back.

Her breathing slowed and her hips rose an inch.

No surprise, if she was remembering that New Year's Eve. They'd stayed in that night, bathed each other, fed each other, bet each other on five-card draw.

They'd played for favors.

And he'd hid a full house, just to let her win.

Blood bubbled hotter in his veins, remembering her bold request. On her knees, her back to him, her panties down, she bent over so her hair spilled over the sheets. *Taste me, Max. Lick me, Max.* She'd spread her legs, watching him upside down, laughing.

Now he inched the sheet lower, revealing the sides of her breasts, and his cock wrenched in response. He squeezed his eyes shut and forced the sexy image away. "You can still taste the lemony flavor of the tea you had with lunch," he said. "You can smell the spice and feel the warm oil on your back. You're back in that moment."

Again, her hips rocked and she murmured his name.

His whole body ached to answer that call. To rip the sheet all the way, to thrust her hips higher and pull that silk lower and slide his tongue along that tiny, taut sliver of skin. To make her scream. And gasp. And come.

Taking a deep, slow breath, he dug for control. "Did you hear the door open, Cori? Do you feel anything?"

"I feel you." The words were less than a whisper and he pressed his fingers into her flesh, clinging to his last shred of self-control.

"Did you hear someone come into the room?" His voice was tight with the effort.

She arched her back, sliding her nipples against the table, like she'd slid them against the sheets that night. Gritting his teeth, he ignored the pressure of his hard-on and forced himself to remember who was hypnotizing whom.

"Remember, Cori. You were in here alone. Then someone came in. What do you remember?"

"I heard something scrape, and then tap."

He scuffed his shoe on the bamboo floor. "Like this?"

"No. Sharper. Louder."

A heel? His were rubber, so he couldn't re-create the sound. "Then what do you remember?"

"Someone breathing. Hard."

"What did you do? Did you try to sit up?"

"I didn't want to look. I wanted to stay . . . with you."

He understood. "Did you lift your head? Look around?"

She was quiet for a long time, her breath quickening. "No. Something . . . hit me. Something knocked me hard on the head, and kept me pressed down."

He could feel the sudden tension of fear in her muscles. "I was so scared. I wanted help. I wanted you."

Guilt tightened his chest. "Did you smell anything? Hear anything?"

"I felt his breath. Heard a raspiness in his voice. He said, 'Give it up.' But he still had that cushion on my head. The voice was muffled." She lifted her head a little, as she probably had the other day, turning so her face was pressed against the suede doughnut hole. "I almost got my head up," she remembered. "My head was high enough that when I turned, he pushed me here." She demonstrated, putting her mouth against the plush covering.

"Think about that voice, Cori. Did you recognize it? Any distinctive cadence or accent?"

"Yes," she said. "I know the voice. I *know* the voice."

"Think Cori. Who was it?"

A little sound of frustration came from her. "I . . . can't . . . get it."

"You're so close, kid. Come on," Max insisted. "Can you remember the feel of his skin? The color of his hands? Jewelry? A watch? Hair on the knuckles?"

She shook her head, starting to sit up. "No, no, no." Her voice cracked in frustration. "I didn't—"

"Wait, not yet." He eased her down, softened his voice, took her back to the trance with a few minutes of gentle massage. "Okay, after he hit your head, after you fell asleep, what did you hear, Cori?"

"My pulse. Blackness. Nothing."

"Did the door slide open right away? Did he say anything else? Make any other noise?"

She was silent, breathing, thinking. He waited, massaging the touchpoints again.

"My handbag unzipped."

Yes. "How do you know?"

"I heard the funny click in the middle, where the teeth don't quite meet."

He walked to the counter, picking up the bag, and eased the wide zipper open. Metal hummed, clicked twice, right in the middle, then zipped smoothly again.

"Yes," she said. "I heard *that.*"

A distinct sound, definitely. So someone wanted something from her purse. He glanced at the contents: a matching wallet, her compact, a comb, a phone, mints, keys. "Then what did you hear?"

"Breezy."

Breezy, yelling at him. He put the purse down and walked back to the table. "Let's bring you out now, sweetheart," he said gently, putting his hands on her shoulders to turn her over. She moved easily, but the sheet slipped low enough to reveal one glorious breast.

He drew it up, covering her. "Now count slowly to ten, Cori."

"One . . . two . . . three . . ." Her eyelids fluttered. "Four . . . five . . . six." She rose up on her elbows. "Seven . . . eight . . ." Their gazes met. "How'd I do?"

"You were great," he said, his hand still on the sheet, holding it in place. "You remember?"

"Yes. My purse. We have to see what's missing."

He nodded. "You'll have to look."

"I remember something else, Max." A strange glimmer lit her blue eyes.

"What?"

"You cheated so I could win that night, didn't you?"

The sheet slipped out of his fingers, but he resisted the urge to look. Instead, he grinned at her. "See? I told you this was an effective crime-solving technique." He picked up her dress and handed it to her. "Here. I'll wait outside while you dress."

When he opened the door, she whispered, "Thanks, Max." He just held up his hand in response, and slipped out into the much-needed coolness of the hall.

CHAPTER
Fourteen

Positioning himself at the long granite kitchen counter that offered a view of both the patio and the cooking area, Max kept one eye on Cori's sleek body enclosed in a white one-piece bathing suit as it sliced through the water with the same wicked precision with which Marta wielded her chef's knife.

He'd much rather be outside with Cori, but he stayed rooted to the counter, popping stuffed olives that Marta had served him from a cold stone dish, and sipping water, wishing it could be beer.

After the day he'd had, he deserved a cold one—not this split-screen challenge that left him unable to concentrate on questioning Marta and unable to truly appreciate Cori swimming.

"You ever meet a guy named Swen Raynor, Marta?" he asked as he chose a black olive sprinkled with red flakes.

She looked up midchop from a Vidalia onion, her ebony eyes sharp. "No, I've never met him," she said, using her wrist to brush back a wavy strand of black hair.

Pepper burned his tongue, but he weathered it, eyeing the pimiento of a stuffed green olive, for evidence of heated spice. His gaze drifted to the pool as Cori pulled herself onto the stairs at the shallow end, and took a long pull on the bottle of water. Behind her, the expanse of her property framed her in palm fronds and the purplish glow of early evening. Like a water nymph, or some kind of goddess rising up from the Aegean Sea, she lifted her face to the sky and drank, bathed in light and water.

He bit on the olive, his gums and tongue prickled by the heat.

Cori propped back on one hand, the outline of her chilled nipples well defined through the wet suit. How much torture could one man take in a day?

"Did he ever . . ." He forgot what they were talking about. Oh, yeah, Swen. "Hot—" He grabbed the water. "Pepper."

Marta chuckled. "Careful. I've seasoned those with red chile flakes."

"No kidding," he said with a half choke.

She gave him a look of victory. "You'd be better off with milk."

"Never touch the stuff." He managed not to tear up.

Marta glanced over her shoulder toward the pool, silently acknowledging the distraction. "She's out there almost every evening before dinner," she said wistfully. "Ever since Mr. Peyton died, she skips what used to be their cocktail hour and she swims." Shaking her head, she scraped the chopped onion into a pile and started on some carrots. "It's so sad."

In the past half hour, he'd learned that Cori and her husband had stopped eating red meat more than two years ago, but Marta hoped the braised beef in red wine she was making for Max would tempt the boss to give up her boring salads. And he'd learned that Marta used to live in northern California, where she'd met Mr. Peyton right before he married Cori. He'd talked her into moving to Florida to be his personal chef and housekeeper, although she hated heat and humidity as much as Max did.

He'd learned equally little from the afternoon's way-too-erotic hypnosis session. A thorough check of Cori's purse had revealed that nothing was missing.

"So, you were talking about Swen Raynor," Max said casually.

"You were," she corrected.

Max smiled at her no-bullshit style. "Did you know his mother wrote a book on herbs?"

Marta slid the chopped vegetables into a silver bowl. "I had no idea."

"But you're quite an accomplished cook. I would imagine Swen was interested in your work. Being raised by a renowned chef, he was probably intrigued by the work of others."

"I'm a housekeeper, not a chef, Mr. Roper." She placed the cutting board in the vegetable sink, and turned up the faucet. "And no, he's never been in my kitchen."

"Never brought you any recipes or any of his famous herbs?"

"No."

"No one ever suggested you incorporate something in particular—a rare spice or an unusual herb, perhaps?"

She looked up at him. "What are you asking me, Mr. Roper?"

Every once in a while, someone nailed him. And that always impressed him.

"I'm just curious," he said with a smile and a shrug to acknowledge her small victory. Outside, Cori lifted her arms in a stretch. The movement pushed her breasts higher, and revealed the toned muscles of her stomach.

"You know . . ." He stalled, watching Cori reach for a towel, water sluicing down her ribs, over her hips, and down her legs.

"Yes?" Marta prodded, her focus on the cutting board.

What the hell had he been talking about now?

"Are you from Latin America, Marta?" That was graceless, but he was totally sidetracked by the view.

"Mexico." She said it with the Spanish pronunciation, and no small amount of defensiveness.

"And you moved here from California for this job."

She gave him a wary look. "I just told you that."

Max forced himself to ignore the view. "That's quite a significant move. Do you have family in California?"

"My sister is here now." She turned to the six-burner stove, hiding her face and giving him a view of the back of her uniform. She wasn't a svelte woman, but her curves had a definite appeal. She had a pretty face, lots of thick curls, ample breasts, a lilting Spanish accent, and she could cook.

Many men would find her attractive.

Including William Peyton, who liked her enough to bring her three thousand miles to live in his house.

"Exactly how did you meet Mr. Peyton?"

She clanged a cast-iron skillet onto a lit burner. "He was a customer at a restaurant where I used to work."

"A customer? You were a chef there?"

She threw him a look over her shoulder. "A cook. Yes, I was a cook there."

"So how did you actually meet him?" Max prodded. "Did you have the opportunity to mingle with customers?"

"I really don't remember," she said, pouring some wine into the pan and causing a loud hiss and burst of steam.

In his mind's eye, he could see the circle of "lovelovelove" around the letter W.

Or the letter *M*?

"You must have been quite trusting to leave California and work for a virtual stranger," he said. "Or did you know him fairly well before you left?"

She spun around, her eyes watering from the steam. "I endured a personal tragedy, Mr. Roper, and wanted very much to leave California. I jumped at the opportunity to work for Mr. Peyton because he was good and kind and fair." Her voice cracked. "If you think to prod any further into my life, I suggest you stop right now."

He studied her. "Why is that?"

"You know why as well as I do, and I . . . I can't do anything about it now."

"Anything about what?" The familiar sensation of closing in on the final moments of an interrogation grabbed him. "You can tell me, Marta."

"I can't. You have all this security. People are coming to install cameras and spotlights. They will interview me." Her voice cracked again, sending Max's heart rate up. Could it be this easy?

"Maybe I won't let them."

"No." Her black eyes burned him like the hot pepper. "I don't want to tell you anything."

"You can trust me," he said, tilting his head a little, drawing her in. "I'm staff here, too."

"You are a legal citizen, Mr. Roper. I am not."

Was that her secret? A missing green card? "Was Mr. Peyton helping you with that?" She turned back to the stove. "Why? What happened?"

Marta held one hand up, the universal signal for *shut up*.

"Did Mrs. Peyton help? Or were you closer to Mr. Peyton," he suggested. "More comfortable with him?"

She gave him an odd look. "He was a saint."

A saint with a stash of rubbers his wife had never seen. "Did you happen to have a chance to clean out his boat, Marta? All of his belongings are gone."

"Mrs. Peyton already asked me that," she said, denial and confusion on her face. "I did not."

"But you know your way around the boat, don't you?"

"I clean the cabana," she said. "I hate that boat. Just like Mrs. Peyton does."

Behind her, the pan flared with fire and she spun back with a gasp, seizing the knob and flipping the flame down. When she turned to him, her face was completely composed again.

"Will you be having dinner with Mrs. Peyton on the terrace tonight, since Mrs. Breezy can't make it?"

Locked down. Max wouldn't get another thing out of her.

"I might," he said, taking the empty bowl and placing it in the vegetable sink. "I'll have to see what I can do about scoring an invitation."

Outside he followed the water drips up the spiral stairs, but her door was locked and Cori told him she preferred to be alone.

So he ate braised beef by himself on the veranda under her room, her absence hitting him as sharply as a knife wound. He stayed there long after Marta came out to remove his plate, refusing eye contact and barely accepting his compliments on dinner.

Deep into the oppressive heat of the night, he sat on Cori's patio, staring sightlessly at the stars. Instead, images flashed before him, some achingly beautiful, some terrible and violent. He knew he should go to bed, walk the property, punch a wall. Something other than sweat and simmer and grow harder and madder that he couldn't change the past.

Can you keep your emotions out of this, Max?

Apparently not.

Around four, he heard the water heater that ran Cori's shower. Funny time for her to bathe. He hustled up the outdoor spiral stairs that led to her bedroom.

Through the tiny cracks in the shutters, he could see a dim light. At the far corner of the sliding glass door, he crouched down to peer through the opening he'd created for this very purpose. And what he saw on her bed turned his blood to ice.

Dan Gallagher hadn't stopped moving since his flight landed in Osaka and he'd boarded a train that took him to Kyoto Station. Why Max's target couldn't be in a city with its own international airport, he didn't know. And he was so freaking tired, he didn't care.

He'd get the information Max needed, and then he'd roll into the top notch *ryokan* he'd just checked into and sleep for two days. Maybe he'd find one of the last remaining geishas in the country to entertain him in style before he headed back to Paris.

He'd made amazing progress so far—which probably meant that the man in hiding wanted to be found.

Using the sketchy data Max had sent, Dan had gone to a local hospital where Dr. Bauer had connections. Three interviews, including one with a very charming and accommodating nurse, gave him the names of some relatives who lived in the northern outskirts of the town.

When he arrived at their humble wood-framed house, a tiny woman opened the door before he'd knocked. Through a frustrating conversation in broken English, bad Japanese, and sign language, Dan learned that he was at the home of Dr. Bauer's uncle on his mother's side, the Tashimoto family. And yes, the

Bauer family was staying there—he thought. The woman, Tanikasan, finally invited him in.

An older woman moved like a ghost behind an opaque sliding door, but Dan stayed focused on his attempts at communicating with Tanikasan. A lanky boy of about fifteen had been sprawled across some pillows, filling up most of a tiny living floor to the right. After a few minutes he unfolded himself, walked through the entryway, and leveled a black-eyed gaze directly at Dan. He wore a white ribbed tank top and sleep pants with SpongeBob SquarePants all over them.

Tanikasan spoke in rapid-fire Japanese to the boy, but he just shrugged and indicated the white earplugs of his iPod. With one more harsh look at Dan, he pushed a lock of black hair out of his face and disappeared into a dimly lit hallway.

Reddening with embarrassment when the boy left, Tanikasan drew Dan into a tiny kitchen packed with floor-to-ceiling cupboards and a square Formica-topped table. Tea was offered with much sign language and repeated *arigato gozaimasu* from both of them.

After an elaborate ritual that Dan knew not to rush, Tanikasan served him tea and led him to a garden not larger than two hundred square feet, cluttered with stone lanterns, ceramic animals, and dozens of plants in pink and blue plastic containers. Stepping over a hose, Dan sat on a stone bench and then nearly fell off it when she turned around and left him alone.

Well, that wasn't very Japanese of her.

Baffled, tired, and rapidly losing patience, Dan

sipped the tea while moist summer air pressed down. Fifteen minutes ticked by, and Dan realized how hungry he was by the tempting, tangy smell of fish and noodles wafting through an open window.

"I understand you're looking for me."

Dan turned at the sound of a female American voice. A petite woman with pretty hazel eyes and short, silky blond hair stepped through the trellis to the garden.

"Are you Dr. Bauer's wife?" he asked.

"I am Adrienne Bauer." She slid her hands into the pockets of khaki trousers, a gesture that was as unwelcoming as it was casual.

Dan set the teacup on the bench and approached her, fixing a smile in place as he took in the wariness in her gaze.

"How can I help you?" she asked.

"I'm Dan Gallagher and I'm trying to find your husband. Is he with you?"

Her eyes widened. "Excuse me?"

He glanced toward the house where Tanikasan could be seen at the kitchen window, watching them. "I had some trouble communicating with . . . is it your husband's aunt?"

"Who are you?" she demanded, the boldness of the question as out of place in this atmosphere as her light eyes and smattering of freckles.

"I'm with an organization of security specialists, and one of our clients is seeking the medical examiner who handled an autopsy in Miami three months ago. That pathologist is your husband and I'd like to talk to him." Dan was too tired to spellbind her with charisma. Besides, something in her eyes and posture told him she wasn't the least bit vulnerable to his easy smile.

She walked by him to the bench where he'd been sitting, and lowered herself onto it. "Why?"

He'd had enough of middlemen. "Mrs. Bauer, I need to have this conversation with your husband. As I'm sure you know, much of his work is highly confidential and I think it would be more productive to talk to Dr. Bauer directly."

"Not really, Mr. Gallagher." She crossed her arms and stared at him. "Since he's been dead for nearly a month."

Dan drew back in surprise. "I'm sorry to hear that." And Max would be even sorrier.

She looked toward the house for a moment, the flash of grief and something else—worry?—evident in her eyes. "I'm afraid I can't help you."

He walked closer, gauging her body language, and trying to decide if he would get further by sitting next to her, crouching in front of her, or looming over her. Max would loom, and he was usually pretty damned effective in situations like this.

Pausing a few feet away, he asked, "Was he ill? Is that why he returned to Japan so suddenly?"

"No, he wasn't— Well, yes, I suppose he was." She folded her hands, her white knuckles revealing far more than her face. "I'm sorry if you've come a long way, but there's nothing more I can tell you. My family and I are still deeply in mourning." She indicated the house. "I need to go inside now."

"Perhaps you still can help me," he said as she headed toward the doorway. "Perhaps he shared some professional information that could help me and my client."

Pausing, she looked over her shoulder. "My husband didn't talk much about his cases and business, so whatever you've come to find out, I wouldn't be able to help you. Again, I'm so sorry."

She disappeared inside, leaving him burning. He hated dead ends and, frankly, he didn't believe her.

Heading back to where his cabbie had indicated he could get a return ride into the city, he pulled out his cell phone and prayed for service. It would be spotty, but maybe he could text message Max. But the screen read NO SERVICE.

More irritation boiled through him as he climbed into a spotless taxi and closed the door. Before he could speak, something thumped on the window.

Dan jerked at the sound, turning to see a flat palm pounding the glass, a sea of smiling SpongeBob SquarePants in the window. He flung open the door and the teenage boy all but threw himself into the car.

"Go!" he demanded, pushing at the front seat as though he could propel the driver into action. "Go now!"

"Wait a second." Dan grabbed the boy's narrow wrist and jerked him around. "What's going on?"

"Go!" he urged again, looking over his shoulder in the direction Dan had just come. "Before my mom catches me."

Gone was the sullen teenage pout. And from the

sound of this kid's voice, he wasn't Tanikasan's son—he was American, despite the Asian tilt to his dark eyes.

"Why did you follow me?" Dan demanded.

The kid tossed another look over his shoulder, then at Dan. "Because I want you to help me figure out why my dad is dead."

So this was Yakima Bauer's son. And Dan had been wrong; he was closer to twelve than fifteen.

"I heard you talking to my mom and aunt," the boy said, tucking his straight black hair behind his ears and revealing that he still wore the iPod earbuds. "I know you're looking for him."

"I was," Dan said. "I'm sorry to hear that he's gone."

"Why did you want to talk to him?"

"I needed some information about his work."

The boy held out his hand, a silver key poised between his fingers. "Then maybe you need this."

Dan looked at it. "Maybe I do. What is it?"

"I don't know. But my dad gave it to me and told me never to give it to anyone. And I want to know why." His eyes closed on a sigh. "I want to know why."

"Why he gave you the key?"

"Why he blew his brains out."

Dan took the key and had a sneaking suspicion he wasn't going to get any sleep or a geisha girl that night. "You're not the only one."

CHAPTER
Fifteen

At the top of the main staircase, Cori took a breath and lifted her suitcase again. If she clunked it down the steps, she'd surely wake Marta. Max must be in the guest house, because she'd made a complete check of the upstairs rooms and William's office before she'd zipped her suitcase closed and grabbed her handbag from the hall table.

Downstairs, she kept the suitcase on the oriental runner and didn't make a sound as she went to the kitchen. She propped a note to Marta by the coffeemaker, knowing that was where her housekeeper would start her day in about two hours.

Then Cori dragged the suitcase over the tile and along the breezeway, glancing at the dark guest house. As soon as she stashed her suitcase in the car, she'd go wake Max up and tell him they were going to California. He wouldn't be thrilled, but at least she'd let him sleep as long as she could. By dawn they had to be at the

Kendall-Tamiami Executive Airport, where a pilot waited for her with the Peyton jet.

She opened the door to the garage and thumbed the alarm pad, blinking into the pitch blackness. From feel, she lugged the bag behind her, clunking it down a small cement stair and guiding her way with one hand extended like a blind person.

Reaching the trunk, she opened her handbag for the keys.

Which weren't clipped to the inside like they always were.

"Damn it," she said, stuffing her hand into the bag and feeling around. "Didn't he give them back?" She checked the back pocket of her denim skirt, then dug into the front purse flap to see if she'd stuck them in there. "Where the hell are my keys?"

"Right here."

She jumped a foot backward and nearly choked. "Max, is that you?"

"Running away, kid?"

She reached out into the darkness to grab the keys he dangled, not caring if she hit Max's face, fury boiling through her. "Give me the keys."

His hand closed over her wrist. "What do you think you're doing?" he demanded.

"I'm traveling on business," she said, letting him hold her wrist. "And maybe you could tell me what you're doing lurking in my garage at four-thirty in the morning."

He pulled her closer and she could finally make out

the whites of his eyes and a shadow of stubble over his face. How was it that this one time, her body hadn't picked up his pheromones?

"Where're you headed?"

"California."

She felt him tense. "And when were you going to tell me?"

"In about five minutes." She jerked out of his grasp. "I thought I'd let you sleep as long as you could."

He closed in, a tower in black looming over her. "You weren't going to tell me."

"Yes, I was," she insisted. "I'm going to the house in Healdsburg and I'm going to see the Petaluma Mall. I wouldn't go without you."

He just stared at her, anger emanating from his very skin.

"You don't believe me."

"You're running away. Again."

"Aw, Max. I knew it was just a matter of time."

"*What* was?"

"Until you threw that in my face. The last time I ran away, I had a pretty compelling reason to get away from you. Plus, here's what you don't know: I came back in a few days and you were gone for good." She let her handbag slide down her arm and hit the top of her suitcase with a thud. "I have a plane waiting at the Tamiami Executive Airport, and if you'll just pack a bag, we can leave in a few minutes."

"It's in the trunk."

"Your bag?"

"When I saw that you were packing, I did the same. Just to be sure you didn't leave without me."

"I'm sorry you didn't trust me. I had no intentions of running away." She pushed his chest, moving him back an inch. "We have a job to do here: we have to find who killed my husband and stay alive in the process. Anything else is out of the question."

He moved right back into her space. "There isn't anything else. Didn't you prove that with your little striptease this afternoon?"

"I was testing you."

"Why?"

"Why?" he repeated and moved an inch closer, filling her nose and lungs with the dizzying, spicy scent of him.

"I didn't ask for you as my bodyguard," she said evenly. "And I still don't know why I got you. So, I wanted to find out if you came here to do a job or to see what it would take to have me again."

"And what if I did what you were teasing me to do? Huh?" He pulled her toward him, right up to his mouth. "What would that prove?" His heart hammered so hard, she could feel his body vibrating.

She backed out of his grasp, hitting the garage door.

He closed the space instantly. "Would it prove that I still want you?" He slammed his hands on either side of her head so hard the garage door shook. "Well, guess what?" He got right into her face. "I do."

He kissed her hard, delving into her mouth with total ownership and command. He slid his hands down her ribs and over her hips, pressing his massive erection against her.

Wild desire ached between her legs, making her moan.

His mouth trailed down her throat, sucking away her sanity and leaving raw, hot need twisting through her.

She grabbed his neck and pulled his face into her, smashing her breasts against his chest to send sparks to the hard peaks of her nipples. Instantly, his hand came between them, sliding inside her sweater and closing over her breast as a sexy sound of desire escaped his throat. He dug under her bra until his palm touched flesh, thumbing her nipple, pinching it gently, then grasping her with a rough groan of helplessness.

He pushed her higher, his insistent erection grinding into her crotch. Blinded by lust and need, she tried to ride him, her skirt digging into her thighs and holding her legs together.

She let out a sob of frustration. He reached down, cupping her rear end, then inching lower to the hem of her skirt.

"I want you," he ground out, his breath jagged. "Okay? I *want* you."

She pressed against him in silent consent. He yanked the skirt up her thighs, freeing her to finally, blessedly open her legs and feel the crush of his hard-on against her wet panties.

"I want you, Cori," he admitted again, growling into her mouth, moaning into her skin. "I *want* you."

His hand covered her crotch, his fingers slipping under the silk, threading her curls, teasing her flesh.

As he kissed her he circled her nub with his thumb, then matched the wicked, rapid thrusts of his tongue with one finger, then two.

She rose up, wrapped her legs around his hips, and let the fire build. He pinned her with his thighs, his hands on her breasts, her throat, her hips. He never stopped kissing her, moaning, murmuring her name repeatedly. His zipper snagged her panties, but she was so wet and needy she just kept grinding against him, wishing he were inside her.

Fire shot between her legs and she dropped her head back and rode him hard, unable to stop. A climax started deep inside and built with lightning speed. Hot, endless waves of pleasure pounded down on her, until she could only sob his name, biting his shoulder, her throat raw from ragged breaths.

Slowly, finally, he let her down.

"Get in the car, Cori." His eyes were hooded and dark and hungry. "I'll take you to the airport."

She opened her mouth, but nothing came out, her whole body still thrumming from lust. She half stumbled away, vaguely aware that he was opening the trunk for her suitcase as she climbed into the passenger seat. In a minute he got in next to her, his face set so hard, it must have hurt his jaw to hold it like that.

She knew that look. When Max went deep into battle with his emotions, he shut down and no amount of talk would open him up.

She had no desire to talk, anyway. Her core

squeezed, her limbs grew heavy. She wanted *more*. More of him. Inside her, deep inside her. On the plane, thirty thousand miles above earth . . . they would make love.

She glanced at him but he stared straight ahead, that tiny scar pulsing, his massive shoulders tense under the fabric of his shirt.

As long as they could keep it on a purely physical level, this would be fine. She needed this.

She closed her eyes and let her orgasm-shaken body float back to reality. God, she needed *him*.

She didn't open her eyes until they parked on the tarmac, where the Peyton Enterprises Gulfstream G450 was lit and powered for takeoff in the misty predawn.

She turned to Max, but he was already out of the car and approaching Capt. Dale Willingham, her pilot, to shake hands.

She hoped to God he was telling Dale they needed complete privacy in the cabin. A shudder of anticipation jolted her. Jorge, her usual copilot, opened her door and she managed some small talk, aware of Max's every move. He climbed into the cockpit, stored luggage and, from what she could tell, conducted a thorough preflight check.

As Cori settled into her favorite sofa in the back, she looked out the window and watched Max on a cell phone, taking the moment to devour his sexy body, and remember the thrill of his incredible mouth and fingers and manhood.

He still wanted her. And, God, she wanted him.

The realization was liberating and she tapped the arm-rest impatiently, ready to take off.

Finally, the pilots disappeared into the cockpit and Max dipped into the cabin.

"All set?" she asked.

He nodded. "He's good. He knows what he's doing and the plane checks out."

"Then buckle up." She tilted her head to the seat next to her, on the sofa.

He didn't move. "Your bodyguard in California is Chase Ryker. He's excellent—former Air Force and NASA astronaut, one of the top Bullet Catchers."

She blinked at him. "What?"

"He'll meet you at the Sonoma County Airport."

Her heart hit bottom with a thud just as the engines fired. "You're not going."

He shook his head. "I'd like to keep investigating people here. You'll be in good hands with Chase."

"But not in *your* hands."

Her look must have been abject despair because his eyes darkened with a little sympathy. "It's better this way. We're combustible." He reached around to the cockpit and tapped on the door. "You can close up now. I'm leaving."

"Max—"

He held up his hand in farewell, then pointed a finger at her. "You be careful out there, kid."

And he was gone.

Through the window, Cori thoughtfully watched him climb back into the Mercedes and drive away. Max Roper could be tough and mean and deadly. He could be soft and funny and kind. But she'd never known him to be scared.

Until now.

As Gifford Jones strode through the underground garage of Peyton Enterprises, he imagined how he looked to others. A fit and handsome man with a gorgeous wife, an excellent career, a beautiful home, expensive cars. True, he'd endured tragedy, but, for the most part he got what he wanted in life and carried himself with the confidence of a winner.

So why, he thought as he pressed the call button for the elevator, had he stayed awake last night considering the merits of a gunshot to the head? After Breezy told him Corinne had decided to go out to California, he'd actually considered it. Desperation could kill a man.

The elevator doors opened, and Giff froze at the person staring back at him.

Billy Peyton could kill a man, too.

"Dude," Billy said, tossing a surfer-blond strand off his face. He grinned, baring his teeth with a scary twinkle in his eye. "You are such a creature of habit. Arriving at the office at . . ." He looked at his watch. "Six forty-five, on the nose. Before most any other executive at Peyton Enterprises. Before most *any*body at Peyton Enterprises."

Icy cold fear clutched Giff's chest as blood drained from his head. Something big had to get Billy Peyton out of bed at this hour. "What do you want, Billy?"

"I wanna talk to you."

Giff tried to slice him with a look he'd perfected on guilty witnesses. "You'll have to make an appointment and, if I may suggest, bring your attorney if this is about the *Peyton v. Peyton* case."

Billy chuckled and stepped into the garage, blocking Giff until the elevator doors thumped closed. "I guess you could say it's about the case. I have some new evidence that might affect the outcome."

"There's a legal procedure for filing evidence," Giff said, proud of the command in his voice. He reached for the call button, but Billy grabbed his arm.

"Corinne Peyton killed my dad."

Giff blew out a disgusted breath. "Yes, I've heard your theory. Even your own attorney advised you to stop making these ridiculous allegations." He managed to extricate his arm from Billy's grasp. "Have your attorney call my office. I have a very busy morning planned." Behind a locked door, doctoring files and databases and covering his trail.

Billy didn't move. "Beckworth Insurance is investigating William's death."

"If that were true, I'd know it already." Still, Giff was intrigued.

"It is true. And she killed him. And they know it but don't know how to prove it."

What a boatload of problems *that* would solve. The temptation to believe was powerful, but Billy wasn't exactly a reliable source. "Beckworth is investigating William's death?" he asked, just to be sure he heard right.

"You know," Billy said, that gleam sparking in his

eyes again. "If she's out of the picture, you are the most likely to be CEO, and I could get my inheritance."

"Being CEO of Peyton Enterprises isn't important to me."

"How about a billion dollars? I'll split the take with you."

Giff choked. "You can't even count to a billion."

Billy's eyes narrowed. "My dad was right. You are a pompous asshole."

Resentment whipped through Giff. "Where'd you get your information, Billy? About Beckworth?"

"From the horse's mouth, I told you. I heard Cori say they are investigating her when she didn't know I was listening."

A chill of hope ran over Giff. If Corinne were indicted on murder charges, every problem he had would be solved. Except for the headaches and blindness. But he hadn't had one since the night in the limo. Maybe it was temporary, stress induced.

The situation with William was fixed . . . at least he thought so. But Corinne—could this actually be the ticket to getting out of this mess? If so, maybe he could help steer that investigation a little. He sure as hell didn't want to go to jail.

"The autopsy showed William died of natural causes," Giff said. "There's no ongoing investigation. Any case against Corinne is closed."

Billy gave him a snide look. "Maybe not, dude."

Giff closed his eyes. Being in any kind of partnership with Billy went way beyond distasteful. "Why are you telling me this, Billy?"

Billy shrugged. "You got a lot to gain with her out of the picture."

Billy had no idea how much.

"Plus," Billy said, his eyebrows raised, "you got a certain amount of credibility I don't."

For a stupid druggie, Billy was pretty smart. "I have no interest in bringing down Corinne Peyton," he said. And that was true. He just wanted to stay out of jail for what he'd done.

Billy shrugged and backed up. "Suit yourself, Giff."

The elevator arrived and Giff got on. As the doors closed, Billy leaned into the opening to hold Giff's gaze. "Do it your way," he said, "and you'll kiss her ass for the rest of your life."

Or commit suicide for what you did.

Except, Billy had just handed him a better option.

CHAPTER
Sixteen

Adrienne Bauer looked a hell of a lot more accommodating the second time Dan showed up at the house. But this time he had her son in tow, and she was damned relieved to see him.

"Joshua, where have you been?" She yanked the boy into her chest, while sparks shot from her eyes at the man she obviously believed kidnapped him.

"At the train station." Josh looked over his shoulder for help from Dan, his friend and accomplice now.

"The *train* station?" She sounded like Dan had dragged him to a Japanese whorehouse.

"Dad gave me a key and it fit a locker at the station," Joshua said. "I think there was money in it. Lots of money. But it's all gone now."

"They clean out the lockers every three days," Dan explained. "I'm going back to speak with someone in authority, but I wanted to get him home before you were worried sick."

"Too late for that," she said, looking at Joshua.

"All we got was some stupid piece of paper." The boy was unable to hide his disappointment. The mother, on the other hand, was pretty adept at hiding any feelings at all.

"Whatever was in that locker belongs to me, Mr. Gallagher." She put her hand on Josh's face and, unlike most thirteen-year-olds, he didn't duck away. "I doubt there was money, Joshua. That's just your imagination. Go inside, honey." She tried to steer him into the house but he held steady.

"Mom," Joshua insisted. "I'm tellin' you. This guy, this guy at the train station. He could speak a lot of English and when he realized who we were, he like totally shut down and pretended he couldn't understand us." He looked at Dan. "Didn't he?"

Dan kept his gaze on Adrienne. "Your son has excellent investigative instincts, ma'am."

"And just what are you investigating?" she demanded.

Dan looked at Josh, angling his chin toward the house. "Go." They'd developed quite a rapport during their adventure. Josh nodded, gave his mom one more pleading look, then disappeared.

"I need to find some papers your husband may have left behind, specifically an autopsy report," Dan told her. "To be honest, there's no formal investigation, but there might be."

She stuck her hand out, palm up. "Show me what you found in the locker."

From his pocket, he pulled out a thin piece of

Japanese writing paper, with symbols on it. "Can you read that?" he asked.

"Yes."

He already knew what it said; the security guard at the train station had told him. But if Mrs. Bauer lied, then his job just got more complicated.

She studied it for a minute, then handed it back to him. "It says: P-E-Y-T-O-N. Peyton. That is meaningless to me." She looked up at him, a thinly veiled defense in her eyes. "Now what do you want?"

He'd use every weapon on this lady to find what Max needed, but usually he had no need for more than a smile and lingering eye contact. So he tried both. "Got tea?"

Even though he could tell she didn't want to, she smiled back. "It's Japan."

"Then the polite thing to do would be to let me in."

She waited a moment, then her shoulders shifted imperceptibly downward and she stepped aside. He removed his shoes and she took him back to the tiny kitchen bathed in a milky yellow fluorescent light.

"Why did you and your family come here?" he asked, pulling a vinyl-covered chair from the table and sitting.

"My husband's mother was Japanese. His relatives live here."

"Are you here on an extended vacation?"

She began opening the myriad cabinet doors. "We're staying for a while. Maybe until Christmas."

Until the heat was off her husband?

"Mrs. Bauer, I have to—"

"You can call me Adrienne," she said turning around and leaning against the counter, her face suddenly drawn with sadness. "If my husband did anything wrong, I think I would have known about it."

"Why do you think he committed suicide?"

"He suffered from severe depression," she said. "He stopped taking all medications when we arrived here."

He gave her a sympathetic look. "Did he bring any copies of the autopsies he performed prior to leaving?"

She struggled for a moment, the battle evident in her eyes. "He left some things." She bit her lower lip and exhaled. "I'll be right back."

Hopefully, whatever the doctor left behind would help Max. 'Cause Max sure as hell needed something to improve his mood. Dan had heard something in the big guy's voice he'd never heard before: misery. He'd handed over the woman of his dreams to another Bullet Catcher and had some harebrained idea that he'd stay in Miami and *investigate*. When was the guy going to listen to that titanium heart of his? He'd scoffed at Dan's suggestion to get Lucy's plane and fly out to California ASAP.

Dan looked around the modest house. If Bauer had gotten a big payoff for a fake autopsy, he hadn't spent it improving his family's living conditions.

Adrienne returned with a metal strongbox that she set on the table with a clunk. "I don't have a key," she announced.

Dan jimmied the high-security padlock and knew instantly it couldn't be picked. "Can we go outside in the garden?" he asked.

She led him out there while he carried the box, which he put in the center of the gravel. With one hand, he waved her off. "Stand back." Pulling out his gun, he aimed it squarely at the lock, pulled the trigger and heard her gasp just as he fired.

"Don't always need a key," he said, replacing the weapon and giving her a quick smile.

Her hazel eyes widened but a smile tipped her lips, turning her from merely attractive to extremely pretty. "Evidently *you* don't."

He flipped open the top and started going through the files, labeled in alphabetical order. Nothing said "Autopsy of William Peyton." No, that would have been too simple. Slowly, he went through every tab again, reading them aloud. "Adams, Cooper, Dawson, Exline, Krebs, Mahar, Ortiz, Paige, Pennington, Roswell, Rucker, Statler, Varn." No Peyton.

His fingers slipped back a file. *Cooper.* He pulled out the file and opened it. The only item inside was a black-and-white newspaper clipping with a four-inch photo of three women standing together, wearing evening gowns and holding drinks. A typical society page snapshot, except one woman had a black circle drawn around her face.

Dan studied the pretty lines of her face, the long dark hair. He'd seen a picture of her once before when he'd been looking in Max's wallet for something. He'd made a joke, and learned she was off-limits to his humor.

Corinne Cooper Peyton.

Why was she circled, and hidden in a file full of autopsy reports? He flipped it over and stared at the words written along the yellowed margin.

She gets it next. Stuck to the paper, a little yellow Post-it note said, "Overlook Glen."

He had no idea what it meant—except now he could call Max and give him what he wanted most in the world: a reason to go get his girl.

Most women would find Chase Ryker drop-dead gorgeous. From the kitchen window, Cori studied the Bullet Catcher securing locks and checking the gates to the neighboring vineyard. Most women would be mesmerized by his serious blue eyes, the set of his wide shoulders, and the military precision of his spare, graceful movements. And surely most women would be captivated by the fact that he was a former astronaut, had commanded the space shuttle, and had literally seen the world from sixty miles in space.

Was Max aware of that when he left her on that plane alone? Did he care that he was sending her to a romantic hideaway tucked in the hills of wine country with a man as attractive as Chase Ryker?

Obviously not.

Chase came in through the back door, stomping dirt from his feet. "Everything is secure, Mrs. Peyton; you can rest easy."

"Thank you, Chase. Since no one knows I'm here, I feel fairly safe."

He looked back through the kitchen door. "Beautiful vineyard out there."

"Isn't it? Luckily, our neighbors are generous with

their fantastic pinot noir. But I love the view. That's where I got the name Overlook Glen for the property." She opened the door to the refrigerator. "Oh. Looks like the cupboard is bare."

He glanced at her. "I'll take you to the market, if you like."

"There's a little place a mile down the road, and a bigger supermarket not much farther." She turned from the refrigerator. "I'll go."

"No can do, Mrs. Peyton. Max was very clear that you are not to go anywhere alone. If you like," he suggested, "I'll go and you can stay here, now that I've changed and secured the locks. If you promise not to leave the house."

She agreed and gave him a shopping list. "Can I go next door and let my neighbors know I'm here?" she asked. "I'll come back with a few bottles of pinot noir."

He smiled, a slow, lazy grin that probably made him a poster boy for NASA. "I don't drink, ma'am. And I'd prefer if you'd wait until I'm back, so I can go with you."

She agreed. "There are keys hanging in the mudroom for the cars in the garage. You have a choice of a Navigator, which holds groceries, or the Carrera—"

"Which holds turns."

She laughed.

"I'll do the SUV." He took her list and winked. "This time."

She heard him leave and headed for the back stairs. After a bath she'd take a glass of pinot up to the turret, to her secret place, and indulge in a pity party for missing Max.

Just before her bedroom, she passed the den that she'd set up as an office for William. She stepped into the room, drawn to the warm afternoon sun pouring over the antique oak desk. She grazed her finger along the bullnose edge of the desk, leaving a trail in the thin layer of dust that had accumulated.

William had spent so little time here, except for the few visits he'd made when the Petaluma property became available. About six weeks before he died, he'd come out with Giff for a town council meeting about the property.

At least, Cori thought with a black ache in her heart, he'd *said* he'd come out with Giff. She closed her eyes and pulled out the chair. She still couldn't get her head around the possibility that William had cheated on her. It was so out of the realm of reality—but there was damning evidence on that boat.

Was there any other evidence of infidelity?

She yanked the desk drawer open, her breath suspended as though she might find a picture, a letter, a credit card receipt. Something that other women found that confirmed their husbands were bastards.

But pencils, a calculator, and some loose change were all she found. She lifted a pad of paper and under it was a small silver key chain, with no keys. No, she realized, picking it up. This was no key chain. This was one of those tiny computer memories—a jump drive. She fingered it for a moment, frowning. There was no computer in this house. They'd brought laptops when they traveled and had never wired this house for the Internet. She'd wanted it to be a true getaway.

But she didn't need the Internet to find out what
was on this jump drive. In a few minutes, she had her
laptop set up on her bed. She slid the drive in and
called up the files, not sure what she expected to find.

Maybe something damning. Maybe something that
would exonerate him. Anything that might connect
her to the man she thought she knew.

The file was called PM Subs. In two clicks, she realized that it meant subcontractors for the Petaluma
Mall. Her heart dropped in disappointment.

Her gaze flittered over the spreadsheet, none of the
names familiar. In fact, no subs were identified by
name, just by specific function. That was strange.
There were premolded membrane designers, window
and glass installers, asphalt and concrete pouring,
lighting, flooring . . .

Already? They'd just broken ground, for God's
sake. They were months away from taking bids from a
lighting sub.

She clicked ahead. Forget bids, these subs had all
been *paid.* She did a quick scan of the dates. Some were
paid well over a year ago. That was patently *insane* in
construction. How could this be?

The answer had to be at the Petaluma Mall site.
Yanking the jump drive out without even clearing the
screen, she stood and peered out the window toward
the driveway. Chase wouldn't be back for a while. And
if she showed up with some big, bad bodyguard,
they'd know who she was immediately. No, she had to
go fast and alone—before anyone at Peyton found out
where she was, and alerted the foreman. She had to find

out what was going on at that mall and why her company was paying subs years before they did the work.

She could get halfway to Petaluma before Chase Ryker realized she was gone. But then he'd worry and call Max, and they'd put out an APB and send helicopters and Bullet Catchers roaming the hills of Healdsburg.

She grabbed some paper and wrote "Visiting neighbors. Be back soon." Snagging the car keys, she slipped the jump drive in her jacket pocket and headed for the garage and the welcome speed of William's Carrera.

When she arrived at the mall site, Cori downshifted and pulled past a six-foot sign bearing the Peyton P, squinting into the afternoon sunlight at the acres of concrete block and rebar, surrounded by an army of dump trucks, front loaders and cement mixers and men moving around like hard-hatted ants crawling around a mountain of red-brown earth.

It was well past "broken ground," but not nearly far enough along to pay lighting subs.

She parked as close as she could get to the trailer marked OFFICE, which was surrounded by mounds of cement blocks and several rows of Porta Potties. A few men stood near the trailer entrance, some perched on the makeshift stairs, drinking water and Gatorades, hard hats tucked under brawny arms darkened by a life in the sun.

They all turned to stare at the car.

Turning off the ignition, she knew exactly what to expect. Unless she was wearing a sign that said WILLIAM PEYTON'S WIFE: DON'T CATCALL, it was never pleasant to visit a construction site alone. She might be wearing jeans and a plain white cotton blouse, but looking at that crew, dirty, hungry, and ready to impress one another, she might as well have been dressed in a bikini.

Maybe the bodyguard would have been a good idea.

She slid out of the car, lifted her chin, and braced herself for the first whistle.

Nothing.

Two of the men looked away, a few studied their water bottles with intense interest, and the others merely nodded. Either she looked really bad, or California bred exceptionally polite construction workers.

As she approached the steps, the two men seated there stood to make room for her. One nodded, the other opened the steel door and held it for her with a quiet, "Mrs. Peyton."

What?

Inside, she came face-to-face with an attractive young woman with frosted blond hair seated at a cheap, pressed-board desk. On it were neat stacks of paper, carefully separated into pink, blue, white, and goldenrod. The place smelled like room-deodorized lavender that barely covered the bitter tobacco odor seeped into the indoor-outdoor carpeting.

The woman flushed and stood up, with a swipe of her palm over her T-shirt before holding it out to greet Cori. "Hello, Mrs. Peyton." She held out her hand. "I'm Sandy."

Cori shook her hand, certain she must look as stunned as she felt. "Hi, Sandy. Did you know I was coming?"

She beamed. "No, but I recognize you."

Was that possible? "Oh." Glancing around at the unnaturally immaculate trailer, she tamped down the urge to argue. Surely they'd been expecting *some-one* here.

There was no shock, no disbelief. No astonishment that the head of the corporation, based three thousand miles away, just waltzed into the construction office that had, conveniently enough, been cleaned within an inch of its life?

The young woman swept a hand over her desk and file cabinets, indicating the two metal chairs with frayed cushions as though she were showing a Park Avenue apartment. "Just a second, Mrs. Peyton. I'll get Mr. Nash for you." She came out from around her desk. "Here, let me take your jacket."

Sandy hung the hooded jacket up on the back of the door with as much care as if Cori had handed her a mink coat. Then she disappeared behind a warped paneled wall and reemerged, followed by a stocky man in his late forties, his few hairs plastered to his forehead and a broad smile stretched across his face.

"I'm Doug Nash, owner of Nash Builders. What a pleasant surprise, Mrs. Peyton."

Pleasant, maybe. But *so* not a surprise.

"Would you like something to drink?" Before she answered, Doug put a hand on Sandy's shoulder. "Is fresh coffee brewed, babe?"

The young blonde nodded enthusiastically and a minute later, Cori was seated in a back office—just as neat—drinking remarkably good coffee from a ceramic mug as Doug Nash proudly showed her pictures of his three children, featured in a family photo on his perfectly organized desk.

A family, Cori noted, with a mother that didn't even resemble the woman Nash had just called "babe." But she gave him the benefit of the doubt; she was overly sensitive on the subject of fidelity.

When he finished, Doug turned to Cori. "Now, what brings you to the site, Mrs. Peyton?"

"You have made surprising progress on this property. I was under the impression we'd barely broken ground."

His eyes widened. "No ma'am. We've really kicked into high gear over the past few months."

Since William died. "Who is the architectural and engineering firm?" she asked.

"A&E's being done by a company down in San Francisco, ma'am. They got a suit up here every coupla days or so. Got another design-and-construct slave driver breathin' down my neck, too." He grinned. "We're just following orders and doing the job they tell us from Miami."

"Who's your contact at Peyton Enterprises, Doug?"

A hint of color rose in his ruddy cheeks. "Well, I . . . I talk to several folks there. Couldn't say if it was just one. You know, we're pretty far removed from the head company. I just run the subs, ma'am."

Far removed? He'd just said they were following orders from Miami.

"What's the status of the sub fulfillment?" she asked.

"Everyone is on board. 'Course, a lot of the hiring

was done before Nash Building took over as the main site contractor three months ago."

"Three months ago?"

He nodded. "The former contractor had to be let go. But you probably know that."

No, she didn't. "Can I take a look at the project management files, Mr. Nash?"

"Absolutely. You can look at everything. Why don't I take you on a site tour while Sandy pulls the papers? Then you can take your time and read them all, with a better understanding of the place."

She'd seen plenty of partially constructed malls in the last four years. "No, thank you. I'm more interested in the documentation. Specifically, I'd like to look at the original planning-and-feasibility statement."

He frowned. "The original? That might be down in San Francisco."

"It should be on site."

"Yeah, you're right about that. Let me have Sandy dig out what we have." He stood and left, while Cori bit back a growing sense of frustration. Maybe she should take that tour—to take pictures and demand an explanation from the board.

When he returned, he was shaking his head. "This'll take a while, but I'll get what you want. Sandy will help you, but I gotta pay some of the workers who are anxious to call it a day. Could you come back tomorrow?"

"You hired day laborers?" She frowned at him. "That's not Peyton policy."

He shrugged. "We're in a rush to meet the schedule."

A rush? "I'd rather not wait for tomorrow, Mr. Nash." By then, documentation could be changed or destroyed. "Just bring me all the files you have. I'll pull what I need and take it with me."

He didn't look happy but nodded, and over the next half hour, Sandy loaded up a corner conference table with dog-eared files. Not nearly as neat as what covered the front desk.

When she'd dropped the last of them, Sandy said, "Would you like me to work with you, Mrs. Peyton? To help you find something in particular? I'm pretty familiar with those files."

Cori considered the offer, studying the girl's pretty face. She reminded her of someone, but she couldn't quite nail it. "You know, I'm not even sure what I'm looking for, so I just want to peruse."

"I'll be right out here until you're done, Mrs. Peyton. I can make copies if you like."

"Thanks." Cori settled into the chair at the table and chose a file. "I would love another cup of coffee."

"Sure. And, if you don't mind, I think you might want to move that car. It's gettin' an awful lot of attention from the guys and I'm worried one of them is going to scratch it or something."

"I'm sure it'll be fine."

Sandy gave her a playful smile. "I'll move it around back, if you like. I'd love to drive it, even twenty yards."

"Sure." Cori reached down and pulled the Porsche keys from her bag. "Here you go."

As she began to read and sift, Cori missed William

with a sharp pang. He'd know what all this meant. Materials management, resource requirements estimates, statistical quality control, and pages and pages and pages of something called critical path management—terms she had barely a working knowledge of.

Running her hand through her hair, she opened the next file and read about concrete pavement strength. She forced herself to think like the lawyer she had once studied to be. What was wrong with the picture? Where were the loopholes, the clues, the evidence . . . that someone . . .

That someone what? *Built a mall?*

Looking up, she realized the trailer had grown quiet and that dusk had fallen. With a start, she thought of Chase Ryker, who'd probably held her pinot noir–making neighbors at gunpoint by now. She lifted her purse to grab her phone, but the slot that normally held it was empty. Right—she'd taken it out on the way to Petaluma to check in with Marta, but there hadn't been any answer. Then she'd tossed the phone on the passenger seat to shift gears.

"Sandy?" she called. "Are you there?"

At the silence, Cori got up and walked to the front of the trailer. It was empty. Sandy's desk was closed up for the night, her computer off, her chair pushed in.

So much for "I'll stay as long as you need me, Mrs. Peyton."

She didn't remember the phone number to Overlook Glen, but it was on her cell speed dial.

Holding her purse, she opened the front door of the trailer and took two steps down. The door slammed behind her just as she remembered she'd given Sandy her keys. Swearing under her breath, she turned and grabbed the knob, but it was locked.

Damn. Maybe Sandy had left the car unlocked. She glanced around the deserted site, then remembered Sandy had said she'd leave it around back. An evening breeze penetrated her cotton shirt, reminding Cori that she'd also locked her jacket in the trailer. She jogged around the other side of the trailer, but the dirt lot was completely empty. Where the hell was her car?

It was dark, deserted, and she was in a construction site with no phone and no car. She returned to the front of the trailer, climbing the stairs to jimmy the doorknob a few times. On her tiptoes she tried to reach the window, but it was impossible.

She turned to look at the abandoned construction site behind her. Set far off the main road against a thickly wooded area, none of her options seemed palatable. She could walk directly through the construction site to the main road, which would be the fastest, but construction sites were inherently dangerous. She could follow the chain-link fence that surrounded the property and it would get her to the main road. Where she would . . .

Figure it out when she got there. She'd find a gas station or something and call Marta, get the number to her house. Or maybe just get the phone number of her neighbor's ranch. . . . Thankful she'd worn jeans and loafers, she started toward the far edge of the site.

After five minutes of walking along the fence, she realized it was more than a mile to the road. A glance around revealed nothing but high walls of concrete, treacherous-looking rebar beams, trenches, and shadows everywhere. Cori picked up her pace, cursing her stupidity for letting that trailer door lock. At the sound of a car she stopped, peering uneasily into the darkness for lights.

There were none.

She quickened her pace, the sound of her feet on the pavement matching the pulse pounding in her ears. Then lights caught her from the left. She turned instinctively toward them, blinded by the halogen beams. The car—a truck by her quick guess—rumbled over a gravel access road. Cori blinked into the lights, her throat tightening.

Should she wave them down for help? The truck picked up speed, heading straight in her direction. Fear paralyzed her for a second as the headlights bore down on her. God almighty, it wasn't going to stop.

She could go left or right, but the truck could follow her. She could hear the rumble of the engine as it got louder, closer.

She turned and dug her fingers into the fence and started to climb, her loafer slipping.

She looked over her shoulder. The truck had picked up speed. Turned on its brights. A scream caught in Cori's throat as she pulled herself up a foot. The horn honked, loud, long, endless, shocking her and making her lose her footing. She slipped back down to the ground just as the truck bore down, closer, closer, then screaming to a stop.

Trapped, terrified, she turned to face her assailant.

If she was going to die, she wanted to know who the hell it was.

The headlights went off, but white spots still blinded her as the driver's door opened and someone climbed out. Slow, menacing and deadly.

Cori sucked in a breath of disbelief. She'd never dreamed it would be him.

CHAPTER
Seventeen

Gifford Jones stumbled into the bathroom and turned the light switch on. But it was still dark.

He kicked the door closed and rubbed his eyes, nearly doubled over from the pain that pounded his temples.

"Are you okay, baby?" Breezy called in a sleepy voice.

Lord Jesus, he was not okay. "I'm fine," he managed to respond, clearing his throat. "Just getting an aspirin."

He waited for a minute. He made lots of trips to the bathroom at night; that wasn't unusual for him and she generally slept through them all. But tonight Breezy was particularly attentive, and when the headache slammed him, his body, as always, malfunctioned.

How long would she stay with a man who needed Viagra and still couldn't satisfy her?

He rubbed his eyes again. Straight ahead, he could see the vanity and sinks, the marble floor, the edge of the bathtub. But the sides were dark. His peripheral vision was gone.

How long would she stay with a blind man?

He knew why he had the headaches tonight. Because he had managed to finagle a meeting that afternoon with Thomas Matuzak. The head of Beckworth Insurance had said just enough to panic Giff.

They weren't investigating Corinne—or, if they were, he wasn't saying. But he could tell they were digging around. Just how deep would they look? And with Corinne in Sonoma . . .

Thank God he'd given Nash plenty of warning. Maybe Corinne wouldn't even go to the site, but if she did, Nash knew what to do. In the meantime, even if she was just taking a break from Miami like Breezy said, he had a chance to really make it look like Corinne killed her husband. But how?

With no body and a clean autopsy, they would need hard evidence. Something he planted and the insurance company found. But how could he do that?

The bathroom door flew open. "What is going on, Giff?"

Tunnel vision forced him to turn his whole head to look at his wife. He could see the concern in her eyes, which suddenly meant much more than the skimpy bra she spilled out of and the tiny lace panties she'd worn to entice him.

He pressed his fingers to his temple. "Headache."

Her features softened as she reached for him. "Oh, baby," she cooed and put her fingers on top of his and started massaging. "You're getting these headaches too often."

He shut his eyes and closed his hands over her bare

waist. "Breezy," he said, pulling her to him. "You're the best thing that ever happened to me."

She drew back, her eyes wide. "Giff! What brought that on?"

"I can't tell my wife that I love her? It's true." They both knew that he married her because she made an incredible accessory to his life: He didn't try to hide that when they met and she didn't try to deny it. But over time, she'd become much more than arm candy. Despite her edgy humor, Breezy had a soft heart.

But was it soft enough to love him . . . blind?

"Giff." She flattened her hands on his cheeks and forced his face to hers. "You have to get help."

He tried to shake his head, but she held him firm.

"Don't be like that," she insisted. "Doctors are not all hacks and quacks. I don't care what happened to your son. You have to go to a neurologist or a specialist. Don't look at me that way, Giff."

He knew the horror that was in his expression. He'd never step foot in a neurologist's office again. They whipped out their knives and opened heads and killed people. Teenage people. He knew that firsthand.

"It's stress," he said. "There's nothing wrong with me that a long vacation wouldn't cure."

"Then take one."

Right. As if he'd leave before he found and hid every sheet in the paper trail. But what if he did go blind? How could he hide anything if he couldn't see it?

He could . . . if the media and company attention

was focused on the trophy wife who'd killed her rich husband. But how could he do that? *How?*

"How what, baby?"

He didn't even realize he'd spoken aloud. "How can I find time to take a vacation? Someone has to run that company."

"You can't run it if you're dead, Giff." Her voice was flat, and he could see her eyes were bright with anger. Or tears.

Tears? From Breezy Jones?

"You love me," he said, as though it just dawned on him. And in a way, it had.

"Of course I do." She slapped his shoulder playfully and grinned. "You think I married you for money?"

If his head hadn't hurt so bad, he'd have laughed. She'd practically audited him before she accepted an engagement ring. But now . . . now things were different.

A wisp of hope wrapped around his chest. Did she love him enough to help save him? Enough to set her best friend up for murder?

He slid his hands up to her breasts, cupping them over her bra.

"You ready now, Giff?" She leaned her hips into him, and he cursed his limp dick. If only he could make love to her, then afterward, in the dark, he could quietly ask her a hypothetical question. To test her.

She'd never been one for postcoital chitchat, but right now she seemed so soft. So compliant. He squeezed her tits again and she closed her eyes, shimmying against his useless cock.

"I thought you had a headache," she whispered, as

though he were raging hard. That was Breezy's gift. She never complained about his problems, she just helped him solve them.

And maybe that's what she could do now.

He inched her away, returning his hands to her waist and looking into her eyes. What would she do? Turn him in?

Of course not. This was a girl from Chicago's South Side. She'd worked too hard to get where she was to let his mistake bring them both down.

"I have to ask you a question," he said steadily.

"Anything, hon."

"Who do you love more? Me or Corinne Peyton?"

She searched his eyes, her clear green gaze clouded with uncertainty. Giff held his breath. Of course she'd say him. It was no contest. He was a man. Sort of.

"Who?" he asked again, the pain tightening in his temples as he waited for the answer.

"I love you both," she said.

He tightened his grasp. "*More.* Who do you love more?"

"Giff." She shook her head and tried to pull away. "She's my best friend; you're my husband."

"Who?" His voice hardened with the demand. Shit, he was backing her into a corner and there was nothing Breezy hated more. But he couldn't stop. He was desperate.

"Well, I love you, Giff," she finally said, with just enough hesitation to worry him.

"If you had to choose one of us—say, to save our

lives—who would you choose?" His fingers dug into her hips and he could feel the bones. She was so thin, he could break her in two. "Breezy, tell me. Who would you choose?"

"I can't believe you have to ask."

The look in her eyes told him exactly what he needed to know.

"I could kill you, Cori."

She finally released her grip on the chain-link fence. "You damn near did, Max."

He closed the space between them, wearing a scowl so deep it cut a slash in his forehead. "I can't believe you would be so stupid as to run around this place by yourself at night. What the hell are you trying to prove?"

"I didn't set out to run around at night." She rubbed her arms as the adrenaline that had just surged suddenly turned her blood icy. "I got locked out of the trailer. Someone moved my car. I don't have a phone. I was looking for— What are you doing here?"

"You left your computer on and the last file was still up." He pulled her into the heat of his chest and she could feel his heart pounding as hard as hers.

But that didn't answer her question. What was he doing in California?

"You scared me," he said gruffly.

"Then why did you try to run me over?"

"To show you how easily it could happen. Plus I didn't want you to tear off into the woods." He hugged her even closer, burying her in the hard muscle of him. "Jesus," he muttered. "I knew I shouldn't have left you."

"No," she said roughly, pulling away to singe him with a look. "You shouldn't have."

"Let's go home. I gotta call Ryker." He started walking to the car, but she resisted.

"I have to get back into the trailer, Max. The jump drive and the files are there."

"Tomorrow."

"No," she countered. "Tomorrow everything could be gone. I need to have the evidence together to confront Giff and the board about why this property has been rushed, and why we're prepaying hundreds of thousands to subs."

"Tomorrow," he insisted.

"Max, something in my gut tells me this is going to lead us to William's killer."

He held open the passenger door to the SUV—the Navigator from her garage that Chase had taken to the store. "All right. Let's get what you need and leave."

"Can you get into the trailer?"

He shot her a look and slammed the door shut.

Like her, he couldn't park closer than about a hundred and fifty feet from the trailer because of the blocks of cement and the temporary bathrooms. As they climbed out of the SUV, Cori suggested he lift her up to climb in the window.

She just got that same look again as he crossed the gravel, took the two stairs in one step, and knocked the door open with one swift kick. "We're in," he said. "Make it fast."

"I just need to figure out what to take," she said, heading to the back office.

"Take everything."

"Can you go look for my car?"

"No. I'm not leaving you." He folded himself into one of the guest chairs as she picked up files.

After a moment, she asked, "Max, why did you change your mind and come here?"

He didn't answer right away, and she looked over her shoulder at him. He balanced his chin on his fist, his elbow on the armrest and his eyes burned with . . . something.

"Dan found something in Japan that worried me."

She dropped the file she'd been holding. "What?"

"A note. In the file of the—" He jerked his head up and looked over her shoulder, at the window. "Get down," he ordered, sliding out of the seat and pulling a gun in one swift move. "Get away from the window."

She fell to her knees, watching his face and not the window. "What is it?"

"Lights. A car." He held her down with one hand, crouching as he moved toward the window. He nudged the blind with his gun and peered out. "I saw headlights."

She stayed low as time ticked by. "Are they still there?"

"Shhh." He put his hand against her mouth, closing his eyes as he listened. "Son of a bitch," he murmured.

"What?" she whispered.

"Listen to me," he said, still looking outside. "You

do exactly what I tell you to do, when I tell you to do it. Do you understand?"

She nodded. "Are we going to stay in here or try to get to the car?"

"*We* are not going to do anything. You are going to stay low to the ground and follow my instructions, which will not be delivered nicely. We're going to— shit."

"What?"

He just shook his head to quiet her. She listened but heard nothing.

"There's someone outside," he mouthed.

Blood pounded in her ears, and every muscle tensed. "It could be Sandy," she whispered. "Or Nash. They work here."

He looked at her, his gaze darting from eye to eye, thinking hard. "Why wouldn't they come up to the door? The lights are on. They know we're in here." He frowned, listening again, sniffing the air. "We have to get out of . . ." He sniffed again, harder. *"Now."*

He seized her by the arm and yanked her to her feet, twisting toward the desk to grab the SUV's keys. "Do the lights flash when you unlock this car door?"

"I think so."

"Then we're not going to unlock it until we're next to it."

As he pulled her toward the trailer door, a whiff of gasoline assaulted her.

"When I say go, we're going to run like hell," he told her. "Stay with me every inch of the way until I tell you to let go. I'm going to unlock the car and open the doors. The minute I do, you throw yourself in the backseat, driver's side. Don't stop, don't look, don't do anything but that. Got it?"

"Got it."

He grabbed the trailer door with the hand that held the gun and pulled her with the other. "Go!" he barked, rushing her down the steps and breaking into a run. The Navigator looked like it was a million miles away, out in the open, an easy target.

She sprinted with every ounce of power she could muster, deafened by air rushing over her ears. Her heels slid on stones and Max pulled her up from a stumble, the car still about fifty feet away. Her feet pounded in rhythm with his, gravel stabbing into the soles of her shoes. Thirty feet.

He held up the key toward the SUV. Fifteen feet, ten, five.

"Wait," he ordered just as the headlights flashed with the keyless entry. She froze and he closed the space to the car, but something moved in her side view. Jerking her head to the right, she saw a man standing between two portable bathrooms.

A red sweatshirt, hood up, arms extended, gun aimed directly at . . .

"Max!" she yelled, hurling herself toward him and pushing him so hard, he stumbled with a vicious grunt. Like a firebrand, heat smacked her arm, a whizzing, tearing noise whipped through the air and burst against the side of the car.

She'd been shot.

He yanked the back door of the SUV and shoved her in so hard, she lurched to the other side. Before she righted herself, he was behind the wheel.

Another bullet hit the back door with a thud. "Get on the floor!" he shouted. She rolled down and the SUV flew forward as he slammed on the accelerator.

"Are you hit?" he asked.

She slapped her hand over her upper arm, expecting to feel blood. But all she felt was the crispy edges of a torn blouse. "No," she said on a breath. "It grazed my shirt."

"Jesus Christ, Cori!" he hollered, pounding the steering wheel. "What the hell were you doing?"

She sat up to defend herself. "Saving your life."

"Get down!" he bellowed, whipping so hard to the right she really thought they were only on two wheels. "I don't need you to save my life, damn it!" He revved the engine until they had to be hitting seventy, cinders crackling like popcorn on the undercarriage.

"He was going to shoot you, Max. You didn't see him and I did. I just acted—I didn't think!"

"Just like your father," he muttered.

Just like her father? Slowly, she rose up from behind the seat, clinging to the leather pocket for stability as he careened toward the site exit.

That wasn't how her father got killed. Just as she opened her mouth to argue, a flash of orange burst in the rearview mirror. Whipping around, she saw the trailer engulfed in flames.

And inside were the files and, oh God, that jump

drive with the subcontractor spreadsheet on it. Turning, she caught his gaze in the rearview. He gave her a hard, closed look.

She'd seen him shut down and shut her out before. She'd begged, she'd pleaded . . . and then she'd assumed she knew what he wouldn't say and why he wouldn't say it.

Just like your father.

Had she assumed wrong?

CHAPTER
Eighteen

Chase Ryker moved through Cori's house with military precision, snapping out orders to another Bullet Catcher and the police officers brought in to patrol the property. From the corner of a chintz-covered sofa in the softly lit den, Cori sipped coffee. An endless pot had been brewing in the hours since her house became overrun with large men bearing handguns.

The former Air Force commander rallied the troops with exactness, telling them where they would be stationed that night and when their shifts would end. The police officers seemed outranked, outsized, and wholly outclassed by Chase and the younger Bullet Catcher, a man named Johnny. Though neither reached Max's height, the two men had the same quiet sense of control, authority, and fearlessness.

Max sat at the game table with a local detective and fire chief, answering questions and giving them information to help them find the arsonist. He paused at the soft ring of the house phone, then continued talk-

ing. Cori picked up the receiver, barely getting a
"hello" out before being interrupted.

"My husband is getting emergency wake-up calls
and I'm sleeping alone. I don't like that," Breezy said
in a harsh whisper.

Cori rolled her eyes. "Sorry, Breeze, but he's on the
crisis contact tree. We woke up quite a few unhappy
employees and spouses tonight."

"What gives? He said there was a fire at the
Petaluma Mall site. Were you there?"

"Yes." She mouthed "Breezy" to Max who responded with narrowed eyes of distrust. "It was arson,"
she said quietly.

"Really? Are you sure?"

She could instantly feel Max's glare on her. She
stood, turning away and walking toward the kitchen.
"It's too complicated for this hour."

"Cori, I have to know." There was an edge of desperation in her voice; this wasn't just hunger for gossip.

"Some things at the job site don't seem right," she
said. "We're going to halt construction for now, for the
company's best interest."

"Cori fucking Peyton, don't you hand me that corporate BS. What's going on?"

Cori stepped into the kitchen, where Johnny, talking to Chase, shot her a friendly smile. Another heart-
breaker.

"Come on," Breezy prodded. "You can trust me."

The fact that Breezy even said those words made
Cori uneasy. "Don't do this, Breezy. Don't put both of
us in the situation."

"What situation?" Breezy sounded insulted. "Are you holding something back because of Giff? Do you think he was . . . involved?"

"Of course not. But the Petaluma property has been under his watch, and I'm afraid he's going to take this mess personally."

Breezy was quiet for so long, Cori thought she'd lost the connection.

"Okay," Breezy whispered. "I just checked. He's in the library on the phone. Tell me what you found, before he comes back."

"Breezy, I just told you—"

"Goddamn it, I'm trying to help you." The urgency in her voice sent a chill down Cori's spine.

"I found a document with William's signature forged on it, dated the day after he died," she said quietly, aware of the men's eyes on her. "And I discovered that subs have been prepaid, some a year in advance."

"Could it be a clerical error?" Breezy asked. "People make mistakes, you know."

"But arson isn't a mistake—and neither is being shot at."

Breezy was dead silent, and Cori reached for the patio door to get some privacy. "I'm in the middle of something, Breeze, and it's not good. I just found out that the guy who did the autopsy on William is dead, and he left—"

A strong hand closed over Cori's shoulder. "What do you think you're doing?"

She turned to meet Max's blistering gaze. "Talking to my best friend."

He took the phone from her and stabbed a button, tossing the receiver on the counter with a clunk. "Not in the middle of a murder investigation."

"We are not—"

"Oh yes we are. Dan Gallagher just called."

Cori braced for the blow. "William *was* murdered?"

Max shook his head. "A witness came forth in Japan. The medical examiner didn't commit suicide. He was shot to death."

Breezy stared at the receiver, then looked up at Giff. "I lost her."

"Lost the connection, or she hung up, or what?" he demanded, rubbing his temples and blinking at her.

"I don't know."

"What was the last thing she said?" His eyes were red-rimmed and all the color had drained from his face.

"That subs were prepaid," she said, lavishing insinuation in her voice. "She's going to find out, Giff."

"Call her back."

"Giff—" He looked so old and decrepit, with a vein throbbing on the bald spot she detested. She put a hand on his arm and added sweetly, "Do you really want me to do this?"

"I need help, Breezy. If they find out how much money I stole, I'll go to jail for the rest of my life."

She closed her eyes. "I'll do what I have to, Giff."

"You better," he said, "or life as we know it is over."

With bodyguards stationed around the property, Max could almost relax. At least, he could think. Cori had disappeared upstairs for a bath, carrying a goblet of red wine. Once the crew had their duties and placement, he'd followed her to the bedroom, but she'd locked the door.

After a moment, he went in search of a guest room and shower. When he opened the last door in the hall, he discovered a set of stairs that ended at another doorway. Opening it, he stepped into the glass-enclosed octagonal room perched high atop the house.

It couldn't have been ten feet across, with a cushion-covered window seat encircling the room and giant throw pillows on the floor. Moonlight bathed the tiny area in white light, illuminating the flowered patterns on the pillows and window seat.

He knew he'd found one of Cori's spots. The whisper of her fragrance was in the air; the essence of her seeped into his flesh. Closing the door, he sat on a window cushion, dropped his head in his hands, and sucked in an agonizing breath.

His chest hurt. His throat hurt. His head hurt.

Just like your father.

He'd lied to her five years ago. He hadn't meant to lie, he just wanted to spare her pain. And he certainly hadn't meant the truth to stay buried this long, but it had. And it cost him everything that mattered. He'd seen the look on her face when he made that verbal slip, greased by fear and adrenaline.

Eventually, she'd ask what he meant. Could he tell her the truth . . . and let her realize he'd lied, and because of it they'd thrown away their life together? Could he not? Would she ever trust him again? Would she ever believe him again? Could she ever *love* him again?

Jesus. *Nice work, Roper. Way to keep those emotions off the job.*

He lifted his head at the sound of a footstep on the stairs. He leaped to the door and whipped it open to find Cori, her glass of wine in one hand, a deck of cards in the other.

"Don't tell me," she said, "you got the watchtower duty."

He smiled, taking in her strappy tank top and tight-fitting sweatpants, bare feet and damp hair. "Come up for a quick round of solitaire with the devil kid?"

She brushed by him and settled on a floor cushion, placed the goblet next to her, and rapped the deck. "Unless he wants to play poker."

Ah, man. Cori Cooper, cross-legged with a deck of cards and a look of pure sin in her eyes. For one moment, he was back in Chicago and life was perfect again.

"You don't have much on," he said, sitting across from her. "I'll have you naked in three hands."

She shook her head. "We're not playing strip."

Disappointment curled in his gut. "Okay. I already have my first favor lined up."

"No favors, either." She handed him the deck to cut. "I like that game we played the other night."

He tapped the top card and mentally cursed himself for inventing *answers*. Now he'd have to cough up a few. "Fine," he said. "You deal."

She did, then looked at her cards, set two down, and

picked up her wine. "Want to taste what the neighbors grow?"

He took the glass, sniffed it, letting one drop touch his lips. "I'd prefer the neighbors to grow some hops."

"When in Rome." She took the glass and took a healthy sip. "How many cards do you need?"

The most ridiculous sense of contentment rolled over Max. Years faded, time evaporated, and they were just a happy couple who spent hours playing cards, making love, and spinning dreams about the future.

"None, I've got two pair," he said.

She dropped her cards with a sigh. "Okay. What's your question?"

"Would you take off your top?"

She laughed easily. "No."

He shrugged and scooped the cards. "It was worth a shot."

On the second deal, he knew she had something good. Her eyes shone, and her transparency twisted something inside his chest.

"What?" she demanded at his look.

"Nothing. Just observing your poker face."

She stuck her tongue out, and he took three cards and got zilch. She laid down three tens with an evil grin, and leaned back against the window seat. He flipped his cards and waited for the inevitable.

What did you mean when you said I was just like my father?

But she didn't say a word.

"You can ask me to take off my shirt," he coaxed. "I'll say yes."

"This is answers, not strip. And I have a question that you can't avoid anymore."

Here it comes.

"Why did you take this assignment?"

"I told you—"

She held her hand up. "I know what you *said*. Now I want the truth."

"I don't turn down assignments. No matter how difficult." That was the truth. Sort of.

"Did you want to get back at me?"

He frowned, shaking his head. "God, no."

"Did you think you'd sleep with me again?"

"I didn't know what would happen."

"Did you tell your boss why we broke up?"

"She never asked."

She opened her mouth, then closed it, regarding him warily for a moment. "It's my deal." She shuffled wordlessly, and then dealt him a brutal hand.

"You sure you don't want to play for favors?" he asked, pulling out a card and flipping it between his fingers. "I have a deuce."

She shook her head. "I have a question."

Her tone piqued his interest. "Shoot."

"Have you . . ." She took a breath, then exhaled. "Have you thought about me . . . much . . . in the past five years?"

The cards froze in his hands. "Yeah."

"How much?"

Why lie? He leaned over, so near that he could smell her shampoo. "Every. Single. Day," he said softly. "Sometimes I would go on Cori binges that lasted hours."

His confession hung in the air, as real and powerful as the heat between them.

Her gaze never wavered. "Me, too."

The admission hit his solar plexus like a power punch, followed by another as she leaned forward to kiss him. He pulled her into him, burying his fingers into her long hair. Their tongues fused, fire licking through his veins as she melted onto his lap.

Greedily, he thrust his hand under her flimsy top and enveloped her breast, groaning as her nipple pressed against his palm.

He eased her back and she wrapped her legs around his hips, arching into him. She lowered his face to her breasts with a soft plea, and he slid the tank top off, then licked, kissed, and gently bit her nipples.

She stretched her arms above her head, her eyes hooded with desire. Her black hair spread over the pillow and floor, and she struggled to breathe evenly, her crotch pressed against his furious hard-on.

"Guess we're playing strip after all," she said raggedly.

"Guess I won," he said, placing his hands over her round breasts, tweaking the buds of her nipples. He kissed one, nibbled the other. The tips glistened in the moonlight, wet from his mouth and pulled taut in an enticing circle.

"If you don't want this,"—he slid his hands down her sides, pulling her hips up so his cock could rub her—"tell me now."

"I do," she whispered. "I want this, Max." She placed her hands over his heart, then curled her fingers into his chest hair. "I want this. Every. Single. Day."

He pulled her back up to kneel in front of him, then started a long, slow skim down her body again. Resting his hands on her hips, he slid his thumbs lower to the V between her legs, and gently spread her flesh.

She arched back, bracing her elbows on the window seat, completely open to him. He reached down for the card at his side, then slid it between his teeth.

She flicked the card so it vibrated in his mouth. "Deuce of spades," she said. "My favorite."

He dipped his head and lightly scraped her protruding nipple with the edge of the card; she breathed in sharply, lifting her chest to increase the contact. His teeth locked over the card, he brushed her nipple again and again, then moved to the other breast. She arched into him, releasing a helpless moan.

He grazed down her ribs to her belly with the card, leaving a trail of goose bumps. Lower . . . lower . . . until the card grazed the tight curls between her legs.

Spreading her flesh, he flicked the card over her pink, swollen nub. Once. Twice. She grabbed his shoulders and quivered into him.

He flattened the card against her wet flesh, then he slid it away and blew on her. Using only his tongue, he jiggled the card. Faster, faster, until it fluttered like the wings of a hummingbird against her delicate flesh. Her body shivered and he felt her slip further and further out of control.

Her fingers dug into his shoulders and her breaths quickened as she ground into the card, into his lips.

Suddenly, he opened his mouth and the deuce floated to the floor. She almost buckled, but he licked her gently, quickly, hungrily, blowing softly against her and curling his tongue into her, again and again as her orgasm gathered strength. She ground out his name, begged him not to stop. Just as she rode up the edge of a climax, he stopped and kissed his way up to her stomach and breasts, ignoring her frustrated whimpers.

Then he stood, towering over her as he unbuckled his pants and undressed, his gaze locked to hers. His quick, ragged breaths matched the rhythm of his pulse. He wanted her. He needed her.

Now.

She reached for him, closing her hands over his insistent erection, opening her mouth for him, but he crouched down, eliciting another frustrated moan.

But he would come if she touched him. If she even *looked* at him. And when he exploded, he had to be inside Cori.

"C'mere," he rasped. Sitting, he pulled her back onto his lap, flesh against flesh this time. He took her face in his hands and kissed her slowly and deeply, invading her mouth with his tongue the same way he was about to invade her body.

He never closed his eyes, and neither did she.

Just as a sob rose in her throat and threatened to escape, he slid his hands under her arms and lifted her, holding her over his erection, almost entering her, burning hot.

"Max," she whispered. "Please."

He eased into her one inch and held her there, his biceps flexed hard, his eyes narrowed with the need to make her understand. He dipped her down a bit more and dragged his gaze to where their bodies met. She followed, mesmerized by the power of his swollen, aroused body, poised to take her.

"I think about this." He entered her completely. "Every. Single. Day."

She gasped as her muscles constricted around him, and he started the slow, steady rocking of his body into hers. A bead of sweat ran down his temple and he moaned, low and long and lost.

He held her waist in a hand grasp, sliding her up and down over him, each thrust intensifying in power and depth and intensity. Blind and crazy, he hammered into her as his aching, burning need finally erupted. He climaxed just as she did, exploding in silent fury, holding in his groans by biting his lower lip until he tasted a drop of blood. As he finally relaxed, finally released his grip on her, she covered his mouth and suckled his lips.

He grazed her cheek with a feather touch, then took her hand and placed it over his heart again.

CHAPTER
Nineteen

Sweetness never worked on the Mexican bitch, so Breezy didn't waste time on a fake smile. "Let me in, Marta. I need to get something from Cori's room."

The demand was met with a distrusting gaze. "I'm sorry. Mrs. Peyton's bodyguard left explicit instructions not to allow anyone in the house."

"I don't think that included me." Breezy put a hand on the door and gave it a push. "Outta my way, *chiquita.*"

For a moment, she thought the maid would actually stand her ground. But she backed off, and Breezy bounded into the house, only to realize Marta was following her up the stairs. Breezy spun around. "I don't need an escort."

"I can't let you go into her room alone."

Breezy looked skyward. "Jesus H. Christ. I slept in that room when her husband died. I'm her goddamn best friend. I can go get a sweater from her closet if I need to borrow one."

"No." Marta took another step, making herself even with Breezy. "I'm coming with you."

Breezy leaned way back, making sure her disgust was visible. "Maybe you have something else you need to do, Marta. Like *time* in jail. For . . . what was it?" She tapped a finger against her cheek. "Oh, I know. In this country we call it prostitution."

Marta just blinked.

"Or," Breezy added, "perhaps you could drop by your sister's new job and mention how she had the same gig out in California."

"Uh, excuse me?" A voice from the kitchen pulled both of their attention. "I'm just about done now, ma'am."

"Who is that?" Breezy demanded.

Marta glanced toward the kitchen, obviously pulled. "The man who is taking Mr. Peyton's boat," she said softly. "I have to help him."

"By all means, go. I know my way around here."

"Miss?" Footsteps accompanied the voice, and a man came from the back of the house toward the stairs. "I'm taking off now. You'll need to—oh, hello."

"You're the new owner of *Peyton's Place*?" Breezy asked, keeping a smile plastered on. "Congratulations, she's a lovely boat."

He nodded. "Thank you. I'm Brad Hamilton. And you are?"

"Just a friend of the family, Brad." She gave Marta a solid tap on the shoulder. "Go take care of him, sweetie. I'll just be a moment."

She tore up the stairs without turning to see Marta's face.

In the room, she shut the door behind her and leaned against the wood as she caught her breath. She could do this.

She had to.

By the time Marta barged into the room, Breezy was stripped down to her bra, an array of gorgeous sweaters strewn over the chaise in Cori's closet.

"I'm looking for one in particular," Breezy said smiling at the woman who would be her witness. "That Versace thing with the pearls on the collar."

"It's at the dry cleaner," Marta said, her eyes still suspicious.

"Oh." Breezy gave a casual shrug. "A shame."

The sun had already risen over Sonoma Valley when Max went downstairs, drawn to the aroma of fresh brewed coffee. In the kitchen he could hear Chase Ryker's baritone. Since there was no response, he assumed the Rocket Man was working the phones, learning what progress the detectives had made on the arson at the construction site.

Arson was obvious. But embezzlement, based on the fact that subs were paid in advance, might be harder to prove. Like Cori, he had a feeling it all led back to Miami—and William—but he needed a nice long session with the contractor first.

No, he needed coffee first. Then more of Cori. Then, Doug Nash.

Chase was looking out the kitchen window as he

spoke on the phone, and didn't see Max enter. They'd never worked a detail together, and Max was impressed by the former commander's focus and attention to detail.

Chase laughed softly. "Define 'well,' Lucy." A pause. "Yes, I'd say they get along very well."

Very attentive to detail. Well, Bullet Catchers were trained to observe.

Max cleared his throat and Chase turned and grinned. "He's here now. You want to talk to him?"

The last thing he wanted to do while he still wore the scent of sex with his principal was chat with Lucy Sharpe. He wanted two cups of coffee, then he wanted to go back to the warmth of Cori's body and bed.

"All right, I'll tell him. Take it easy, Luce." Chase flipped the phone closed and gave Max an apologetic smile. "She was worried. You didn't answer your cell."

Max looked toward the ceiling. "Like I need a mother."

"Lucy Sharpe doesn't have a maternal bone in her body," Chase said dryly. "But her calls are expected to be answered, as you know."

"I've worked for her longer than you have, Commander," Max replied, opening a cabinet. "I know the drill."

"Then why didn't you take her call?"

"Why don't you mind your own business?"

He continued to search for coffee cups and heard the sound of a chair scraping the floor as Chase pulled it from the table.

"You know," Chase said, "this is in direct contradiction to everything I've ever heard about you."

Max found a shelf full of white ceramic mugs. "What? That I'm not a morning person?"

Chase laughed. "The way you're acting. Dan says you've got ice water in your veins, and Alex—"

Max slammed a mug on the counter. "Romero? I don't give a rat's ass what that hothead thinks of me. He doesn't have a brain, anyway."

"Like I said," Chase continued, unfazed, "I didn't expect you to be so . . . involved."

"I get involved in every assignment," Max said, pissed that he had to defend himself. "It's part of the job."

Blessedly, Chase didn't answer. Max continued his task, eyeing some fruit in a basket, then opened the refrigerator. Maybe she'd like yogurt or—

"Actually," Chase said, "Alex does have a brain."

Max closed his eyes. He didn't feel like discussing his least favorite colleague, he wanted coffee, food, and more sex. Maybe not in that order. He did not want to get into the mysterious folklore that surrounded his legendary rivalry with another Bullet Catcher. He had no intention of telling anyone why he hated Alex Romero, and he knew the Latin lover certainly wasn't going to spill the rice and beans.

Still, Chase had been a huge help and Max had no issues with *him*. "Maybe being married will activate Romero's dormant gray matter," Max said, slipping a little humor in his voice. "At least it should keep him out of the bed of every woman he protects."

As soon as he said it, he could have kicked himself. With a wry smile, he turned to Chase. "Go ahead. Give me shit. I deserve it."

But Chase just grinned. "No sir. This is obviously more than casual lust. Which brings me back to my original comment: I heard you were a pretty detached kind of guy."

He couldn't even remember how *detached* felt. "Is that what you were talking to Lucy about?"

"Don't worry. I covered for you."

"Thanks, but don't be so sure you succeeded." With two well-placed questions, Lucy probably got far more information out of Chase than he realized. She was a former trained CIA operative and an expert in elicitation. And if there was such a thing as mind control, she'd probably qualify for expertise in that, too.

Max picked up the coffee and grabbed a peach. Sharing that could be interesting. "Any news from the arson investigator?"

Chase nodded. "They found Nash last night and he has a rock-solid alibi for the time of the fire."

"Can you get me a home address for him?"

"Got it already. Courtesy of Raquel, the Wonder Girl."

Max grinned at the mention of Lucy's assistant. "Our secret weapon."

"She sure as hell is," Chase agreed. "You going to talk to this guy today?"

"That's the plan."

"I heard you're very good at interrogating," Chase said.

"Is there anything at all you don't know about me, Ryker?"

"Don't know why you hate Alex Romero."

A swift pounding at the side door sent Chase to open it, finding Johnny Christiano holding a laundry basket full of magazines and papers.

"Mail call," Johnny said as he entered.

"What's that?" Max asked.

"The neighbor picks up Mrs. Peyton's mail." He dropped the basket on the table with a thud. "Nice lady. Makes wine, too." Johnny shook his long, dark hair off a face that looked like a Roman gladiator's. "Just like my grandmother did. Although I get a feeling this Napa stuff is better than Nonna's Dago Red."

Chase, his dark blue eyes twinkling, glanced at Max. "*Dago* Red? Isn't that a little politically incorrect?"

Johnny shot him an incredulous look. "*Guinea* Red would be politically incorrect."

Max merely raised an eyebrow.

Johnny dumped the basket over on the table, sending envelopes, postcards, and coupons flying. "She's a nice lady and I promised her I'd bring her laundry basket back."

"Making friends with the neighbors?" Chase asked.

Max chuckled. "Don't even try to stop him. Once we were on a diplomatic detail in Hong Kong and this one"—Max indicated Johnny with his coffee cup—"spent all his downtime teaching the Chinese housekeeping staff how to make red sauce."

"Gravy," Johnny corrected, a serious look in his hooded dark eyes that he'd no doubt perfected as a young wiseguy on the streets of New York City. "It isn't Ragù from a jar, man. It's *gravy*."

"I'll remember that," Chase said.

Max just smiled. Lucy'd saved Johnny from the clutches of the mob and made a hell of a Bullet Catcher out of him. He was tough, smart, and could outcook them all.

"You want to take any of this mail up to her?" Chase asked. "Or will you be too busy eating peaches?"

Johnny choked a laugh. "Whoa. Harsh."

Max glanced at the envelopes strewn over the table. "There's nothing that can't wait until after breakfast." He picked up the coffee cups and peach.

Chase retrieved an envelope that had fallen on the floor. "You might want to give Lucy a call when you have a minute," he said, dropping it faceup on the table.

"I'll do that," he said, turning toward the door. "After I—"

He froze in place. What had he seen on the table? Spinning around, he stared at the envelope Chase had just picked up. Foreign postage, strange handwriting . . .

Coffee splashed out of the mugs as he dropped them onto the table, then seized the envelope to stare at the postmark.

Kyoto, Japan.

Addressed to Cori Peyton, care of Overlook Glen, Healdsburg. In the left-hand corner, instead of a return address, were the initials Y. B.

He tore the envelope open, vaguely aware of Chase and Johnny staring at him as he yanked out a piece of paper. He knew from the embossed seal from the Office of the Medical Examiner, Miami–Dade County, that it had to be an original. He scanned it, processing as fast as he could read.

Decedent William George Peyton . . . age sixty-three years . . .

Height, weight, sex, race, medical terms and findings, toxicology results . . . then his gaze landed on a line in the middle of the page.

Manner of death: homicide.

"'She gets it next.'" Cori slapped the envelope and the incomplete autopsy on her lap. "Maybe that's all the note that Dan found means. That I get the autopsy report next."

From the driver's seat, Max gave her a look that said that was *not* what the note meant.

"But why send it to me here in California?" she mused. "Why not Miami?"

Max shrugged. "And why only the top page of the report? Why not send the whole thing?"

Cori dropped her head back and closed her eyes. "You know what's funny, Max?"

"Nothing, at the moment."

She smiled. "I feel better." She didn't open her eyes, even when he reached over and closed his fingers over her hand. "Closure."

"Nothing's closed until you know who, how, and why."

They hardly talked for the next hour, but he held her hand for the entire drive to Vacaville, where Doug Nash lived. Once in town, he pulled out the directions Raquel had e-mailed and handed them to Cori to read. "We're looking for the intersection of California Drive and Los Robles Court."

They found it easily, passing modestly upscale homes built on cul-de-sacs with Spanish names. On a Monday afternoon, the little neighborhood hummed with professional landscapers and moms doing errands. According to the address, the Nashes lived in a well-maintained two-story stucco house with a welcoming, bright red door.

"It's as neat as the office was," Cori said. "Maybe I was wrong. Maybe he just runs a tight ship and really was surprised to see me yesterday."

"Maybe not." Max rang the doorbell. When it opened they were greeted by the wary, dark eyes of a woman who'd fought the onslaught of her fifties and mostly lost, with sun-weathered skin and wiry, dark hair wisped with a few grays.

She looked from Cori to Max. "Can I help you?"

"Are you Mrs. Nash?" Cori asked.

"I'm Donna Nash. Who are you?"

"My name is Corinne Peyton and I'm looking for your husband."

"Try his new condo in Napa and be sure to look for the blonde named Sandra," she said bitterly. "He moved out a month ago."

Max felt Cori's shoulders sink, but he wasn't disappointed. A woman scorned was a woman who would talk.

"Have the police been here about what happened last night?" he asked her.

She frowned, a few lines setting around her mouth. "No. What happened?"

"There was a fire at the mall being built in

Petaluma. Do you know where we can find him, Mrs. Nash?"

She stuffed her hands into the pockets of her pleated jeans, concern showing in her eyes. "Is he okay?"

Cori nodded. "He's fine. Can you give us his new address?"

"Honestly, I'd swear the mob is involved on that job or something."

Cori glanced at Max. "Excuse me?"

"I'm kidding, but that job has been weird from day one."

"In what way?" Max asked.

She shifted from one sneakered foot to the other as she considered her words. "For one thing, it was way bigger than anything Doug's company ever handled before. It was since that job started that Doug got all weird and sneaky on me."

"Was that where he met Sandy?" Cori asked.

Mrs. Nash closed her eyes. "Yes."

"He was very proud of his children," Cori said, a note of sympathy in her voice. "He showed me their pictures at the construction trailer."

"If he cared about the kids," she said, "he wouldn't have moved in with his secretary."

Max leaned toward her. "Mrs. Nash, I'm sure you would like to avoid the publicity that would surround this if we had to subpoena records. Is there any chance your husband left files or records pertaining to the Petaluma Mall here?"

She tilted her head toward the hall behind her.

"You're welcome to look at his home office. I've dumped everything he left into cartons and was just about to pitch it. I'm remodeling the room for my thirteen-year-old daughter."

She led them into the house, which was a cheery contrast to the unhappiness on her face. Off the center hall, she indicated a small room with mover's boxes stacked against one wall and samples of fabric and paint chips laid out on the desk.

"You're welcome to take this stuff or look through it. I don't know what you're looking for, but this is what I took out of his desk and files."

If he had anything incriminating, it would be long gone. "Any phone bills that come to the house that you might have kept, records of his calls?" Max asked.

"Oh, I have those," she said dryly. "That's how I caught him. Hang on, I'll get them."

When she left the room, Cori lifted the edge of a carton. "What exactly are you looking for, Max?"

"I'll know it when I see it." Max opened the top box and started sifting through files and bills. The cover of a magazine seized his attention. "For instance, this."

He held up the magazine and watched her reaction.

"William," she said softly.

It was the same cover Lucy had shown Max: William Peyton, smiling from his glorious Star Island home, one happy billionaire. One cheating, happy, about-to-be-murdered billionaire.

Cori started leafing through the magazine as Max continued examining the pieces of Doug Nash's messed-up life.

When Donna returned, Cori asked, "Did your husband keep this magazine because of the story on Peyton Enterprises? Because it's nine months old."

"I'm sure he meant to take it," she said. "There's a picture of his girlfriend in there. See?"

Max turned to look at the picture with Cori.

"Her father is the guy who hired Doug," Donna said. "The one who gave him the job and came out here to supervise everything. That guy, right there."

Cori looked up at Max, confused. "That's Giff."

"You know him?" Donna asked. "I could kill the SOB for introducing my husband to his daughter."

Cori turned to her and shook her head. "But he doesn't have a daughter."

CHAPTER
Twenty

When Cori stepped out of the Peyton jet, she paused at the sight of the most arresting woman she'd ever seen. Easily six feet tall, she wore pure white right down to her stilettos, with long silky black hair billowing around her shoulders and down her back. A thin streak of silver ran down the front of one side of her hair, and her exotic, tilted eyes were such a dark brown they were nearly black.

Bathed in the night lights of the Kendall-Tamiami Executive Airport, she looked like a black-and-white photograph, a shock of burgundy lipstick the only color.

She moved like a panther, smooth and liquid. Before Cori reached the bottom step, Lucy had crossed the tarmac and extended her hand. Long, cool fingers with deep-red nails closed around Cori's hand.

"I'm Lucy," she said simply. "It's a pleasure to meet you, Mrs. Peyton."

"Cori. And the pleasure is mine."

Lucy Sharpe wasn't beautiful in a traditional sense. Her face had so many outstanding features that any one could be the focal point on another person. But with Lucy Sharpe, you almost didn't know where to look— except you couldn't look away. She was mesmerizing.

Max joined them at the bottom of the steps as the engines quieted. "Luce," he said with a nod. "What a nice surprise."

She smiled, revealing straight, white teeth and a hint of warmth in her eyes. "I decided to meet with Thomas Matuzak at Beckworth to bring him up to speed, and it made sense to stay and talk to you." She indicated a limousine that waited at the far end of the tarmac. "We've been assimilating information and doing some background work."

Max put his arm on Cori's shoulder to guide her forward. "The pilot will deal with the plane and bring our luggage."

Before they could take a step, Lucy stopped him. "You deal with the luggage, Max. I want to talk to Cori alone."

They shared a look, then Max said, "I'll meet you at the limo."

"You seem to be holding up well, Cori," Lucy said. "Discovering embezzlement in your company and suspecting your corporate attorney is responsible can't be easy for you."

Not to mention the fact that her husband's death was a covered-up homicide. "That's a fairly major leap you're making, Lucy. It appears that there are problems with the books regarding the Sonoma property, and I've yet to figure out why Mrs. Nash believes that young woman is Gifford Jones's daughter, but—"

"Because she is his son's sister."

Cori stopped completely. "Excuse me? Galen had a sister?"

"Galen was a twin," Lucy said, a light hand on Cori's back to get her moving again. "He was adopted, didn't you know?"

"Yes, but I *didn't* know he had a twin. Only that he passed away from a rare neurological disease when he was seventeen."

"Gifford Jones didn't know his son was a twin until just before Galen died, from what we can determine. We've been digging through his computer files via your company. I hope you don't mind the invasion of privacy."

"Of course not. Do what is necessary." Did Breezy know Galen had a twin? Wouldn't she have told Cori if she did? At the thought of her friend, Cori's heart sank for the twentieth time that day. She ached to share everything, but they needed time to investigate Gifford's role in the misappropriation of funds. Once they had proof in hand, they would go after Giff. Then, and only then, could she enlighten Breezy.

Keeping this from Breezy made her sick, but so did the possibility that Giff had siphoned funds for . . . for what?

"He makes three or four million dollars a year," she said to Lucy, thinking out loud. "I can't imagine why he would embezzle ten million dollars."

"Max said his wife is high maintenance."

"His wife is my dearest friend, and Max doesn't like her for some reason."

As they reached the limo, Lucy asked, "How are you doing with Max?"

Cori just smiled. "Max tells me you know everything, Lucy."

Lucy laughed and opened the door. "That's just Bullet Catcher folklore."

"What is?" A man sprawled across one of the long, leather seats sat up and rubbed sleepy eyes as the interior light came on. "I love Bullet Catcher folklore."

"The rumor that I know everything," Lucy said, indicating for Cori to precede her into the car. "I believe you've met Dan Gallagher before."

Even in the dim light, Cori was blinded by the smile she remembered. Bottle green eyes danced sleepily, but were so inviting that leaning forward to accept his kiss on her cheek seemed like the most natural thing in the world.

He held her shoulders afterward, his expression a mix of sincerity and tease. "She does know everything. And she tells me. Don't forget that."

She took a seat across from him. "It's nice to see you again, Dan."

"Ditto. And how's fun Max?"

"Still fun."

He ran his hand through his hair, tousling the brown and gold locks, then shaking them back. "Wish I had a better report from Japan."

"Did you find out any more about the ME? Max told me it wasn't suicide."

"I started with security at Kyoto Station and that led to the Japanese authorities. Apparently, a reluctant witness came forward and called it a cold-blooded assassination. And we found a trail to some money. Big money."

Cori divided a look between Dan and Lucy. "I have to tell you: I don't know why Giff embezzled from Peyton, but I believe in my heart that he didn't kill my husband." Nothing could change her mind about that. "He might be a thief, but someone else killed my husband."

"I spent the past few hours with Thomas Matuzak of Beckworth Insurance," Lucy said. "It seems Mr. Jones has already been sniffing around, wondering what the insurance company knows. They didn't tell him anything, but why would he be suspicious if he's innocent?"

Cori's gut burned certain on this one. Still, she hadn't known that Giff's son had a twin sister. And what was their relationship? There was no reason for Giff to have contact with the young woman; Galen had been dead for five years. And wouldn't Breezy have told her if Galen's biological twin suddenly turned up?

"I realize you are conducting an investigation, but I want to talk to Giff directly."

Just as Cori spoke, the car door opened.

"Not alone," Max said, folding his long body into the limo and sitting so close to her you couldn't slide a hair between them.

Lucy kept her expression blank, but Dan grinned as he reached out to punch knuckles with his friend. "Mad Max. 'Sup?"

Max gave him a once-over. "You look like hell."

"I love you, too, honey." Dan winked.

Ignoring him, Max turned to Cori. "I mean it. You won't talk to the guy alone. I will."

"Max, I've known him for years. If he stole money from the company, then he had a good reason. And maybe he can shed some light on William's death, now that we know for sure it was not natural causes. I can get him to tell the truth."

"*I* can get him to tell the truth."

"What about Breezy?" Cori asked. "I have to tell her."

"After we arrest her husband." As Cori started to argue, Max held up a hand. "This is a multiple homicide situation, and your life has been threatened more than once. You'll do this my way."

She sighed, leaning back and closing her eyes. Max lifted his arm and pulled her even closer, dropping a soft kiss on her hair. "It'll be okay, kid."

When she opened her eyes, her gaze landed on Lucy who stared at Max with an expression so clear, even Cori could put words to it.

I told you so.

Not for one minute did Cori doubt that Lucy did, indeed, know everything.

"Why aren't the new security lights on?" Rain had started to fall, and Max peered through the blurry limo window as the gates to Cori's house opened. "I know they were installed, and the installer gave detailed instructions to Marta."

"Wednesday's her night off, so she might have forgotten to put them on," Cori said. "Though when I'm out of town, she usually stays and has her sister over."

Dan and Max shared a look as the car moved up the dimly lit driveway. They'd dropped Lucy off at her hotel and then driven to Star Island.

"It's almost midnight," Dan observed. "No doubt she's in bed."

"There's doubt," Max said. Grilling the housekeeper was first on his list. Her background was murky; even Raquel couldn't find much information on her.

They unloaded the car, agreeing that Cori would wait outside with Dan while Max searched the house. Drawing his gun, Max entered through the kitchen door and began a room-to-room security check, yielding nothing. The place was dark and empty.

No one answered when he knocked on Marta's door.

Confident the house was secure, Dan went off to a guest room while Max took his and Cori's luggage up to her bedroom.

When Cori didn't immediately follow, he jogged back downstairs and found her in the kitchen.

"What are you doing?" he asked, stepping behind her and laying a possessive hand over her stomach.

"Brewing tea."

"Come upstairs and don't leave my sight again for thirty seconds. Bodyguard's orders."

She laughed softly. "I need my lemon balm. I'm still on West Coast time."

He dipped into the waistband of her jeans, the feel

of her warm, tight flesh shooting blinding arousal through him. "I'll make you tired."

She turned her face toward his and he kissed her instantly, making no effort to hide the effect the kiss and physical contact had. God only knew what tomorrow held. Tonight, he wanted to touch, taste, and own every inch of her.

The teapot whistled, ending the kiss. He kept his arms around her and his body pressed against her, as she opened a ceramic container full of loose tea. She escaped him to open and close a few drawers, shuffling their contents in search of something. "Where's my tea ball?"

He reached into the sink and lifted a metal ball with holes in it. A few drops of water dripped from it. "This it?"

"That's strange," she said, taking it. "Marta never leaves anything out. She must have been in a rush to leave."

"I'm in a rush," he reminded her, taking his cozy place at her back again. "Hurry up."

She filled the container with loose tea and tapped it a few times. "Relax."

Relax? He was growing harder by the second. He took a deep breath of her, and got a whiff of citrus mixed with something pungent and sweet brewing in her cup.

"That stuff won't make you too sleepy, will it?" he asked, pressing a kiss against her neck.

She chuckled. "No."

She leaned back into his chest and Max kissed her

hair while he ran his hands over her breasts, fingering her nipples and smiling at her moan of response. "How many more minutes until that's ready?"

"A few." She lifted her head and looked outside. "Look. The boat's gone."

"The buyers must have come."

"That was fast," she said. "I thought the broker said later this week." She turned to him with a sly smile. "Feel like a game of favors tonight?"

He grinned. "The game where no one loses. Let's go upstairs."

"My favorite deck is down in the cabana. Can you go get them? I want to try something new on you."

He let out a soft groan. "Evil woman. Okay, come on, let's go. I'm armed."

She plucked the metal tea holder out of her cup and dropped it in the sink. "You're always armed, Max. Your hands are weapons of destruction."

She held the cup to her mouth just as he squeezed her backside. "And this is the target."

She laughed, the tea missing her mouth. "Damn you, Roper," she said, wiping her chin. "You're gonna pay for that."

Outside, even at this hour, the heat pressed. The moon waned, but the security lights made rounding the pool and heading toward the stone path that led to the dock easy. As they took the three stairs to the lower lawn, Max tucked her under his arm.

"So why did you lose your balance that first night?" he asked, bringing her first sip to a halt.

"Excuse me?"

"When I found you, right here." He motioned to where she'd been standing the night he arrived. "I saw you trip when Breezy mentioned my name."

She gazed at him over the rim of her cup, the rising steam causing droplets of water to form on her upper lip. He wanted to taste them. "You need to ask?"

"I need to hear." He lowered his face to hers.

They stared at each other over the mug, the connection as powerful as ever.

"Max."

There it was, that sweet note in her voice that always preceded *I love you*.

"What?"

"Let's go get the cards."

For a moment, he didn't move.

"Listen, kid." He touched that upper lip just because he couldn't help himself. "I have to tell you something. It's something . . . I never told you before."

"Then instead of favors, we'll play for secrets. You can tell"—she grinned—"when you lose."

"Okay." He guided her to the dock, thinking of how to tell her. She wasn't going to like this secret.

"Who put a light on in the cabana?" she asked. "Did you?"

"No." Instinctively he pulled her behind him and reached for his weapon. "Stay here."

A wave lapped against a dock piling, and a fish jumped about thirty feet away. He made no sound as he approached the cabana, his Ruger drawn. The boarded front window cast an eerie shadow over the empty sofas and the end table, where a coffee cup rested, along with some CD jewel cases and a picture, turned facedown.

He tested the door, and it slid open. No one would leave it unlocked. Not after his instructions—

He froze at the sight of a woman's body lying on her side, and cursed as he recognized the thick, black curls and body.

"Marta." He reached her in two steps and crouched down, lifting the hair from her neck as he felt for her pulse. He couldn't find it. Around her lay books and maps and a baseball cap with the words "Peyton's Place" embroidered on it. Tucked under her side was the statuette of a palm tree.

His gaze darted around the room. What had happened here? His attention fell on the mug on the table. Grabbing it, he sniffed, the pungent lemony smell wickedly familiar. He leapt up just as Cori came to the sliding door, her cup tipped toward her lips.

"What is it—"

He lunged forward and whacked the mug out of her hand, sending ceramic exploding against the wall and tile floor.

"Did you drink it?" he asked.

She shook her head, too stunned to speak.

He turned toward the body as he whipped out his cell phone and handed it to her. "Call 911. I think Marta's been poisoned."

"The stupid maid wouldn't leave me alone, Giff. Honest. I couldn't do it."

"Stop whining." Giff seized his drink and followed

her to the patio. "It makes my teeth itch when your voice hits that pitch."

She mumbled something that sounded suspiciously like "fuck you" but he didn't respond. Instead, he stared at the misty midnight rain and downed a solid slug of Scotch.

Getting Breezy to plant evidence had been a stupid idea, anyway. How would they know what to plant? He had no idea what the hell killed William. "There has to be a better way," he mused.

"You could come clean," she said over the cigarette she was lighting. "Cori would undoubtedly forgive you."

"Like we could cough up ten million dollars to pay her back for what we did."

Breezy choked on her first drag. "What did you say? *I* didn't do anything. You stole the money, Giff. You're the one with the soft heart, promising the sun and moon to your kid on his deathbed."

His fingers tensed around the glass, fighting the urge to fling it in her face and chip her twenty-three-fucking-thousand-dollar porcelain veneers.

"If you ever had a child," he said around a clenched jaw, "you would realize that no value can be put on their lives."

She sighed. "She isn't your child, Giff."

"She's Galen's flesh and blood, Breezy. She's his twin sister and—"

"You didn't even know she existed when you and Orca adopted her!"

He slammed the glass on a table, and the first burst

of pain shot through his temples. Damn it! "Don't call her that, Breezy. She has a thyroid problem."

"She has a lot of problems, Giff. But none of them is as big as the one I've got right now." Breezy threw her cigarette on the wet fieldstone and let the rain douse it. God, he hated when she treated this house that way. "You basically screwed my best friend out of ten million dollars to pay for medical costs that haven't even been incurred yet."

"She'll get it, Breezy. They have very similar DNA and if it killed Galen, it could kill her." He froze as he realized the outer edges of his vision were already growing dark as Breezy approached him. "Son of a bitch," he muttered.

"Precisely. Your son was adopted, Giff. *A-dop-ted*." She poked his chest with each syllable. "I realize that you loved him. But the long-lost biological sister he scraped up from an Internet search is *not* your child, Gifford Jones, and *not* your responsibility. Whatever obscure-disease gene they were born with killed Galen, and that is a damn shame. But his sister is not your problem."

He swallowed, placing his fingertips on his temple. "I made it my problem."

"And now you're making it mine!" She took a deep breath and raised two hands. "Listen, Giff. You cannot get out of this with some convoluted scheme to make it look like Cori killed her husband, and I don't give a damn what that drug addict Billy told you. We can't let it come to a murder investigation." Her voice cracked with the strain of trying to modulate it. "We can't. It will ruin Peyton." She waited a beat, just as he would have if he'd been in front of a jury. "It will ruin us."

He blinked, hating the onset of darkness and the drill-like pain shooting in his head. Breezy put her hand on his cheek, instantly cooling his skin. "Listen, baby. It's time to come clean. She called me this afternoon, they were getting on a plane to come home from Sonoma. She should be back in Miami by now. Let me get her over here, and we can talk about it."

He closed his eyes and covered her hand with his. That was his Breezy. Always looking for a solution. But this time, there was only one solution.

It was going to hurt, but this was what she deserved.

For the first time in months, he felt the early stirrings of a hard-on. Great—he was about to end a life, and that finally made him horny.

"Breezy," he whispered, closing his fingers over hers tightly. After all, it would be the last time he held her. "I have to tell you something. And you're not going to like it."

"Whatever it is, I can fix it."

"No, you can't," he told her. Closing his eyes, he pulled her against him as his dick stiffened slightly with the first hard pump of blood and arousal.

Finally. He could have her now, one last time. Before he had to say good-bye. "Come upstairs with me, Breezy."

CHAPTER
Twenty-one

"I'm going with her." Cori tried to push Max aside as the paramedics slid Marta's stretcher into the back of the ambulance.

Max didn't move and glared at her. "No, you're not. She's unconscious. She won't know you're there until they pump her stomach and then she'll just sleep. I want you safe in the house with me."

"Safe? In the house?" She plucked at the tea stain on her shirt. "I don't think I'm safe here."

"I'll go," Dan said. "I'll follow them to the hospital and if—when—she wakes up, I'll find out what happened. In the meantime," he looked at Cori, "stay here and don't eat or drink anything in the house."

"You think that tea was meant for me," Cori said, blinking into the red and blue flashing lights.

"I think we have to consider every possibility," Max said.

"Such as?"

"Maybe she tried to kill herself," Dan suggested. "But why?"

Max watched as the ambulance doors closed. "Maybe because the man she loved died. Maybe because she killed him. Maybe because she knows who did."

Cori just closed her eyes. "She wasn't in love with William, Max."

"No? Then why did she follow him across the country?" Max asked. "And why did she surround herself with his belongings?"

"That stuff might still have been in the cabana. She was cleaning," Cori insisted. "She drank *my* tea."

"You know," Dan said, "maybe she was going for a murder-suicide the night she killed your husband, and failed. Now the guilt or loneliness got her. The loss of his boat, the place where they—"

"Stop it!" Cori shouted. "I've lived in the same house with them for years. Don't you think I'd know if my husband was sleeping with the housekeeper and all this *drama* was going on under my nose?"

The look of pity that Max gave her sent a wild fury through her. "Do you think I'm that stupid?"

Dan put a gentle hand on her shoulder. "Not stupid, Cori. It's easy to ignore clues you don't want to see."

Cori looked down at her hand, still clutching the palm tree she'd seized from the cabana. Who had given it to whom? Marta to William, or William to Marta?

"Go, Dan," she said, looking up and swallowing the lump in her throat. "Go to the hospital and find out what you can. I'm going to call Breezy."

Max clasped her arm. "No, you're not."

She jerked out of his grip. "Yes, I am. You don't get it, do you?" She narrowed her eyes at him. "You are so cavalier about my husband and whether or not he cheated on me. He was my rock, Max." She pounded a fist into her chest. "He was my grounded, stable, dependable, supportive partner. So stop painting him in this black, awful light. I refuse to believe it."

"Take your blinders off, Cori. I understand that you loved him. And that you trust Giff and Breezy and Marta and even Billy, for God's sake. Not everyone is what they seem."

She stared at him. "No, I guess they're not." She started back up the driveway and Dan left for his car.

"I didn't mean to be so harsh," Max said, walking next to her without touching. "You were raised by a drifter, and security and stability are important. Your friends are—"

She stopped in place and just shook her head. "No. It's much simpler than that. I love Breezy; I loved William. I love Marta, regardless of what you think she did to me. I loved my father and I loved you. I don't want to lose what I love anymore—" Her voice cracked. "Some things are irreplaceable. Like my father. And my husband's reputation. And my friendships."

When he didn't say anything, she blew out an exasperated breath. "Okay, you can probably blame that on my whacko mom who can't hold a job, husband, or hairstyle for twenty minutes, but frankly, I don't want to blame anyone. I'm a big girl and I'll take the responsibility for how I turned out."

She marched toward the house. As she reached the door and opened it, he put his hand on her shoulder.

"How about a compromise? Wait until tomorrow to call her, until we have a plan for interrogating Gifford and Marta wakes up and tells us what happened."

"No." She pulled the door open and continued toward the stairs. Behind her, she heard the dead bolt and locks. She'd reached the fourth step by the time he grabbed her arm.

"Stop, Cori."

She tried to wrench out of his powerful grip, but he didn't let her go. "I need my friend," she said through clenched teeth. "I need to talk to my friend."

"I am your friend. Talk to me."

He was a step below her, so they were eye level when she turned to him. "I can't trust you, Max. You are so quick to put the screws to my husband, my housekeeper, my attorney—"

"He's the one who created fake contractors and deposited ten million dollars to accounts he owned." He loosened his grip. "And you're the one who's suspected your husband's death from the moment it happened. Or did you forget that box of condoms? And that." He pointed to the gold sculpture in her hands.

"I didn't forget. Circumstantial evidence, both of them."

"I'd bet not."

She flipped the statuette from one hand to the other and looked at Max. "You'd bet not? You want to know what our problem is, Max?"

He looked at her. "*Our* problem?"

"Our whole relationship was built on betting and games and the need to win."

His brow crinkled with disbelief. "What are you talking about?"

"We met at a poker table. We played for a year. It was all about who had the better hand, who called the shots, who won, who bluffed, who called."

He leaned forward. "I wasn't bluffing when we made love. I wasn't bluffing when I asked you to spend the rest of your life with me. And I'm not bluffing now when I tell you that someone—someone on that list of people you love—might have killed your husband. You know it and I know it."

"And what about my father, Max?"

He jerked back. "What about him?"

"Were you bluffing to win the night we told him we wanted to get married and he went ballistic?"

Color drained from his face, telling her she'd hit a nerve. She powered on anyway, sick of holding it all in. "When he slammed his bedroom door shut and you punched a hole in the wall, I heard what you said, Max. I *heard* you."

"What?"

"He said he'd do whatever was necessary to stop us. Including have you shipped away to some remote assignment." She paused. "And you said, 'He won't win this. Nothing can stop us.'"

"Cori." His face contorted as he shook his head. "That was just an expression. There was a lot of emotion that night. Things were said by all of us. You were the one who stomped your foot and said you'd follow me to the ends of the earth. Or were you bluffing?"

"And then you took matters into your own hands."

The look on his face was even more pained than the night in Chicago when she had first made the accusation.

He lowered himself one more step, putting more distance between them and actually forcing her to look down on him. The position made him seem vulnerable, as did the look in his eyes.

"I did not take matters into my own hands, Cori." He spoke so softly, she leaned forward to hear him. "Your father did."

"Pardon me?"

"I know what you *think* happened. But believe me, I didn't have a chance to take matters into my own hands." His throat moved as he swallowed. "Coop did that for me."

Disbelief squeezed her heart. "What do you mean?"

"I mean that . . . I lied."

Cori reached for the wrought-iron banister. "What did you lie about, Max?"

"I lied about the O'Hare drug bust. I lied to you, and the DEA." He closed his eyes. "And I've paid for it ever since."

Oh, Lord. "What really happened that morning, Max?" she asked quietly.

"I didn't freeze and let Coop take that bullet." He swallowed again. "He dove and took it for me."

Her eyes widened. *Just like your father.* "On purpose? He did that on purpose?"

"He saved my life . . . for you." He put his hand on

top of hers on the banister. "Before he died, he told me to watch out for you, to take care of you. He gave us his blessing."

"Oh." It was more of a sound than a word. "And I blamed you. And ran away."

"And I didn't watch out for you or take care of you. Until now."

"That's why you took this assignment, isn't it? Not to nail me for murder. Not to get back at me. Not to rekindle anything. It was to keep a five-year-old promise."

"I really loved your dad." His voice cracked at the same moment her heart did. "And he really loved you."

"Well, that was some stupid way to show me," she whispered, tears in her eyes. Her father had given his life for her, and they'd blown it. Both of them.

He took a step up, bringing them closer again. "He just wanted you to be happy."

She closed her eyes. "And he thought I'd be happier with you than him."

He nodded.

"Why didn't you tell me, Max?"

"I wanted to, but not when the pain was so raw. I thought . . ." His eyes were dangerously moist. "When some time passed. When I came back to Chicago . . ."

"And when you came back, I was already married to William."

"I lost that bet."

"Oh, Max." She put her hand on her chest, trying to quell the pain. "I blamed you. I blamed us. I never thought he'd . . ." She closed her eyes.

"That's what I wanted to tell you tonight," he said. "Before we found Marta."

Irony strangled her. "The very act that was supposed to bring us together drove us apart," she said sadly. "I bet he's looking down from heaven, mad as hell."

Max smiled. "Coop? I doubt it." He touched her cheek. "I bet he's laughing his ass off because it took us so long to get it right."

She looked into his eyes and could see her reflection in their dark depths. "You think we got it right, Max?"

He leaned into her mouth and brushed his lips over hers. "I think we're finally gettin' there, kid."

The kiss was whispery soft at first, then flared hard and hot. He pushed her up the next few steps, and the statuette fell out of her hand and clunked down the stairs. She grabbed his shoulders and let him guide her up the stairs, their mouths still connected in a heated kiss.

Arousal slammed from her head to her toes, so strong it buckled her knees. They both gave in to the weakness in their legs, collapsing on the top step together. He tore at the buttons of her shirt, she stabbed her hand into his pants, closing over him and eliciting a grunt of pleasure.

He kissed her again, opening her blouse and sliding his hand behind her back to unsnap her bra. As he did, he rolled over and pulled her on top of him. Her hair fell into his face as her clothes fell onto the floor and he palmed her breast.

She fumbled with his buckle and freed him, shoving

his pants away to stroke him. They rolled again across the top landing, blood singing, breath rasping, sweat prickling their skin.

"This isn't what I want," he ground out.

He pulled himself up, closed his pants, and scooped her up in his arms. "Not here. Not rolling around in the hall."

Carrying her, he strode toward her bedroom, determined and unstoppable. He kicked open the door and laid her on the bed. There he straddled her half-naked body, lowering his head to kiss her gently, deeply. He slowly ran his hands down her arms to her fingertips, threading their hands together, and drew her arms over her head, holding her wrists together with one hand.

Then he brushed her lips with a kiss. Flicked the hollow of her throat with his tongue. He looked at her again, his jaw taut with the fight for control. Excited by his relentless study, she lifted her hips in invitation.

"Look at you," he murmured raggedly. "*Look* at you."

She slid her fingers under the headboard as he licked her cleavage, one long, slow stroke with the tip of his tongue. He trailed a path to one breast, circling the bud, gently teething her, then suckling while he claimed the other with his hand. She let go of the bed and buried her fingers in his hair, moaning his name, asking for more.

He rose to his knees, stripping off his clothes, the sight of his mighty erection dizzying her. She curled her fingers into the bedding, staring.

He took off her jeans and panties, then burned her from top to bottom with his eyes.

Her lips parted and she closed both hands over his erection, unable to find her voice. He grunted with the kick of pleasure, sliding in her fingers, letting her caress him.

Then he pulled her higher on the bed, placing himself between her legs, where arousal had left her moist and ripe for him.

"I'm lousy with words, Cori," he said, poised to enter her. "You understand that, don't you? Words and feelings . . . I can't."

"But you are, right now." She touched his cheek.

"Only with you."

He plunged into her, deeply, completely, owning her body. He pushed to the hilt with a raw, lusty groan, sliding in and out with a slow, achy rhythm.

Her body tightened around him, constricting with the pleasure and intensity of their connection. He drove into her, grinding and helpless as though a dam had broken, releasing so much pressure that it had control of him.

She clasped his hips with her thighs, planted her mouth against his shoulder and shuddered his name as she spiraled into an orgasm, losing her sanity and grip on everything except Max.

He came the instant she did, burying himself into her with a deep growl of pure bliss.

Then he fell on her, rasping for air, heavy and spent and exhausted.

"You want to know why I took this job?" he whispered.

"Because you promised my father you'd take care of me."

"No." He breathed the word into her ear. "Because I have never, ever stopped loving you."

Max woke when Cori sat up. "Where are you going?"

"Don't you hear the phone?"

"I didn't hear anything. What time is it?"

"Just after three. You were dead asleep." She reached for the cordless on her dresser. "Maybe Marta is awake and this is Dan."

"Dan would call my cell," Max said ominously.

She stared at the caller ID and looked up at him. "It's Breezy."

"At this hour?"

Cori shrugged and answered. "What's the matter?" she asked Breezy without saying hello.

"Help." The word was a breathless sob. "Cor, I need help."

"What? What happened?"

"It's Giff." Her voice cracked.

"What about him?" Cori demanded, reaching for Max's hand.

"He's . . . he's lost his mind. He's threatening me. I ran outside to call you, and I'm scared. I'm really, really scared."

"Where is Giff? Does he know where you are?" She started climbing out of bed, reaching for clothes. "She's in trouble," she whispered to Max.

"I'm hiding in the backyard, in the gazebo. Oh, God, Cori. I'm so scared. He's gone crazy."

"Call 911. We'll come over, but you need to get the police there."

"No. No. I need someone to talk sense into him. He just needs to be calmed down. You could do that. Come over and talk to him."

"What happened?" Gifford never lost his cool. "What started this?"

"Cori, please. Just come over and talk to him. He always listens to you. Talk to him about William. That'll help him."

"I'll be right over."

Max gave her a hard look.

"*We'll* be right over," she corrected.

"Don't bring that bodyguard!" Breezy said quickly. "It'll freak Giff out."

The connection died and Cori pulled on her discarded jeans. "My friend needs me," she said. "She needs me to talk to Giff."

He pushed the covers back. "All right. Let's go."

They were dressed in less than thirty seconds and jogging down the stairs. As she reached the bottom step, Cori's foot hit the gold statuette that had fallen to the floor. Maybe Giff knew why William had it. Maybe Giff knew her husband better than she did.

She scooped it up in one move, then grabbed the handbag she'd dropped near the front door and left.

CHAPTER
Twenty-two

Cori was silent, except for the occasional direction for the fastest way to Coral Gables. Silence suited Max fine. They'd said enough for one night.

She knew, now. About her father. About his feelings. The rest was up to her. He focused on the rain-slick highway. Even at this hour—especially at this hour—a few crazies were recklessly weaving and flying on US 1. He concentrated on the traffic, not the fact that they were headed directly toward the *suspect's* home in the middle of the night.

"Turn left here, on LeJeune," Cori instructed.

"What's the security situation?" he asked.

"They live in Cocoplum. Gated, guarded, waterfront. Their house backs up to a marina that leads to the bay."

He had agreed not to call the cops because if they showed up, Giff might clam up. If Max could get him alone, he could probably get a confession. "Who else lives in the house?" he asked. "Any staff?"

"No one. Her housekeeper comes in the daytime."

For a few minutes, the only sound was the rhythmic thump of the wipers and the hiss of tires on the wet pavement.

"Max," she finally said, quietly. "I can look at my dad's choice in one of two ways."

He glanced at her, listening.

"I can choose to believe that he was a hero who saved your life."

He cruised through a yellow light. "How can you look at it any other way?"

"Or I can think of it as a betrayal. That he killed himself."

He shook his head. "One of us was going to die that morning, and Coop decided it would be him. It was a selfless act of love. Stupid as hell, but heroic." He reached out and closed his fingers around her hand. "He loved you. And he was so proud you were in law school—destined to argue your way right to the Supreme Court, he told me."

She turned and looked out her window. "I guess I wasted his sacrifice, didn't I?"

"If we're doling out blame, I deserve some. I should have told you. And I shouldn't have stayed away almost a year."

"Why did you?"

He lifted a shoulder. "Guilt, I guess. Anger. Work. General stubbornness." He stopped at the red light and looked at her. "And I never dreamed you would marry someone else."

"It happened fast," she said. "He was there at the

right time, in the right place, and I took the comfort and support he offered." Then she squeezed his hand. "I loved him, too, Max. In a different way than us. I loved him and he . . ." She shifted the statuette she held on her lap. "I never had any reason to doubt he loved me."

"I'm sure he did," Max said gently.

"No, you're not. You're placating me." When he didn't disagree, she dropped the statuette in her bag. "What about the tea Marta drank? When do you think the analysis will be back?"

"Not soon enough."

"You know, I can see the suicide theory," she conceded, "but it doesn't explain who shot at me or attacked me in the spa."

"I have a feeling we're about to find out."

"Giff?" She shook her head. "Oh, Lord, I hope not."

He shot her a quick look. "He embezzled ten million dollars, we're virtually certain of that. He may have killed your husband."

She dropped her head back, closing her eyes. "And you think he paid off the ME to file a false autopsy report, and then had him killed?"

"It's possible. And he probably arranged for the trailer to be burned at the mall site. Now it sounds like he's gone off the deep end." He rounded a traffic circle and slowed down at the marble, gated entrance to Cocoplum.

"I'm on the list," she told him. "Just give them my name."

A minute later, they were cruising down the main road, past uplit palms and sprawling palaces of stucco and glass. She told him to turn into a cul-de-sac where a few of the homes were tucked behind walls, but most were visible from the street.

Nearly every one was darkened for the night—until they got to the pink monstrosity at the end, where every light blazed from an array of arched windows and Roman columns.

"That's weird," Cori said. "Why are all those lights on?"

"Any chance you have a key?"

"It's on that ring in the ignition," she told him. "But let's knock first. They're obviously home."

Nothing was obvious. "If there's no answer, I'll go in."

Cori took a few steps toward the side yard, squinting toward the back where sailboats and motor yachts bobbed in the marina.

"Breezy said she was outside. Should we go back there first?"

He took her hand and tugged her toward the door. "If she was hiding from him, he might be out there. Waiting for you."

They rang the bell twice, with no response. Max held the key chain out and she plucked the correct key and gave it back.

"Listen," he said. "If Gifford is really panicking, he's probably weak enough to give me a confession. Let me handle him, okay? You take care of your friend."

"What if he really hurt her?"

"Then I'll really hurt him," he said quietly. "Is there an alarm?"

"Yes. To the left of the front door. The code is 7936."

He pulled out his gun, then slid the key in the door, holding up a hand to keep her back as he stepped in and looked around. He turned the alarm off and listened for a moment.

"Anybody home?" he called out. He motioned for Cori to come in and took her hand.

"Breezy?" she hollered. "Are you here?"

Silence.

"Their bedroom is upstairs, but let's try the back patio first."

Just as they started in that direction, they heard a low rumble. Max held a hand up as he listened. "Garage door?" he suggested.

Instantly they heard the whine of an engine. Max leaped to the front door and Cori followed, just in time to see a late-model Jaguar catapulting out of the garage and flying down the driveway. As it passed Cori's Mercedes, the left side of the Jag scraped the other car, tearing off the side-view mirror and making a horrendous screeching noise as metal scraped metal.

Cori turned and started toward the back of the house. "Breezy? Are you here?"

Max grabbed her arm. "What the hell are you doing?"

"Maybe she's here. Maybe she's hurt. That was Giff's car."

"Call her on her cell," he said, handing her his phone.

She punched in Breezy's cell phone number. Instantly, they heard a mechanical tone from the kitchen. Cori took off with Max right behind her.

The phone sat on the dark granite counter, bright

pink and trilling the digital version of "Hello, Dolly."

"Damn it," Cori muttered, picking it up.

A movement of light caught his eye outside. "What's that?"

Through the wall of French doors, he could make out a bright orange dot glowing in the middle of an elaborate gazebo.

"She's out there smoking," Cori said, rushing toward the door.

Max beat her there in an instant. "Me first."

She was on his heels as they crossed the wet flagstone around the pool and approached the covered gazebo. Although the landscaping lights weren't on and the rain clouds had obliterated the moon, the house was bright enough to shed a yellow aura over Breezy as she sat facing the marina, puffing away as though her only care in the world was getting that nicotine in her body.

"Breezy," Cori called softly as they got closer. "Are you okay?"

Breezy sucked in a drag, and blew it out slowly.

"Breezy!" Frustration colored Cori's tone. "What's going on?"

"He's going blind and shouldn't be driving."

"What? What are you talking about?" Cori reached the gazebo and dropped onto the curved stone bench next to Breezy. She reached toward her friend, but stopped, probably because of the stone cold expression on Breezy's face.

Breezy's lifeless gaze slipped past Cori to Max. "Would you go get him, please?"

"Excuse me?" Max burned her with a glare, then stepped into the gazebo out of the misty rain, his gun still in his hand.

"He's in no condition to drive. I just told you, he's going blind." She puffed again and finally looked at Cori. "I'm sorry I got hysterical. He's having a very hard time with his illness and, frankly, he scared me."

"I had no idea he was ill, Breezy." Cori closed her hand over Breezy's. "Are you okay?" she repeated.

She flipped her cigarette into the wet grass. "I'm fine. But I'd rather my husband's bloodied remains were not strewn all over US 1 tonight so, would you please"—she looked up at Max again—"go and get him?"

"Call the police," he said, his voice as icy as hers. "That's their job."

"He's ready to confess. He's on his way to the Peyton offices to write up his letter of resignation."

Cori glanced at Max, then asked, "Confess to what?"

Breezy looked skyward. "You know as well as I do, Cor, that he sucked millions out of the Peyton coffers. What you don't know is that he had only the most noble and altruistic motives." She flicked her hair back and revealed her earrings. "It wasn't so I could have more of these."

"Why did he do it?" Max's question held no sympathy.

She looked at Cori when she answered. "He promised Galen before he died that he would help Galen's twin sister in California—whom he didn't even know about when they adopted, mind you—if she came down with the same disease. She hasn't, but he told me tonight that not only is he going blind, but that all the money is gone. *Pffft.* Spent. He tried to ease the blow of that with sex but, what a surprise, it didn't work." She shrugged and laughed humorlessly. "Then he threatened to kill me if I told you, and that's when I called you."

"You said you were scared."

"I was, but I handled him. When I told him you already knew about the money—I figured you do, based on that brief conversation when you were in Sonoma—he calmed down." She gave Max a tight smile. "I assured him that he wouldn't go to Alcatraz, just some country club prison for bad executives."

There was no minimum security for murderers—but now wasn't the time to tell her.

"Why didn't he tell William about Galen's sister?" Cori asked. "We would have covered her medical bills, or whatever she needed. Surely he knew that."

"Pride. And now the irony is after paying for all those medical tests and bills, he's the one who's really ill."

"We'll take care of him, Breeze," she said softly, then turned to Max. "I want to stay with her. Please, please do me a favor and go find Giff. You know where the office is, on Biscayne Drive. Please, Max. Go get him. There's no danger here."

He wanted to nail Giff, wanted to be the one to yank a confession out of him, but not at the price of leaving Cori. "No."

She stood up, approaching him. "I'm begging you. This is really important to me. Giff may have stolen money, but he's Breezy's husband and he was my husband's closest friend. Regardless of what's happened, I want to help him, but I need to stay here." She shot a pointed look at Breezy who did look borderline nuts at the moment. "Please. Go get him before he has an accident and kills himself. Or someone else."

"He may have already killed someone else. William Peyton."

Breezy choked. "Oh, please. *That* I would know about."

Cori looked from one to the other. "He didn't kill William, Max. I know that like I know my name."

"Then who did?"

She bit her lip. "Marta?"

For a long time, he didn't speak, all his instincts locked in a battle with one another. Finally, his gaze shifted to Breezy. "You better not be lying."

Breezy snorted. "Like I could make this up."

"Don't leave this property," he said to Cori. "Keep her cell phone next to you. And program my number into it now."

"Okay," she agreed.

He held out his hand to Cori. "Come inside. Both of you."

Breezy shot him a look of pure loathing as she pulled out yet another cigarette. "You're not babysitting me, stud. Go get my husband before he kills someone."

"I'll get the phone, Max," Cori said. "Just please hurry and find him."

Breezy stayed in the gazebo as they crossed back to the house. When they entered the kitchen, he kicked the French door closed with enough force to rattle the panes of glass. "You know something? I hate her."

"I can tell." She picked up the phone and flipped it open. "Turned on, with a full battery. Hers was the last number dialed on your phone. Just hit redial if you need me."

"I always need you." He reached out, sliding his hand under her hair and pulling her closer. "Someday you're going to realize that." He dipped his head and kissed her hard. Then he turned around and left.

Cori stood in the kitchen for a long time after she'd heard Max lock the door and drive away, the taste of him still on her lips, the sound of his confession still in her ears.

I have never, ever stopped loving you.

"Me neither, Max," she whispered to herself. "And my dad did not die in vain."

She dropped the phone into her handbag and slid it over her shoulder, then headed out to the gazebo. Her footsteps slowed when she reached the grass. Breezy was gone.

"Breeze?"

In the distance, waves slapped against hulls, and something skittered through the bushes. Where did she go?

"Breezy!" Cori called. "Where are you?"

The yard was empty, with slow, steady rain whispering over the palm fronds and hibiscus trees. Cori reached the gazebo, her heart thumping.

She turned back to the house, imagining Breezy's path. Had she gone into the house through another entrance?

Behind her, a shoe scuffed on the gazebo floor. Sucking in a breath she turned, but the full weight of a man threw her to the ground, and a strong hand slapped against her mouth. When she gasped for air, she tasted mud.

Something sharp and cold pierced the skin under her ear.

"Where is the palm tree?" The voice was low and gruff, nearly incomprehensible.

She squirmed and fought, and the metal dug deeper against her skin.

"Tell me." He loosened his hand over her mouth, but his whole body pressed her into the ground, a belt buckle jabbed her lower back and his knee painfully stabbed the back of her thigh. "Where is it?"

"Where is what?" she managed to say.

One hand twisted her hair, the other raised a blade high enough to glint in the light from the house. "The golden palm tree. I want it now—or someone else is going to die."

The *palm* tree?

Her bag was propped under her right hip, knocked off her shoulder in the fall. The palm tree was right under her.

"Where is it?" He yanked her hair hard.

"Where's Breezy?" she managed to ask.

He swore in her ear.

That voice. That voice was so familiar. She tried to look back and instantly felt the same explosion of blinding pain she'd felt in the spa.

Just as she lost consciousness, she realized who it was.

CHAPTER
Twenty-three

As Max peered along the side of the road, looking for a Jaguar that might have rolled over or crossed the median strip, he whipped his phone out and hit the speed dial.

Dan answered on the first ring. " 'Sup, mad man?"

"How's the patient?" Max asked.

"Groggy, but alive. She hasn't talked to me yet. How's Cori?"

"She's at Gifford Jones's house in Cocoplum. Coral Gables. You know how to get there?"

"What's she doing there?"

"Jones evidently had a meltdown, confessed to his wife that he stole and spent the ten million bucks. He is currently headed into downtown Miami to write his resignation letter. The wife is either in shock, on drugs, or playing serious head games, but she called Cori for help."

"And where are you?"

"Tracking Jones to Miami."

"What's the address in Cocoplum?"

He gave it to Dan.

"I'll head over there."

"Hurry." Good—Dan would be there in half an hour, tops. Max slowed down where two police cars had pulled someone over, but it was a white van with teenagers, not a Jag with a crazed blind man driving.

The only way into the Peyton office at this hour was a direct executive elevator in the Peyton Building parking garage. He'd used this entrance when they'd come to the board meeting. Climbing out of Cori's Mercedes, he fingered the key chain, trying to remember which one worked the elevator.

There'd been more keys before. He looked at the ring, mentally tallying the ones he'd used and seen. When they'd taken the elevator to go to the board meeting, there was one more key on this ring.

But the first one he tried fit the elevator, and would fit the office. In a moment, he was in the elevator, headed toward the executive offices on the eighteenth floor.

The elevator opened to a hushed, darkened reception area. The soft buzz of white noise, a powered-down computer or the air-conditioning, was the only sound he heard after the elevator quietly dinged. He paused for a moment, getting his bearings. The boardroom was across from the reception area and he distinctly remembered the direction Jones walked after they'd had a conversation in the hall. Max re-traced those steps as far as he remembered, to a T in a darkened hallway. He stood motionless, listening for any sound.

And he heard one. The distinct double-click of a semi-automatic hammer being cocked. He flattened against the wall, his own gun raised. He inched down the wall toward the last office, ready for any movement, any threat.

He moved closer to the open door, the office beyond it even blacker than the hallway. He didn't know the layout and had no idea where Jones could be hiding. But he was in there—or someone was. And he had a gun.

His shoulder touched the doorjamb and he inched his head into the opening.

A sudden sucking of breath broke the silence and Max jerked back, only to hear a whimper as soft as an injured puppy and just as pathetic.

Max lunged into the doorway, his weapon straight ahead, braced with two hands. "Don't move!"

Metal thunked against wood as the crack of a gunshot blasted Max's ears.

He crouched, aimed, and heard the whimper turn to a scared sniffle. "Oh, fuck. I can't even do this."

Holding perfectly still, he asked, "Jones?"

A leather chair squeaked and Max debated sliding to the wall to find the light switch, but he let his eyes adjust to the darkness instead of dividing his focus.

"I'm trying to kill myself, if you don't mind."

Max slowly lowered his gun an inch, now able to see the outline of a person in the chair. "I do mind. And so does your wife. She sent me for you."

"My wife." He snorted a dry, soft laugh.

"She thinks you're here writing up your resignation letter." At least, that's what she told him and Cori.

"In a sense, I am."

The shadow moved and Max straightened his gun again. "Don't," he barked. "Don't touch that weapon." He slowly entered the room, his night vision improving enough to see a sheen on Jones's bald spot and tears in his eyes. "I'm going to take that gun, Jones. Don't move, or I'll commit your suicide for you."

Jones rolled the chair back away from the desk. Not the move of a man who really wanted to die.

Max closed the space and lifted a compact Beretta from the desk, checking the safety and stashing it in his waistband. He still didn't take his Ruger off Jones.

"Turn on the light," he ordered.

"No. It hurts my eyes."

"Too bad. Turn it on."

After a second, a desk lamp clicked and bathed the room in soft white light. Jones blinked and covered his eyes.

"Your wife says you're going blind."

He kept his head cradled in his hands. "She should know."

"All this just for some embezzlement?" Max asked dryly. "Or are you in even deeper than that?"

Jones lifted his head enough to gaze at Max. "Isn't that enough?"

"Did you arrange for the construction trailer to be torched and send some thugs to shoot at Cori?"

"Doug Nash wasn't about to give up his gravy train." Jones sucked in an unsteady breath, closing his eyes. "I was trying to do the right thing. It was stupid."

"No kidding. And how about William Peyton?" Max asked. "When did he find out?"

Jones closed his eyes. "A few months before he died."

"Before you killed him, you mean."

He shook his head violently. "No, no! I didn't. I wouldn't. He was trying to help. We were trying to figure out . . . never mind. The money's gone. William's gone. Everything's gone."

Max widened his stance but Jones didn't seem to notice. Hell, he really didn't seem to be able to see. "So if you didn't kill him, who did?"

"I guess we'll never know," he said. "The answer is cremated and deposited into Biscayne Bay."

No, someone knew the truth. Max eased into a chair, scrutinizing Jones's expression as the man squeezed his eyes repeatedly, forcing yellowish tears from the corners and into his crow's-feet. This guy really was blind.

He wasn't interrogating a suspect; Gifford Jones was a victim.

"Did you know William was having an affair, Giff?"

Despite the eye problems, Jones looked up with dismay that turned into a short laugh. "I hope the insurance company isn't basing its investigation on that bullshit." He shook his head. "The man loved his wife and wouldn't cheat on her if you pointed that gun at his dick and threatened to blow it off. He thought the sun rose and set on Cori."

"I have evidence to the contrary."

"Whatever you have won't hold up in court against

an impressive list of people who will testify that William was faithful."

"William was murdered. It's a fact; the only thing missing is proof. No one seems to be able to find anything but the cover sheet of the original autopsy report." Max lowered the gun and leaned forward. "Any idea where the rest of it might be?"

"No." The single syllable, Max knew, was the truth.

"You want to help figure out who murdered him?"

Jones managed to open his eyes. "Would it save my ass?"

Max shrugged. "Couldn't hurt."

"I have no idea. Honestly."

"What about Marta Gaspero?"

Jones frowned. "Their housekeeper? She loved William."

"Precisely."

"No, no. She loved him for saving her. She was a prostitute in California."

"Did she service him?"

Jones just shook his head. "You really don't get it. William Peyton was the real deal. One of the last good guys. He found Marta doubled over in the parking lot of some restaurant in Napa Valley, took her to the hospital, paid her bills, and gave her a home. That's the kind of man he was."

Or the kind of man he wanted people to believe he was. "The night before he died, he went down on his boat to get it ready for fishing. Did you know that?"

Jones nodded. "We were going off-shore the next morning."

"Why would he keep condoms on the boat?"

"Condoms?" He dropped his hands from his temples and frowned. "I thought they were trying to have a baby."

"And, yet, the last of the great American good guys had a box of Trojans in his Dopp kit and a pricey gift engraved 'love W' that his wife had never seen." Max leaned back in the chair. "Sounds like he was doing something other than fishing, on board."

"I doubt it. You could dust that place for prints. He wasn't entertaining women on that boat."

"Too late," Max acknowledged. "The new owners picked it up."

Jones's eyes flashed. "No, no they didn't. I would have been called since I have Cori's power of attorney."

"The boat's gone," Max told him. "I was on the empty dock."

Max's phone vibrated in his pocket and he grabbed it, hoping it was Cori, but was almost as glad to see Dan's number. "Where are you?" he asked without preamble.

"I'm just leaving the hospital now. Marta woke up and got chatty. It was not suicide. She made tea, using Cori's favorite stash, then went down to the cabana to pick up some stuff the new owners had taken off the boat. Anything else you want to ask?"

"Can you put her on?"

In a moment, Marta said, "Is Mrs. Peyton okay? You mustn't let her—"

"When did the new owners pick up the boat?"

"Today," she said. "He came this afternoon."

He shot a look at Jones. "Was the broker there? Mendoza?"

"No. Was he supposed to be? This man just showed up and said he was there to take the boat. He had a key."

Of course he did—the key that was missing from Cori's ring. The key that somebody took from her bag while she was out cold in the spa.

"Was he alone, Marta?"

"Yes."

"Can you describe him?"

"Tall, like you. He had light hair and a big diamond earring. I could hardly understand him, his English was very . . . thick. You can ask Miss Breezy," Marta said hopefully. "She met him."

"She did? How?"

"She wanted to borrow a sweater. She went to Miss Cori's room and made a holy mess out of that closet while the man was there to pick up the boat."

What a coincidence. "Were either one of them alone in the house, Marta?"

"I'm sorry, Mr. Max. I know I promised you I wouldn't let anyone in, but I had to help that man get stuff off the boat. So yes, she went to Mrs. Peyton's room alone."

He looked at the miserable expression on Gifford Jones's face as the older man dabbed at his eyes and rubbed his aching head.

What could make a man get headaches and go blind like that?

He didn't know, but he knew someone who sure as hell did. Someone with special knowledge in the art of healing . . . and the opposite. Then someone close to Jones could have administered the poison in small doses, enough to make him think he was going blind.

Enough to make him think he was going crazy. Enough to make him think the only way out was suicide—freeing ten million dollars socked away in some Swiss bank account. Or a *Finnish* bank account.

"Marta, tell Dan to leave *now*."

Flipping the phone shut, Max leaned toward Jones. "How long has your wife been screwing the masseuse?"

Jones dropped his head. "Awhile."

Cori opened her eyes, but everything was still dark.

Her throat thickened with the feeling that came right before she was sick, and she gagged and swallowed the bitter, metallic taste back down her esophagus.

Her body undulated again. What was underneath her? A water bed?

No. A boat.

She was on a boat. With supreme effort, she lifted her head and stared at the strands of navy and gold thread in front of her face.

She was on *Peyton's Place,* and this was William's bed and she was alive and—

The stateroom door slammed against the wall and someone grabbed her shoulder and flipped her over like a pancake.

She stared at him. "Swen. Why—"

He thumped his hands on either side of her head

and jammed his knee into her stomach. "It's not on this boat," Swen said, his eyes burning with fury and determination. "Where is the palm tree?"

The golden palm tree that William had received or given as a gift to a woman. Where was it?

Wherever her purse had landed. If her purse had made it with her to this boat, it was only a matter of time until Swen got what he wanted. As soon as Max called her and "Hello, Dolly" trilled into her handbag, then Swen would find the palm tree.

And then, she knew, she'd be dead.

"Where is it?" he growled in her face, increasing the pressure on her stomach. "Tell me!"

"Where's Breezy?" Her voice scraped like sandpaper. "Did you hurt her?"

The boat rose over a swell and Cori's stomach rolled with it, but she willed herself not to retch as Swen leaned over her, his hand closed over her throat. "Tell me where the palm tree is, Cori."

"Why?" She managed to choke out the word.

He smacked her face, rattling her brain. "If you don't tell me, they will find it anyway. And you'll have no alibi, no excuse. No one will believe you didn't grind up that oleander from your very own yard and feed it to your husband. You had so much to gain. Billions, Cori. There is no one with a motive like yours."

A motive. What was *his*?

"All I want is the evidence. I'll hide the evidence and disappear," he said quickly. "And you can live fat and happy with your billions. Doesn't that sound good, Cori? Huh?"

"Why did you kill him?"

He lifted a menacing eyebrow. "In truth, he did himself in. The poison wasn't intended to give *him* the heart attack."

This wasn't meant for me.

She closed her eyes, her heart as sick as her stomach.

"Please tell me where Breezy is," she whispered again.

He jabbed his knee into her ribs. "Where's the palm tree?"

She looked up at him, plans formulating and dying in her head. As soon as Max called her, the minute that phone rang, she lost her bargaining chip. She needed to get off this boat. At least then she had a chance.

"It's . . . it's in my house. I hid it in the safe room."

"Good." He gave her a smug smile. "That's exactly where we're headed."

They were headed somewhere? But the boat wasn't moving now; they were still.

Before she could answer, she heard one piercing tone, then the familiar digital melody that now sounded like a death knell instead of a Broadway tune.

"Well, hel*lo* dolly." The voice came from the doorway. "Lookee what I found."

Cori looked past Swen into the face of her best friend.

Breezy held the statuette above her head, a wild and victorious light in her eyes. "I'd like to thank the Academy." She grinned at Swen. "My incredible lover, Swen." She shifted her gaze to Cori, and her expression turned hard and cold. "And most of all, my dearest friend, Corinne Peyton."

This wasn't the face of her best friend. This was the face of a stranger. A liar. A killer.

"I'm so sorry Cori couldn't be here tonight." Breezy wrapped both hands around the golden palm tree and hugged it to her chest. "But she had to join her husband at the bottom of Biscayne Bay."

CHAPTER
Twenty-four

Gifford leaned forward straining the seat belt and squinting through rain that had nearly stopped. "I can almost see again."

Max floored the Mercedes as he hit the highway, holding his cell phone to his ear with his shoulder and listening to the fourth ring. Where the hell was she?

He swore silently when the line clicked to voice mail and a sultry smoker's laugh greeted him.

"Hey hey hey, it's Breezy Jones. You can leave a message or not. If I like you, I might call you back."

He threw the phone on the console and tossed a disgusted look at Jones. What kind of a fool would marry a woman like that? "So she knew you were stealing money? Do I understand this right?"

Jones squirmed in his seat. "That's what she told me tonight. She told me . . ." He paused. "It doesn't matter."

"Yes, it does."

"Look, I'll come clean and I'll pay the price for taking the money from Peyton Enterprises. But leave Breezy out of it. All she's done is . . . what any normal woman would do if she had a husband like me."

"You still don't get it, do you?" Max practically banged on the steering wheel, frustrated at the red light and the moron next to him.

"It's not just about my going blind," Jones insisted. "I have other problems. Personal problems."

Max ran the light. "And you don't think it's all related? You don't think this sudden onset of blindness and *personal problems* might be the result of something you're taking—"

"I'm not taking—"

"Or being given."

That shut him up. Max barreled down the highway and slid into his turn at damn near a forty-five-degree angle. He grabbed the phone again and hit a speed dial. "Where are you?" he barked.

"On my way," Dan said. "Did you talk to Cori?"

"No. She's not answering the phone."

"Are you sure she has it with her?"

He wasn't sure of anything. "She should."

"I'll call Raquel. She can institute a satellite search for the location of the phone. What's the number?"

Max gave it to him and rolled through a stop sign. He'd welcome Miami PD at this point; they could run all the lights for him. When he hung up on Dan, he stole a glance at his passenger, whose jaw was slack with realization.

"She put it in my Scotch."

Ya think?

"Every single time I had a headache, or lost my vision, or . . . anything . . . I'd had a Scotch that Breezy made."

"You can thank Helsinki's finest herbalist for the mixer, pal."

Max practically ran the gate at Cocoplum, grabbing Jones's collar and jerking him forward so the guard could recognize him. The gate opened and Max whipped toward the house that remained lit up like a night game. "Why all the lights?" Max asked as he screeched into the driveway.

"I was trying to see."

To his credit, Jones kept pace with Max as they jogged to the front, through the house, into the kitchen, and out to the yard.

The rain had stopped but the grass was wet and muddy. Max bolted to the empty gazebo, but found nothing but a half-dozen cigarette butts on the ground. He looked around, a foreign sense of helplessness tugging at his chest.

Cori. Something punched his throat and stung his eyes. *Something?* How about destitution? Emptiness? Devastation? *I can't lose her again.*

He clenched his fists, squinting into the shadows, staring at the house, willing her to appear. All he wanted to do was howl.

Helpless and furious, he punched his phone again, hoping to hear it ring and find her nearby. But he heard nothing. She was gone, along with the phone and a woman he knew not to trust.

"The gate to the water is open," Jones said, running

toward the marina. Max followed him to the cement dock, his gaze flitting over the fifty or so boats tethered to wooden docks.

"Our boat's here," Jones said, jogging down a dock and standing in front of a thirty-foot Sea Ray made for cruising. "So they didn't take it out."

Max grabbed his cell phone the second it vibrated and read the ID. "Raquel?"

"Dan's stuck at a drawbridge." The familiar New Jersey accent of Lucy's right-hand girl echoed in his ear. "But I have info for you on the phone location. You're not going to like it."

"Where is she?"

"Not far from where you are, in Biscayne Bay. Moving very slowly, if at all. Looks like they might be headed northeast, but the progress is slow."

Max's fingers closed around Cori's key chain in his pocket and he frowned. She was on *Peyton's Place* with two people who'd murdered at least once and wouldn't hesitate to do it again. The horizon was invisible in the predawn, and only a smattering of red and green running lights dotted the water where pleasure craft anchored for the night.

Was Cori on one of them?

"Should I contact the Coast Guard?" Raquel asked.

Max thought about that. An approaching Coast Guard boat or helicopter could scare them into doing something very stupid. And stupid, scared people were the most dangerous kind.

"Get them on alert, but don't move in." Jones's Sea Ray could get him there quickly, but not quietly. His gaze moved to the row of tenders and dinghies lined up on a smaller dock, and he asked Jones if one was his.

"That one." He pointed to a sizeable Zodiac.

Max peered at the plastic hull and miniature console. He could take the Sea Ray close enough to row the Zodiac the last couple hundred feet and surprise them. "Do you have precise coordinates?" he asked Raquel.

"To the square inch, Max."

"I'll be in touch." Max flipped the phone closed and looked at Jones. "Your wife have a gun, Giff?"

"Yes, of course. And she's taken shooting lessons." His expression shifted to a sickening realization.

"One of those compact nine millimeters that women like, right?"

"Yes, a Smith and Wesson."

The ballistics report had come in while he was in California, and that was exactly what had been shot into Cori's cabana.

If he didn't get there, fast and silent, Cori would be dead. If she wasn't already.

"Get back up there and watch the depth finder," Swen barked at Breezy.

"I don't like to drive in the dark." Breezy leaned against the bulkhead, the hard glint in her eyes matching that of the mysterious palm tree she held. "I can't remember if the red buoy lights are supposed to be on the right or the left."

Cori managed to lift herself up on her elbows since Swen had eased the pressure on the knee jutting into her ribs.

"Breezy," she gasped, still fighting for a breath, "what are you doing?"

"I'm covering my well-toned tush, my dearest." Her smile was as wide as it was phony.

"Covering . . . for what?" But then she knew. The betrayal hit her with a fistful of pain to the gut. "How could you?"

Breezy looked at her as if she'd asked an inane question. "Very cleverly, that's how."

Swen straightened, releasing Cori, but she was too stunned to move. "We've got to get over the deepest part of the channel, then get this boat back to her house. We don't have time for a girl chat."

But that was what Cori wanted. She might die tonight, and she damned well wanted to know why.

Breezy brandished the palm tree. "Darling, do I really have to give this up? It's so ingenious."

"It's incriminating evidence."

She made an unhappy face at Cori. "It's engraved with my special initial." She held it upside down to show the letter and the circle of love. "He calls me Mariah—like wind, get it? And see?" She fingered the windswept fronds. "Swen's the tree that can bend, but never break, in the breeze. Isn't that downright poetic? I thought I'd cry when he gave it to me."

Not a gift to William. Not evidence of his infidelity. How could she have doubted him?

The cell phone rang "Hello, Dolly" again, this time from the tight jeans pocket where Breezy had tucked it.

That had to be Max.

"And see?" Breezy twisted the tree top and separated it from the base, revealing a cuplike dish at the bottom. "A secret hiding place. How cool is that?"

Then she turned the tree over and put the palm leaves inside the statuette base. "And look at this," she said coyly. "A mortar and pestle. Specially made for crushing herbs, and spices, and . . . other stuff."

"Give it to me," Swen barked and reached for the tree, but Breezy swiped it back with a chiding *tsk*.

"I'm showing it to Cori, if you don't mind."

Was Breezy going to act like nothing was wrong? Like this was a pleasure cruise, and they were about to pop champagne and gossip about Lulu Garrey's divorce settlement?

She managed one word. "William?"

Breezy sighed, shaking her head. "Bad timing, babe. We were onboard to spike the Scotch Giff would drink the next day. Then he'd keel over miles offshore. But William was so upset with us, he drank it instead."

Cori closed her eyes, the heartache of mourning fresh again.

Swen pushed off the bed. "I'm going up to the helm. Give me that." This time, he succeeded in relieving Breezy of the palm tree. "I'll make our guest a drink."

As he walked out, he and Breezy shared a knowing look. The room suddenly seemed too close and small, but Cori held herself steady, her eyes on Breezy.

"God, we had so much to clean up that night," Breezy continued, moving through the stateroom like it was a stage for her soliloquy. "The whole freaking boat had our fingerprints all over it, and Swen said William wouldn't make it to morning—if he even made it up to your room. We couldn't find the palm tree and we knew that was evidence. William had hidden it while we were in the back."

He'd come upstairs from the boat and never told her that Breezy and Swen were onboard. Why in God's name not? He'd just said, "It wasn't meant for me," and "Be careful, cara."

"I thought we'd actually gotten away with it—even though it cost me a small fortune to get the little half-Jap doctor to go along. But then you started dropping hints and I knew you were suspicious of how he died. That's why I sent him your picture with the note to send you the autopsy next. If the report showed up, it would look like you were hiding it."

Every piece that snapped into place took a bigger chunk out of her heart. "You did all that?"

Breezy choked back a bitter laugh. "Oh, please. I've been working overtime to keep you out of this. I tried to get you to focus on that Foundation, and to worry about Billy and make it look like he was after you. I tried to keep your nose out of Sonoma so you wouldn't find the missing money. I tried to remind you, daily, that your husband died of natural causes." She punctuated each statement she'd made with a dramatic extension of a fingertip, enumerating her efforts.

"The attack in the spa?"

"Swen's idea. But you were just on a tear to figure this out, weren't you? And I still had to unload Giff, but I couldn't get rid of him the same way." She set a hand on her hip. "I mean, how obvious would that be?"

"Breezy," Cori rasped, pushing herself up from her elbows. "Did you do this . . . for money?"

"The money started me thinking," she said, as calmly as if they were discussing the cost of a new pair of shoes. "When I caught Giff's whole embezzling thing a while ago, it got me going. I mean, there he was stockpiling millions for some twit who isn't his kid. That pissed me off, you know?" She meandered to the dresser, studying herself in the mirror. "He gave me carte blanche to his accounts, thinking I wasn't smart enough to figure out how to move his money around. But I was and I did. And now he thinks he spent it all."

How could she have not seen this in Breezy? "If you needed ten million dollars, I would have given it to you."

That earned her a disgusted look. "Of course you would, Saint Cori. You'd do anything for anyone. You're perfect."

Cori ignored the sarcasm. "And Swen? Do you . . ."

Breezy pulled her hair off her face and made a model's pout into the mirror, as if she were checking out her lip liner. "He's smokin' good in bed, and he has that to-die-for BlackBerry full of the most interesting and valuable people. He's pretty smart, too. I knew Giff was going to figure out what I did with the money, so Swen came up with this concoction that can cause heart attacks. But then William . . . I couldn't kill Giff—not yet, anyway." She looked at her watch.

"Hopefully he's done that himself by now. After all, what's the best way to keep someone from seeing something under their nose?" She glanced at Cori in the mirror with an expectant look. "Make them go blind. My idea, but Swen knew how. And he added a little extra something to make sure I was only getting "it" from him and not Giff."

Cori fought a retch in her stomach. "Stop, Breezy."

"How could I? Now, I was smart enough to send that doctor to Japan but when he wanted more money, Swen got rid of him with one phone call. So, all in all, he's a good guy to have around."

Cori fell back on the bed, unable to look at her anymore. "What did you use to kill William?"

"Oleander. Right from your own backyard, doll."

Rage forced Cori up again. "You stood by me at that funeral, Breezy. You slept in my bed the night after he—"

Breezy made her disgusted face. "I can't believe you didn't get a whole new bed after he died in it."

"Breezy, listen to you!"

"I'm sorry, Cor, but he really shouldn't have barged in on us. Though I guess if we hadn't decided to test the bed after we doctored the Scotch, the whole mess could have been avoided." She pointed to the bed. "But he walked right in on us while we were . . . You should have seen the look on his face."

She had seen it. Just before he died. Under her, Cori felt the boat engines rumble to life, but her mind had gone back to that night. Of course William hadn't told her that he'd caught Breezy having an affair. He'd have known how that would hurt, that she'd be disappointed in her friend.

"I didn't care that he saw me fucking Swen. I wouldn't have killed him for that," Breezy said, her tone defensive. "He just shouldn't have helped himself to Giff's Scotch afterward while we were getting dressed and stashing our stuff."

Like condoms. In William's toiletry kit.

"Why, Breezy? If not for love or money, why did you do this?"

Breezy put her hands on the sides of her breasts, turning left to right and checking out her curves and cleavage like she did anytime she was in front of a mirror. "You know, I don't think you've been listening to me."

"I have been, Breezy. But I just can't believe—"

"Not tonight. For the past five years. What have I been telling you?"

Cori searched her brain.

"What do I say?" Breezy prompted, spinning around to peer at Cori like a teacher demanding the right answer, propping her breasts as high as they could go. "What do I tell you all the time, day after day, night after night? I say . . ."

" '*I hate you, Cori Peyton.*' " Cori whispered the words she'd heard Breezy say so many times, they'd become a meaningless, teasing phrase.

"And I do." Breezy dropped her pretenses, her pouty face, her puffy bosom. She leaned closer to Cori, her eyes tapered with evil and envy. "You got the whole package, didn't you? With no compromises.

The über-rich man, not the corporate lawyer who makes a few million. Real beauty, not bought from a plastic surgeon. Real class, real brains, real style—and real love."

Breezy was *jealous* of her? "That's crazy, Breezy. You have so much. Giff loves you."

"Trust me, Giff never loved me the way William loved you. Our deal was a marketing merger." Breezy shook her head. "That's what really rankled me. You really *weren't* a trophy wife." Breezy reached behind her and pulled out a sleek silver gun. "And you weren't a merry widow."

The sting of betrayal dissolved into horror as Cori looked at the gun. "Breezy, Marta knows the boat was taken. Max will figure this out in no time. You'll never get away with it."

"The former hooker can be bought or gotten rid of. And no one will figure this out, because I've covered all my tracks." She pointed the gun right between Cori's eyes. "And to celebrate, Swen whipped up a special cocktail just for you. Come and drink it, and then you can go swimming. That's why we're sitting here at the deepest point of the Bay. It will be a long, long time before they find your body."

Cori dug her fingers into the silken bedspread. "I'm not moving. Shoot me if you have to."

"Trust me, even if your blood splatters all over this boat, we have a back-up plan. Swen can get this thing repainted and renumbered and your boat will be considered stolen property. And as soon as I've handled the grief and loss of my husband and the disappearance of my best friend, I'll join my lover and drink martinis to your memory. I'm not going to get caught. And you're not getting off this boat alive."

What was her best chance at escape? Fighting Breezy for the gun, or following her into the salon and faking that she was drinking something? What would Breezy expect her to do?

"Fine," Cori said, sliding to the edge of the bed. "I can't fight you on this."

"You can, but you won't."

And that's where Breezy was wrong. With the gun jammed into her back, Cori proceeded into the dim salon. On the table close to the galley was the gold palm tree, open in two pieces. A poison cup, not a lover's trinket. Her gaze darted around the room. The glass door to the darkened deck was closed, and the window treatments were pulled tight so no one could see in.

"Here's your drink, darling." Breezy stepped in front of Cori, blocking her from completely entering the salon. She reached for a cobalt blue water glass on the galley counter and lifted it. "To best friends."

Pushing the drink into Cori's hand, she backed away and aimed the gun at Cori's heart. "Your choice, babe. Nice and neat, or a filthy mess. I couldn't care less which way you go."

Slowly, Cori lifted the glass to her mouth. "I'm so sorry you're doing this, Breezy. After all we've been through."

"You have no idea what I've been through." She tapped the glass with her gun as the boat motors died. "Drink. We must be over deep water now."

Cori opened her mouth, put the drink to her lips and took a long, hard pull, lifting her tongue and letting her throat move.

Breezy lowered the gun slowly, disbelief on her face. "You're such a coward. I thought you'd at least put up a fight."

Cori spat the foul-tasting liquid directly into Breezy's eyes. Swearing, Breezy jerked her hand up to her face and Cori dove, her weight knocking Breezy backward and sending the gun across the polished teak floor, landing in the fringe of the oriental carpet.

"Swe—" Cori clamped her hand over Breezy's mouth and jammed her knee into her ribs. Breezy grunted and sank her teeth into Cori's palm, flailing wildly but unable to shake Cori off.

She had only seconds until Swen threw open that salon door and killed her. Seconds to get to a gun that lay ten feet away.

Breezy kicked Cori's shin with a pointed shoe, shooting pain up her leg, but Cori held her hand tight over Breezy's mouth, despite the agony of the teeth in her palm.

Breezy mumbled and screamed into Cori's hand, then jerked so hard, she nearly rolled Cori. But Cori held firm, pushing them farther into the salon.

She glanced at the door, and Breezy managed to get a hand free and yank Cori's hair to the roots, sending white stars through her head. They rolled again and Cori came out on top, with Breezy lying over her own free hand. Cori pinned her other hand down with a knee, still keeping one hand over Breezy's mouth. She was still miles away from the gun.

But the end table was only inches from her eyes, and she smelled the poison in the secret cup.

Breezy bucked again, but Cori held her mouth firmly with her right hand and pinned her skinny hips to the floor with her knees. Keeping Breezy's face pushed to the side so she couldn't see, Cori licked her free hand, then reached toward the small golden bowl. She swept her wet fingers over it, hoping to pick up a lethal dose.

Once again Breezy thrust her body up, but she was too thin and small to be effective. Cori leaned back, letting Breezy up into a half-sitting position.

"Do you promise not to scream?" she asked Breezy, still covering her mouth.

Green eyes flashed in fury and panic.

"Do you?" Cori rasped. "I'll let you free if you promise not to scream."

Breezy's eyes softened but Cori didn't let go.

"So we can talk."

Breezy nodded.

"We really need to talk." Cori forced her voice to be gentle, even weak. "This is crazy, Breezy. We're best friends. We can figure this out."

Breezy's eyes darted over Cori's face, trying to psyche out the bluff.

"I promise to listen to you if you'll listen to me, okay?" Cori braced her other arm, ready. "So I'm going to take my hand off your mouth and you're not going to scream for Swen. We can work this out. Between us, Breeze, we've got a shitload of money."

She felt Breezy almost surrender.

"Billions. And no husbands. Just us. We can travel the world together, have everything we want. Anyone we want."

Breezy's eyes flickered.

"I'll cover for you, Breeze." Cori slowly lifted the fingers covered with poison. "You're my best friend."

She loosened her grip on Breezy's mouth as she brought her other hand up, holding her friend's gaze. "We're best friends," she said again. "Right?"

Breezy nodded twice.

"Okay, then. Let's talk." She took her right hand away and Breezy instantly opened her mouth wide. Before she could take a breath and scream, Cori shoved the poison-covered fingers deep into Breezy's mouth and scraped the flakes onto her tongue and against her teeth.

Breezy started to spit, and managed to get her hands around Cori's throat as Cori held her mouth shut. She squeezed, stabbing her thumb into the middle, closing the esophagus. Cori tried to pry Breezy's fingers away, but her one hand couldn't do it. If she used both hands, Breezy would spit the poison right back at her.

Breezy pressed with all her strength, cutting off Cori's air completely. She tried to suck in a breath, but she couldn't. Still, she forced Breezy's mouth closed, determined to get the poison in her. Breezy squeezed harder and spots of light flashed in Cori's eyes. Her head got heavy. Her lungs felt so full they had to burst. Her ears rang and her muscles spasmed.

She jammed her hand over Breezy's mouth, but

blackness danced in her peripheral vision. The pin-points of light started to fade.

Oh, God, she was dying.

She couldn't hold on. She started to collapse as the salon door was smashed in with a deadly whack and a gunshot reverberated through the salon.

The bullet hit Breezy in the chest, but she didn't let go of Cori until bright red blood oozed over her blouse. As she did, her eyes delivered one last message.

I hate you, Cori Peyton.

Cori rolled off, and Max caught her before she hit the floor.

CHAPTER
Twenty-five

Cori gasped for air, sucking in deep breaths as her head lolled from near unconsciousness. Max turned her on her back, opening her mouth for her. She was breathing, but he tilted her head to open her bruised airway. Cooing to her, whispering her name, he watched the color slowly come back to her face and lips, and her eyes flutter open.

"She killed William," she rasped.

He nodded. "She had help. He's on the deck, lucky to be alive."

"I tried to poison her," she managed to say, lifting her hand and showing him the flakes of black dust on her palm. "I almost did."

"How?"

She gave him a humorless smile. "I bluffed."

He squeezed her into his chest again. "Good work, kid."

"What about Giff?"

"He's on his boat, waiting for my signal to come closer. I got to him before he shot himself." He smoothed her hair. "William didn't cheat on you. He loved you."

"I know," she whispered.

"And I love you, too."

She tried to smile. "I know."

A thud on the deck separated them. Max shot to his feet, blocking Cori and aiming the Ruger.

"Breezy?"

"It's Giff," Cori said. "Don't let him see her like this!"

But it was too late. Jones threw himself into the salon, and stared at the lifeless body of his wife. "Breezy!" he moaned, dropping onto her.

He scooped up Breezy and cradled her, tears streaming down his face. He murmured her name, rocking his wife slowly.

"Giff, I'm so sorry," Cori said, reaching to him.

He looked up from Breezy's body, his eyes cold.

"Come on," Max said, taking Cori's hand and pulling her up. "Let's call for backup."

On the deck she glanced at Swen, slumped on a leather seat. "So much betrayal. So much deceit." She shook her head, then took a deep breath, facing the soft breeze on the bay. "I guess I was blind about the people around me, after all. I had no idea she hated me."

Max stood behind her, and folded her in his arms, pulling her into him. "She was a consummate actress, Cori."

"And I was her biggest fan."

He dropped a kiss on her head, closing his eyes as relief and adrenaline and love washed through him. "I'm just glad you're safe. If anything had happened to you . . ."

She turned, looking up at him with that familiar fire lighting her eyes. "Max."

He smiled. He recognized that tone, knew what was coming next. "Yeah?"

She smiled and stood on her toes, and he reached down and kissed her.

"I love you," they said at the same time.

"Well, I loved my wife." The hatred in that voice yanked them apart, and they spun around just as Jones bounded through the doors, Breezy's blood all over him and her gun aimed directly at Max. "You killed her!"

Max stepped away to get Giff's shaky aim away from Cori, and Jones followed him with a jerky move of the little revolver.

Max lifted both hands to show Giff he was unarmed. "She killed William, and tried to kill Cori. She was poisoning you, too, Jones."

"You know, I had nothing to live for when you found me a few hours ago." The hand holding the revolver trembled, and Max knew when a man was about to shoot. "And I still have nothing to live for. So you're first." He looked at Cori. "She's second. And I'm third."

He lifted the gun, straightened his arm, and gritted his teeth.

Max shoved Cori away and reached for his gun.
Cori pushed him as well, sending them in opposite directions. Jones fired into empty air, and before the
echo died, Max had tackled Jones's legs and pulled
him down.

Cori tore the revolver from his hands while Max
contained him with one hand, his Ruger jammed into
Jones's neck.

In the distance a motorboat growled toward them,
the lights of a Coast Guard cutter slicing through the
blackness. As the spotlight shone on their faces, Max
looked at Cori, who kneeled in front of him holding
the revolver. Her chest rose and fell with each breath,
matching Max's.

"I know." she said softly. "That was just like my father."

"Better, actually. You managed to stay out of the
line of fire."

Cori gave him a bittersweet smile. "I wasn't trying
to be a hero."

"Neither was he," Max said. "But he was."

"You can do this, Billy. You're stronger than your addictions."

Cori's stepson shoved a silky blond strand out of his
face, just enough to shoot her a lethal look but not lose
control of the Gallardo. "Don't talk like a freakin'
shrink, Cor. Nothing's stronger than my addictions."

They'd made some progress in the past few weeks.
He'd dropped the lawsuit, and she'd given him a

chance to run the day-to-day operations of the Foundation. But they were still a long way from affection.

She knew it would have made William happy to know she was trying though—that they both were. Billy had promised to get clean and sober, and Cori would do everything possible to help.

"So where's your bodyguard these days?"

"He took Swen Raynor to Helsinki to handle some legal issues there, before standing trial here. When he's done with that, we're going to meet in California for a while."

Billy shot her a quick look. "You two are good together."

"I'll always miss your father, Billy. He was a really, really good man. No matter who I spend my life with, I will always love your father."

He tried for a casual shrug. "Yeah. Me, too."

For the rest of the trip to the Kendall-Tamiami Executive Airport, they talked about the Foundation and the work she'd given him to handle from Miami. Billy might never realize his father's dream of running Peyton Enterprises, but at least he could have a purpose there. Time would tell.

The Peyton jet waited with the engines whistling, the door open, and the steps down.

"Thanks, Billy," she said as he parked. "I'll call you this week."

"I'll be here."

The pilot took her bags toward the taxiway, giving her details about weather, arrival time, and the menu.

She was nearly at the top of the stairs when the sound of another plane arriving grabbed her attention. It was an unmarked Gulfstream screaming in too fast, and Cori froze to watch it make a spectacular but dangerous landing, then taxi to fifty feet from where she stood.

The door popped open and a man with long black hair lowered the stairs and stared across the space that separated them. He tapped his forehead in a salute and called back into the plane, "I told you we'd make it."

He trotted down the steps and crossed the taxiway, a stunning, muscular man with a silky black mane that whipped in the wind and ebony eyes. She went down the steps to meet him.

"I'm Alex Romero, with the Bullet Catchers." He held his hand out, and Cori hoped she shook it—she couldn't process more than his spectacular good looks. Didn't Lucy Sharpe hire anyone who wasn't breathtaking?

"Am I supposed to have a bodyguard on this trip?" she asked.

"No. But my wife and I were returning home from Finland, and I got stuck with a hitchhiker."

Her heart tumbled, and she looked over Alex's impressive shoulder to see a woman with spiky red hair climbing out of the jet, and behind her . . . the most gorgeous sight of all.

Max shot a menacing look at Alex as he ambled down the steps. "Bad enough you almost got us killed on the landing, Romero. Would you please get away from my woman?"

Alex's grin was high voltage and just as deadly. "Congratulations, Cori. I believe you are the one to have melted the abominable snowman."

She laughed. "He melted me."

Max was headed straight for her, arms open, smile beaming, and she flew into his embrace.

"I thought you couldn't get back for a few more days!" she exclaimed as he twirled her.

He pulled back, gazing at her with a tease in his eyes. "I just spent ten hours on a plane with Alex Romero. If that doesn't prove I love you, nothing does."

Alex had headed back to his plane where the red-haired woman stood, looking at Alex with the same tender expression he gave her.

Max quickly introduced Cori to Jazz Adams, Alex's wife, then grabbed his bag, said good-bye, and guided Cori into the Peyton plane.

As she sat on the long sofa in the back, he stuck his head into the cockpit to talk to the pilots, most definitely requesting privacy in the cabin. Cori shivered with anticipation.

"If you're tired," she teased when he joined her, "you can sleep all the way to California."

He reached into his pocket, pulled out a deck of cards, and dropped them on her lap. "Yeah, right."

They buckled their seat belts as the engines whined. They kissed during takeoff, and cuddled all the way to cruising altitude. By the time they were above the clouds, Cori was all but begging Max to un-button her blouse.

He stopped the foreplay and picked up the cards.

"All right," he said, opening the deck and clearing some space between them on the leather sofa. "Let's play."

"Okay," she said. "Though I think it's pretty obvious I'm willing to lose the first hand."

"Oh, we're not playing strip."

"Favors?"

He grinned. "Are you that desperate to get me naked and take liberties with me?"

"Yes."

That made him laugh. "I have a better game in mind."

"Answers?" What could he want to know that he didn't?

"Promises," he said, splitting the deck.

"That's a new one." She tucked her legs up and tapped the deck when he offered the cut. "When you win, do you elicit a promise from the other person?"

"No." He dealt, looking at her with eyes the color of sweet maple syrup. "You make one."

She smiled. "Really."

"Really. How's your hand?"

She had a pair of jacks, a four, a five, and a two. "Deuces wild?"

"If you have one, and want them to be." He looked at her. "And from the expression on your face, I'd say you have at least one and a few royals to boot."

She laughed. "How do you do that?" She took two

cards, getting another jack and using everything she had to remain expressionless.

"Oh, boy," he said. "That's the face of a winning hand."

"Max!"

"All right, all right." He turned his cards over and folded. "Now you make me a promise. But be warned, I'll hold you to it."

Oh, the things she could promise. "I promise . . . to make love to you tonight."

He barely nodded. "Your deal."

She won again. He patiently waited while she bit her lip and tried to come up with something clever. "I promise . . . to take a bath with you when we get home."

He gave her a dubious look. "You're mind is really on sex, kid."

She reached over and squeezed his thigh. "Hey, I haven't seen you for a few days."

When he dealt again she couldn't read his reaction, of course. She had a lousy hand and her draw cards didn't help, so she folded and waited.

"I promise," he said slowly, "never to leave you again."

"Thank you, Max," she said mistily.

He dealt again, and won again.

This time he pushed the cards to the floor and folded her in his arms.

"I promise to spend the rest of my life playing cards with you. And while I'm at it, I promise to honor," he kissed her forehead. "Cherish," he kissed her nose. "And love you." He kissed her mouth so softly that she barely felt his lips. "Till death do us part."

The plane banked, but it might as well have been the world slipping sideways on its axis as Cori's heart shifted.

He smiled. "And by the look on your poker face, you like that idea."

She laughed, tunneling her hands into his hair for another kiss. "I like the idea."

Max laid back against the armrest, pulling her on top of him.

She kissed him again, tasting the sweetness that was Max, the familiar lips of the man she loved.

"So," he said, pulling her against him. "Is that a yes?"

"I thought we were playing promises, not answers." Closing her eyes, she reached down to the floor and grabbed a card. "Oh, look what I got. An ace."

He lifted his eyebrows. "Now you get to make a promise *and* get a favor."

"Lucky me. All right . . ." She looked into his eyes. "Max Roper, I promise to love, honor, and cherish you till death do us part."

Their kiss was long, slow, and easy, as if they had forever. When it ended, she laid her head on his chest and listened to the steady beat of the heart of gold buried in his chest of steel.

"Don't forget your favor," he reminded her.

She smiled. "That's easy. My favor is that I get to sleep right here for the rest of my life," she whispered, patting his chest. "I love this spot. I love this heart. I love this man."

"I love you, too, kid." At the strange tightness in his voice, she looked up. He tried to smile, but that just forced out a tear from his eye.

"Aw, Max." She kissed the teardrop, then his lips. "You're just so emotional."

Epilogue

Lucy hung up her office phone and inhaled a whiff of something amazing floating up from the kitchen. Johnny Christiano was working magic again. She stood, still smiling from Max's news. She'd never heard him sound so . . . animated.

Eager to share the announcement with the little gathering downstairs, she followed the aroma of basil and the sound of laughter that accompanied it. Only a few of the Bullet Catchers were free to attend her little Christmas soiree, but those who had were definitely having fun.

"The West Coast office just checked in," she told them as she entered the living room, her gaze automatically seeking out Dan Gallagher next to the Christmas tree.

His green eyes sparkled. So, he already knew.

"How's Mad Max?" Chase asked, standing as she entered the room.

"Not mad at anyone," she said, taking the glass

of champagne Raquel handed her. She smiled at her assistant. Just hours earlier, they'd finished her annual review and Raquel's eagerness to take her skills into the field had been the only point of heated discussion. The party, it seemed, had put Raquel back into a good mood. And something else would soon, too.

"He's doing a great job running the operations from Healdsburg," Chase said. "Stroke of genius to station him permanently in California, Luce."

It was that or lose him. She raised her glass. "Thank you, Chase."

"Strokes of genius are Lucy's specialty," Dan said, approaching the group, his gaze warming her. "Are we toasting the news?"

"We are," Lucy agreed, still holding her glass. "The sonogram says it's a boy and they are going to name him Maximillian Phillip Roper . . . the fourth."

That elicited another round of laughter, cheers and an "awww" from Raquel.

Johnny trotted in from the kitchen, carrying a tray of simmering shellfish. "We call this *vongole oreganate,* which is baked clams to the rest of you." He placed the tray on the table and wiped his hands on his white apron. "Now, what am I missing?"

"Baby Roper is a boy," Raquel told him. "Max Junior."

Johnny grinned. "I knew they wouldn't name him Alex."

Dan chuckled. "That's a safe bet."

"What's the deal with that, Lucy?" Raquel asked, taking a clam. "I've heard so many different theories, but neither one of them will talk. Why do Alex and Max hate each other?"

"Has to be a woman," Johnny insisted. "Nothin' else could get under their skin like that."

"They're both married now," Raquel mused. "If it were a woman, they'd let it go."

"Then it's work." Chase looked at Lucy. "Has either one ever lost a principal?"

Lucy shook her head. "No Bullet Catcher has ever lost a principal."

"I'm tellin' you," Johnny said, popping a clam. "Gotta be a chick."

"A sports bet?" Chase said. "Max is a diehard Steelers fan."

"A family thing," Raquel suggested. "You know how Alex is about his Cuban clan."

"A woman," Johnny repeated. "Has to be."

Raquel turned to Dan, who'd been uncharacteristically quiet. "Do you know?"

He lifted one shoulder. "All I know is they had their first assignment together, not far from here in Westminster, and it didn't go well."

"Come on, Luce," Johnny prodded. "You know, don't you?"

"Juicy Miss Lucy knows everything," Dan said, sipping his drink and winking at her over the rim of his glass.

"Not everything." For instance, she didn't know what Dan Gallagher was thinking . . . most of the time. And, God, that intrigued her. "But I do know what happened between Alex and Max."

The group erupted with more questions and she quieted them with a smile and one hand. "It was a woman."

"Told ya." Johnny nudged Raquel. "Go study history. From Adam on, they're the downfall of every great man."

Raquel rolled her eyes and looked at her boss. "Come on, Luce. Spill."

Lucy took a sip of her champagne and let the sweetness of the moment wash over her. This little group, her Bullet Catchers, were her family now. She absently touched the thin streak of white in her hair, a reminder that she once had another family. But this group was her grounding now. And she'd do anything for any of them.

Including keep secrets.

"What was her name?" Chase asked.

"I can't tell you exactly what happened . . . or I'd have to kill you all."

Dan chuckled. "I know her name was Reagan."

"Really?" Raquel's eyes lit up. "Who was she?"

"She was a world-class beauty," Lucy said. "She had long, golden hair and eyes the color of that sky. She moved like poetry and, quite literally, stopped traffic. And, God in heaven, she knew it."

"They always do," Johnny muttered.

"Was she a principal?" Raquel prodded.

Lucy nodded. "They both were assigned to her, because she was very high profile and needed round-the-clock protection. Suffice it to say, Max Roper approached the assignment with detachment and logic, and Alex Romero displayed his usual passion and emotion." She shrugged. "They clashed."

"How?"

"They were both madly in love with her," Lucy said. "But she trotted off with another man."

"No!" Raquel said.

"And," Lucy added, "she took Best of Show that year."

They stared at her.

"A dog?" Johnny choked.

She almost didn't hear the soft beep of her house phone over their roar of laughter. She picked up the receiver, recognizing the number. Grigori Nyekovic, former KGB and current multimillionaire. A brilliant double agent and longtime friend.

"Raquel," Lucy said, holding the phone to her. "Could you handle this, please?"

As Raquel left the room, Lucy looked at Dan. "She has no idea what's about to hit her," she said under her breath.

"Ms. Machiavelli, up to her old tricks again," he said, coming closer.

She tucked that strand of hair behind her ear. This is what she lived for, these days. The orchestration of challenges. The vicarious thrills. The pleasure of managing the lives of the men and women who beat the world's bad guys.

"Watch your back," she warned in a friendly whisper, locking on his Irish eyes. "It'll happen to you when you least expect it."

He shot her his most endearing crooked smile. "I can't wait, Juice."

"Neither can I, Danny boy. Neither can I."

Pocket Books
Proudly Presents . . .

Take Me Tonight

The next novel in the Bullet Catchers Series
by Roxanne St.Claire

Turn the page for a preview of
Take Me Tonight. . . .

Earbuds to obliterate any warning of approaching danger. *Check.*

Long flowing ponytail for an easy take down. *Check.*

Low-slung running shorts to give even the clumsiest rapist easy access. *Check.*

A midnight jog, an abandoned park, not so much as a key in hand for self-defense. *Check. Check. Check.*

Didn't this woman have a mother who taught her any common sense?

Hey. Not his problem. Johnny Christiano slipped deeper into the shadows of the Public Garden and waited for her to make her next pass. When you had a guardian angel named Lucy Sharpe, common sense could take a vacation and let a Bullet Catcher do the clean-up.

She approached at an impressive clip and Johnny

sank farther into the flowered hedge, gauging how long it would take until Hot Legs got herself kidnapped.

He'd figured on four more minutes, but the first time she'd passed him, he realized she was stupid, reckless, irresponsible, and fast. So, maybe three. Following her at a safe distance, he matched her speed.

She rounded the pond, veered into the dim beam of a decorative lamp, then slowed her step. Changing her mind? Rethinking her foolish plan? Or maybe just buying time? Johnny held back, waiting. She looked toward the footbridge to her right and the Charles Street gate to her left. He crouched under a low willow branch to watch her sports bra rise and fall with slow, even breaths. She wasn't even winded.

When a squirrel rustled along the tree trunk, the woman whipped around, her eyes narrowed, her posture suddenly transformed from clueless to alert. Then she fiddled with her iPod and started into an easy jog.

He stayed fifty feet behind her, close enough to get hypnotized by the pendulum swing of her ponytail and mesmerized by the hip-hugging shorts that barely covered a marathon-toned ass. It would have been nice if Lucy had told him she was a runner; he might have planned this differently. But his boss had been short on particulars and long on demands. He only knew what to do; he had no clue why.

One minute.

How hard up could a woman be for a cheap thrill? Well, not so cheap. The cost of a plain vanilla fantasy kidnapping and quick release was a thousand bucks.

Fifteen hundred for a simple rescue. Two G's for something called the "deluxe," which he assumed included stud service from your white knight.

Evidently, male strippers were *so* last millennium for today's fun-loving girls.

Not your problem, man. Just do the job Lucy gave you. That's what Bullet Catchers did: no judgments on the shortcomings of the principal.

She neared the gate and adjusted her earbuds, clearly back in her home state of oblivion. She ambled slowly, bopping her head to the tunes, tightening her ponytail, then stopped, silhouetted against the pale beam that illuminated the swan-shaped row boats moored in the pond. She bent over and stretched to touch her toes, long hair grazing the ground. On an exhale, she flattened her hands on the pavement, curled as gracefully as the swan boats behind her.

With a sudden flip of her hair, she straightened, squared her shoulders, clenched her fists, and headed for the open iron gate that led to Charles Street—and her appointment with a kidnapper. Which either took the cake for stupidity, or proved that somewhere in those sexy curves, she hid a set of titanium balls.

Dumb as dirt or gutsy girl, it didn't matter. A greater force than her desire for an adrenaline rush was at work tonight. And when Lucy got involved, all bets—and thrills—were off.

She lingered near the gate as a few cars passed on Beacon, the next intersection to the north. A white

BMW zipped along the far lane across the one-way street; otherwise Charles was as deserted as most of Boston's streets at midnight on a Tuesday. She walked slowly in the same direction as traffic, drumming her fingers against her bare thigh.

Johnny waited just behind the open gate, stealthy and quiet, but the woman's focus was on the road. The muscles in her back tensed, even though she was trying to look relaxed and unprepared. She glanced over her shoulder at the sound of a car approaching. Scratch that—a van. Dark, older model. Parking lights only.

Show time, baby doll.

She stepped toward the curb, slowing down near the crosswalk. Johnny counted to five, then broke into a light jog. The van veered into the left lane, dropped to about three miles per hour, slowed at the crosswalk, then stopped just two feet from her.

She froze, then started to run. Not nearly as fast as she could, but fast enough to make it seem real. Johnny kicked his speed up just as the back door slid open and a man's leg extended toward the street. She looked over her shoulder and stumbled a little.

"C'mere, honey," the man called. "I need some help."

She hesitated for a moment and looked to the van.

"C'mere," he repeated.

She took one step closer, then Johnny swooped in, grabbed her by the waist and lifted her right off the ground, never missing a beat of his stride.

"Hey!" She squirmed in his arms, kicked his thigh, and gave his back a solid swat. "Not yet!"

He hoisted her higher and the man barked from the van.

She whacked him again. "I haven't been kidnapped yet!" She punctuated that with a knee that barely missed his own titanium set.

"Come on, princess," he growled as he charged toward the Camry he'd parked hours earlier. "This is how it works."

He reached the car in less than ten strides, held her immobile with one hand, yanked the back door open with the other, and shoved her in.

"Not . . ." He slammed the door and barely heard her muffled "Yet!" She pounded the window in protest.

Yes, yet. He dove into the driver's seat and stabbed the keys in the ignition as she grabbed a handful of his hair and pulled like hell.

"I can't believe you did that!" she shrieked.

Shaking her loose, he started the car, threw it into drive, and flew across three lanes to turn right on Beacon. Though he doubted it, the *real* Rescuer could be close by and they might want to find out who was muscling in on their business. Just in case, he blew out of there.

She smacked her hand against the back of his seat so hard, he felt it in his chest. "That was too fast! I didn't even get kidnapped! I paid to get kidnapped, you son of a bitch!"

He snagged her gaze in the rear-view mirror, seeing the fury sparking in her eyes even in the darkness. "You're welcome."

She choked and threw herself back. "That's not what I paid for," she spat. "I didn't get a *thing* out of that." She kicked his seat with a frustrated "Ooh. Damn it all!"

What the hell kind of buzz was she looking for? Was climbing into a van with some creep for pretend danger really a good time?

"You paid to get rescued," he said, looking at her in the mirror again. He hadn't seen a picture, the way he usually did. On a normal job, Lucy would have given him a dossier an inch thick, with every detail down to bra size. He adjusted the mirror slightly south. A decent—very decent—B or B-plus. "I am just doin' my job, miss. Where to?"

"Where to?" She sounded incredulous. "I didn't flag a cab to cruise Beacon Street. I paid to get *abducted*, thank you very much. And I did *not* get two thousand dollars worth of abduction services."

"Two?" He coughed. "You bought the deluxe?"

Her eyes sharpened. "Don't you guys communicate at that company?"

"I was told it was a standard rescue operation," he said, hoping that was the right term. "No deluxe."

She crossed her arms, her creamy complexion darkened with fury and frustration. "I was very clear in the application. I wanted the most amount of time I could possibly have before the rescue. My contact promised me at least an hour of kidnapping. An hour with the guy who's supposed to be the best there is."

"An hour? For what?" The question was out before

he could stop himself, and he backpeddled fast. "I mean, isn't the whole reason you sign up for this the rescue part?" He gave her his most endearing grin. "From a knight in shining . . ." he glanced at the dash. "Toyota?"

She rolled her eyes. "I wanted the whole package." She turned to the window, lost for a moment. Then she looked back into the mirror and burned him with a questioning gaze. "How long have you been at this?"

Five minutes. "A while."

"Do you do a lot of the rescues? Are you a regular?"

"Oh, yeah. Rescuing is all I do, sweetheart." A bodyguard could certainly be considered a rescuer.

"And do you only work for takemetonite.com, or are you a freelancer?"

How many sites were there, where chicks paid for fantasy adrenaline rushes? Was this really a booming business? "Just this one."

"Do you talk to them much? The girls you save?"

"If they want." He had to give it more than this, or she'd never believe he worked for the site. And Lucy said she *had* to believe him. "I'll talk if they, you know, bought the deluxe package."

She leaned forward, pressing her fingers on his shoulders. "Let's be clear here, pal. Is that deluxe business straight sex or something kinky?"

He stopped at a light and shrugged. "Hey. It's your two grand, babe."

"You need to turn the car around."

"Huh uh, we're not going back to that park. You've been rescued. The first part is over, whether it lasted long enough for you or not. No do-overs."

"I know the rules," she said. "But you need to turn around anyway."

"Where do you want to go?"

She smoked him with a look that said it all. "I live off Chestnut Street on Beacon Hill. These are all one way streets past the State House."

He zipped into the left lane to hang a U. "Home? You want to go home?"

"Yep. I want my money's worth." She reached back and whipped her hair out of the ponytail, shaking a thick blond mane around her shoulders, her expression fairly detached for a woman who'd just discussed straight or kinky with a perfect stranger.

Lucy had been uncharacteristically vague about this assignment, but it was a damn safe bet it didn't include a gigolo gig. All she had said was, don't let her go through with the kidnapping, and be sure she was safe. Nothing about deluxe services.

"What did you say your name was?" she asked.

He had to play along. She had to think she had a bona fide Rescuer from www.takemetonite.com, a thrill specialist. "Whatever you want it to be, doll."

She looked skyward again. "Enough with the nick-names. What's your real name?"

"Johnny. My name's Johnny Christiano. What's yours?"

"I'm Sage Valentine."

"Sage." He'd liked the name the minute Lucy had told him about the unorthodox assignment. "Tasty stuff, sage."

"I'm not named for the spice," she told him, looking out the window.

"Actually, it's an herb."

"Whatever. I'm named for wisdom."

Oh, yeah? She sure wasn't demonstrating any of *that* tonight. He watched her closely, seeing the wary, worried look deepening in her green eyes. Or maybe they were brown—hard to tell in this light. But like the rest of her, they were real pretty. Kind of tilted up at the sides and wide. Nice cheekbones, too. His mother always said you could tell a classy girl by her cheekbones.

Of course, Ma hadn't met a woman who paid a couple of grand to be kidnapped, rescued, and screwed for a good time. On second thought, with that family? Maybe she had.

Sage leaned her head against the glass and closed her eyes. "I still can't believe you wrecked my kidnapping."

"Was it your first time, Sage?"

"First, last, and only," she sighed.

He couldn't believe it; he actually felt guilty for saving her ass. "Maybe I can make it up to you."

"You better."

He looked into the mirror, an idea occurring to him. He knew just the thing to put a smile on her face. It worked with every other woman he'd ever known.

"Don't worry, angel. I have something special in mind for you."

At least one thing she'd read on that web site had been true.

Guaranteed safe release, courtesy of hot, handsome hunks specially trained to make your every rescue fantasy come true.

But she hadn't waltzed half-naked through the Public Garden, tripped all over Charles Street, and behaved like a hare-brained blonde just for a flipping rescue fantasy. And forget about the money. That was half her fee if she sold even the idea to an editor which, without the chance to interview the "master kidnapper," was probably moot anyway.

Worst of all, she hadn't had the chance to find out anything about the night Melissa had been kidnapped. Now all she had was a boy toy who used pet names and had screwed up her only chance at getting some facts straight. Her only hope was to keep up the charade and try to get something out of him.

She studied the breadth of his shoulders, the way his black hair carelessly fell over a dark T-shirt. Strong neck, but not thick. Gorgeous eyes. She couldn't see much more than that, but he didn't really seem like Melissa's type. This guy would have been too . . . earthy for Melissa.

Still, maybe he'd met her roommate. Maybe he'd rescued her once.

Would she actually have to sleep with him to find out? That last thought sent something scorching and unholy through her veins. Well, she would do whatever it took, like she always did.

"You can park there, behind that Dumpster. You might get a ticket, but since the car's a rental, who cares?"

He shot her a quick look of surprise in the rear-view mirror. "How do you know that?"

She pulled the Hertz card from where it had peeked out of the back pocket when she'd kicked his seat, and waved it into his line of view. "Dead giveaway. I don't own a car, either. If you're smart, you don't need one in Boston."

He barely shrugged one of those impressive shoulders and zipped into the spot, getting out of the car before she could even figure out where the handle was. He opened the door for her with the flair of a limo driver.

Half a step above a male prostitute, but a gentleman. She climbed out and rocked back on her Nikes, finally having the opportunity to see what they'd sent her. Yep. Truth in advertising. About six feet, rock solid, and built to please the most demanding female customer. Broody dark eyes, silky black hair, a full mouth, and a nose with just enough of a bump to prove he'd been in a fight or two, but healed well. Too bad his timing sucked.

"Whatdya think?" he asked with a half-smile, his

eyes glinting in the streetlight as he checked her out, too. "Will I do?"

If she'd shelled out cash expecting quadruple orgasms at the hands of a blistering, dark, dangerous stranger, yeah. He'd do very nicely. "We'll see," she said.

But would he do for what she wanted? Answers, information. Hopefully, proof. She'd have to butter him up, get him to talk, take down his defenses.

Might only be one way to do that. Ah, well. She *had* paid for the deluxe package.

She indicated the street in front of the alley, "It's just a few buildings down."

He put a protective hand on her shoulder. "Nice neighborhood," he commented. "I like the gaslights and cobblestones."

"Have you been to Beacon Hill before?" Like the night her roommate died, perhaps? "Ever have any other customers here?"

"Hard to remember," he said. "There are so many."

She shot him a look to see if he was kidding, but his hooded eyes gave nothing away.

"Who do you work for?" she asked pointedly.

There. That got the flash of response she wanted. "Takemetonite.com. You know that."

"I mean, at the actual company. Who do you report to? Is there a hierarchy? Are you in, say, the customer relations department?"

He stifled a laugh. "It's sort of a loose corporate structure."

This wasn't going to be easy. But even if he didn't

know Melissa, maybe he'd heard who had handled her rescue that night.

She pulled a key out from the hidden pocket of her running shorts and paused at the three stone stairs leading up to her apartment. "So how long has the web site been in business?"

"I couldn't say."

Stepping up to the door, she slipped in the key, then hesitated. Was this the right thing to do? What if she had sex with him and he didn't answer her questions? Then what?

"You're still not sure, are you?" he said, leaning a little closer to her. He smelled sweet, like the flowers blooming in the Garden. Like he'd . . . hidden in the honeysuckle.

"Were you waiting on Charles Street?" she asked.

"I've been fifty feet behind you since you left home about an hour ago."

She sucked in a breath, her stomach flipping. "You followed me?"

His gaze slid over her like hot liquid mercury. "Down Chestnut, across Beacon—you shouldn't jaywalk, by the way—around the Common, past the little group of homeless people you said hi to, through the Public Garden, all the way to your last stretch by the swan boats. You were never alone."

She stared at him, unable to speak. He'd followed her, through the dark, through the shadows, through the night.

Damn, she hated what that did to her. Hated the

way her nerves tingled and her thighs tightened. Hated the way it *thrilled* her. Wasn't she smarter than the women who signed up to buy that kind of thing? Wasn't she smarter than Melissa, who'd ended up dead the night she'd signed up to be kidnapped?

"What's the matter?" He grazed her chin with his knuckle, hot as a matchstick on her skin. "You're not having second thoughts, are you?"

She still stared at him.

"There's no rule that says you have to do this."

"I'd just like to talk . . . first." *Interview* would be what they called it in journalism school. "Is that okay?"

"Of course. Most women do." He put a hand over hers to help her turn the key, and electricity shot through her. "But I like to do something else, first."

Oh, God. "What's that?"

He dipped so close his breath ruffled her hair; his warm, possessive hand on her back seared the bare skin between her running top and shorts. "It's a surprise."

She turned the knob slowly. "I hate surprises."

"Really." He nudged the door open and guided her in. "Pretty strange way to spend a Tuesday night then, trolling for an abduction."

She'd left the apartment dark, and shadows ate up every corner.

"I wasn't. I'm not in this just for an adrenaline rush." She reached for a lamp, but his hand closed over her wrist, drawing her close enough to feel his chest, his stomach, his hips and thighs through her pathetically thin clothes.

"Then you're in luck," he whispered. "'Cause I deliver way more than that."

She closed her eyes. She could do this, for Melissa. She could do . . . whatever it took.

Who says romance is dead?

Bestselling romances from Pocket Books

Otherwise Engaged
Eileen Goudge
Would you trade places
with your best friend if
you could?

Only With a Highlander
Janet Chapman
Can fiery Winter
MacKeage resist the
passionate pursuit of a
timeless warrior?

Kill Me Twice
Roxanne St. Claire
She has a body to kill
for...and a bodyguard
to die for.

Holly
Jude Deveraux
On a starry winter night,
will her heart choose
privilege—or passion?

**Big Guns Out
of Uniform**
*Sherrilyn Kenyon, Liz
Carlyle, and Nicole Camden*
Out of uniform and
under the covers...three
tales of sizzling romance
from three of today's
hottest writers.

**Hot Whispers of
an Irishman**
Dorien Kelly
Can a hunt for magical
treasure uncover a love to
last a lifetime?

Carolina Isle
Jude Deveraux
When two cousins switch
identities, anything can
happen. Even love...

POCKET BOOKS
A Division of Simon & Schuster
A VIACOM COMPANY

POCKET
STAR BOOKS
A Division of Simon & Schuster
A VIACOM COMPANY

Love a good romance?

So do we...

Killer Curves
Roxanne St. Claire

He's fast. She's furious.
Together they're in for the ride
of their lives...

One Way Out
Michele Albert

Suspense crackles as two
unlikely lovers try to outrun
danger—and passion.

The Dangerous Protector
Janet Chapman

The desires he ignites in
women makes him the most
dangerous man in the world...

I Hunger for You
Susan Sizemore

In the war between vampires
and humanity, desire is the only
victor.

Close to You
Christina Dodd

He watches you. He follows
you. He longs to be...close to
you.

Shadow Haven
Emily LaForge

She followed her heart home—
and discovered a passion she
never dreamed of.

AVAILABLE WHEREVER BOOKS ARE SOLD.

www.simonsayslove.com

11903